Pokémon™ X•Y

STORY
Hidenori Xsaka

ART
Satoshi Yamamoto

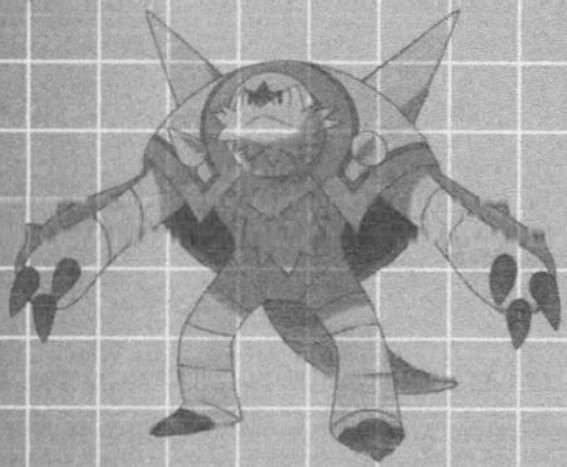

12

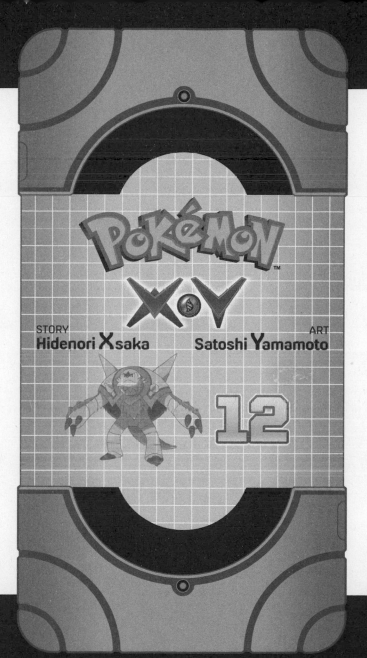

CHARACTERS

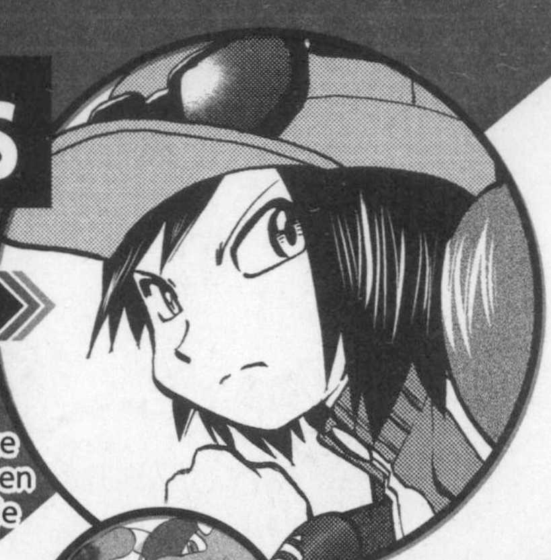

X

The main character of this chapter, and one of five close childhood friends. He was once a highly skilled Trainer who even won the Junior Pokémon Battle Tournament, but now...

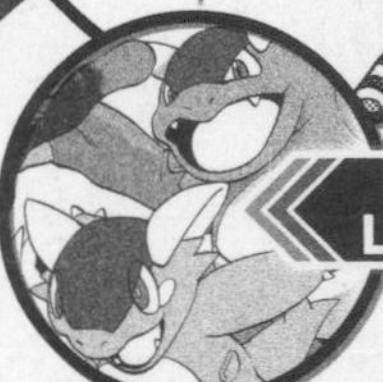

KANGA & LI'L KANGA

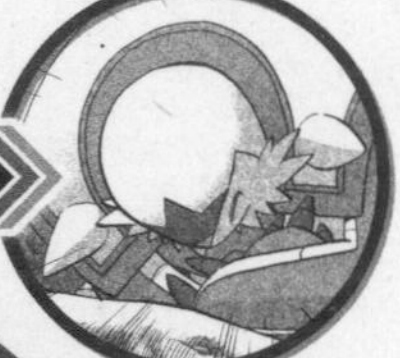

MARISSO

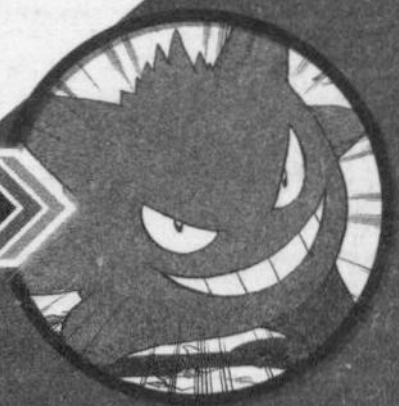

GARMA

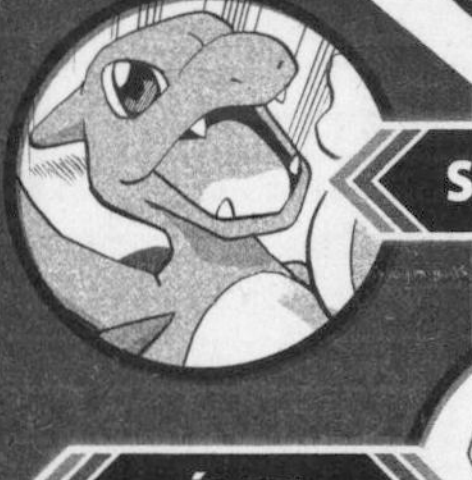

SALAMÈ

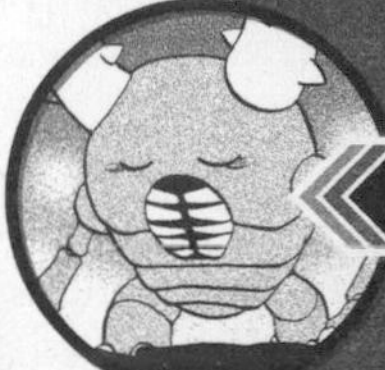

RUTE

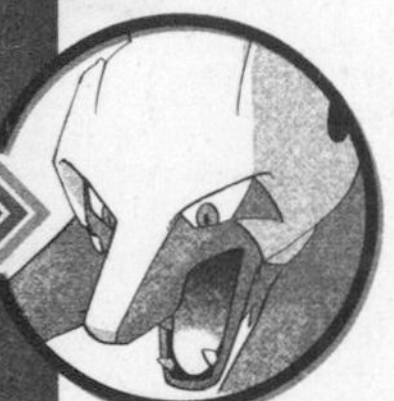

ÉLEC

OUR STORY THUS FAR...

In Vaniville Town in the Kalos region, X is a Pokémon Trainer child prodigy. But then he falls into a depression. A sudden attack by the Legendary Pokémon Xerneas and Yveltal, controlled by Team Flare, forces X out into the world. He and his closest childhood friends—Y, Trevor, Tierno and Shauna—are now on the run.

Y receives a Mega Ring and becomes a Mega Evolution successor. Then X and his friends learn the whereabouts of Team Flare's new hideout and head there for a showdown. But along the way they are ambushed by five scientists from Team Flare...!

MEET THE

Y

X's best friend, a Sky Trainer trainee. Her full name is Yvonne Gabena.

TREVOR

One of the five friends. A quiet boy who hopes to become a fine Pokémon Researcher one day.

SHAUNA

One of the five friends. Her dream is to become a Furfrou Groomer. She is quick to speak her mind.

TIERNO

One of the five friends. A big boy with an even bigger heart. He is currently training to become a dancer.

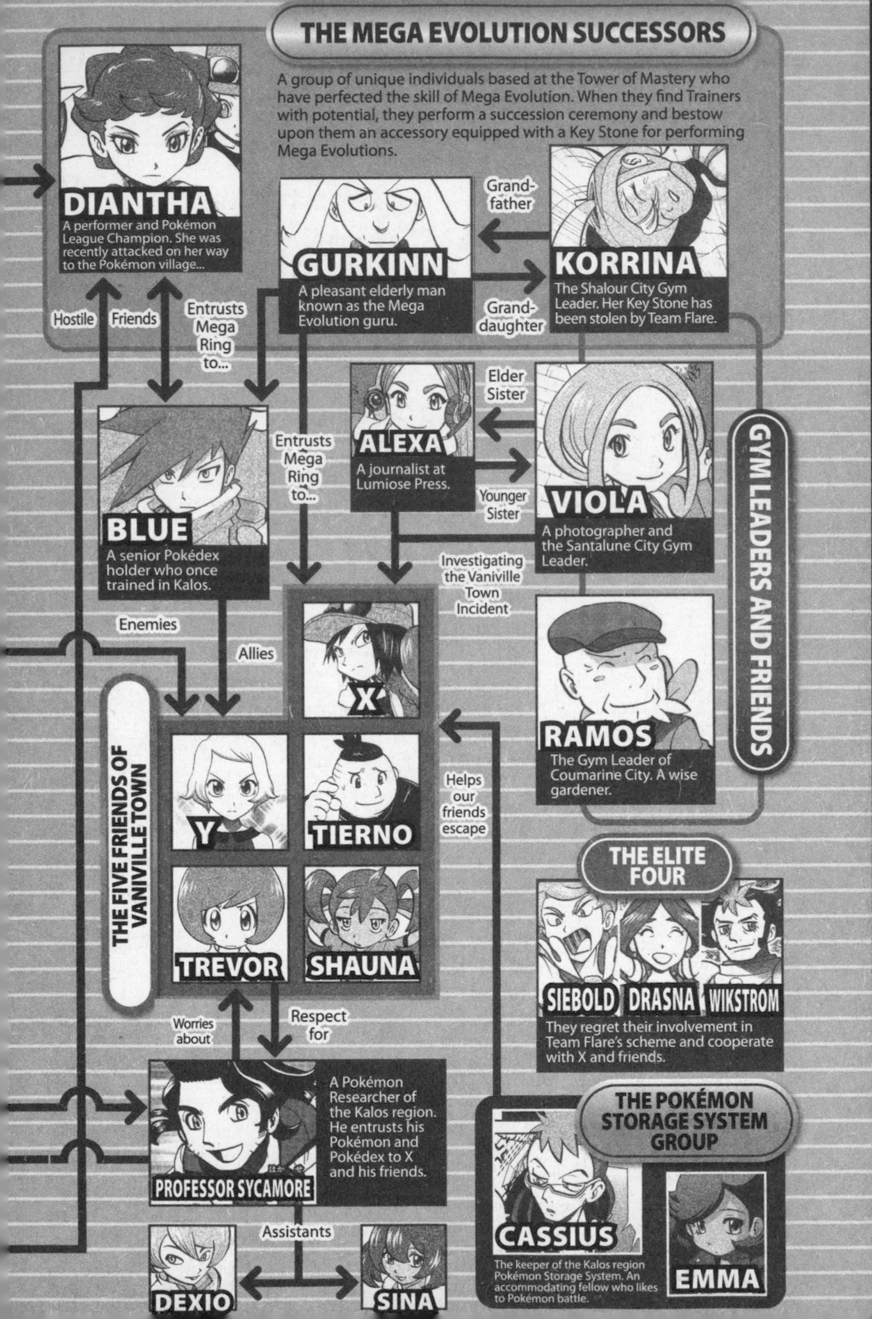
THE MEGA EVOLUTION SUCCESSORS
A group of unique individuals based at the Tower of Mastery who have perfected the skill of Mega Evolution. When they find Trainers with potential, they perform a succession ceremony and bestow upon them an accessory equipped with a Key Stone for performing Mega Evolutions.
DIANTHA
A performer and Pokémon League Champion. She was recently attacked on her way to the Pokémon village...
GURKINN
A pleasant elderly man known as the Mega Evolution guru.
KORRINA
The Shalour City Gym Leader. Her Key Stone has been stolen by Team Flare.
Grand-father
Grand-daughter
Hostile
Friends
Entrusts Mega Ring to...
Entrusts Mega Ring to...
BLUE
A senior Pokédex holder who once trained in Kalos.
ALEXA
A journalist at Lumiose Press.
Elder Sister
Younger Sister
VIOLA
A photographer and the Santalune City Gym Leader.
GYM LEADERS AND FRIENDS
Investigating the Vaniville Town Incident
RAMOS
The Gym Leader of Coumarine City. A wise gardener.
Enemies
Allies
X
THE FIVE FRIENDS OF VANIVILLE TOWN
Y
TIERNO
TREVOR
SHAUNA
Helps our friends escape
THE ELITE FOUR
SIEBOLD
DRASNA
WIKSTROM
They regret their involvement in Team Flare's scheme and cooperate with X and friends.
Worries about
Respect for
A Pokémon Researcher of the Kalos region. He entrusts his Pokémon and Pokédex to X and his friends.
PROFESSOR SYCAMORE
THE POKÉMON STORAGE SYSTEM GROUP
CASSIUS
The keeper of the Kalos region Pokémon Storage System. An accommodating fellow who likes to Pokémon battle.
EMMA
Assistants
DEXIO
SINA

CHARACTER CORRELATION CHART

Track the connections between the people revolving around X.

TEAM FLARE

An organization identifiable by its red uniforms that has been working hard behind the scenes in the Kalos region. They tried to activate the Ultimate Weapon in Kalos, but X and his friends prevented them. What is their Plan B at Pokémon Village?!

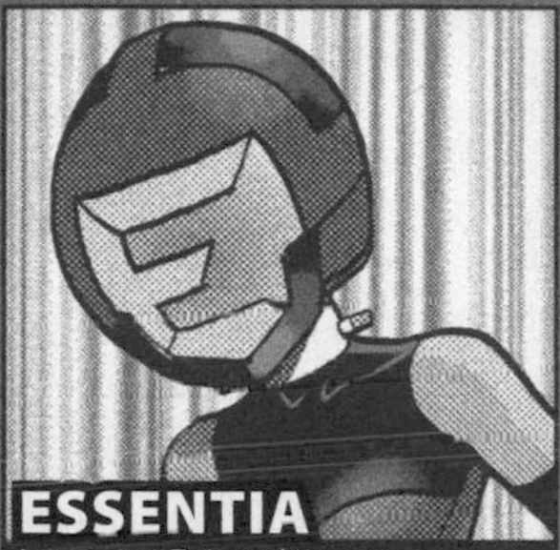

ESSENTIA
A mysterious Trainer who wears an Expansion Suit. She has gone missing since being injured in battle.

Development
Obedience to

TEAM FLARE'S SCIENTIFIC TEAM

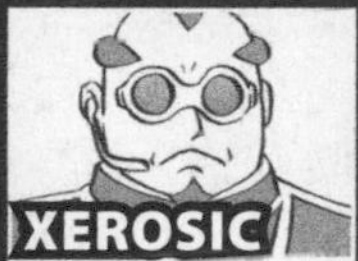

XEROSIC
Member of Unit A. Developed Team Flare's gadgets and the Expansion Suit. Currently fighting X and his friends on the mountain.

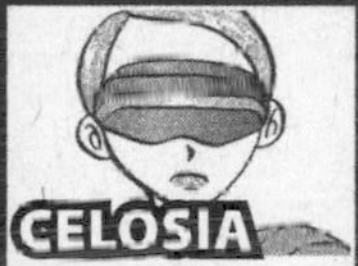

CELOSIA
Member of Unit A. A vengeful woman who somehow always bounces back from failure.

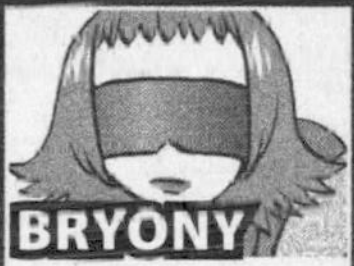

BRYONY
Member of Unit A. A quiet bookworm and military scientist who studies battles.

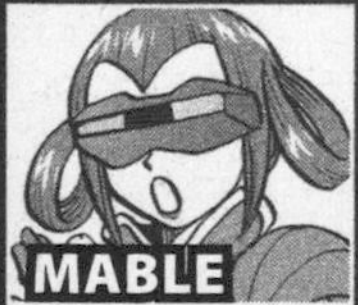

MABLE
Member of Unit B. Outspoken and emotional.

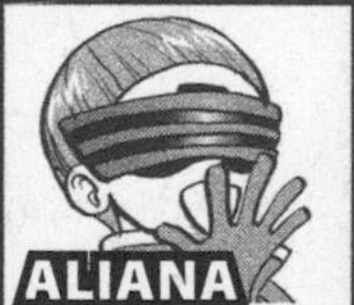

ALIANA
Member of Unit B. Charged with obtaining the Mega Ring.

Old Friends

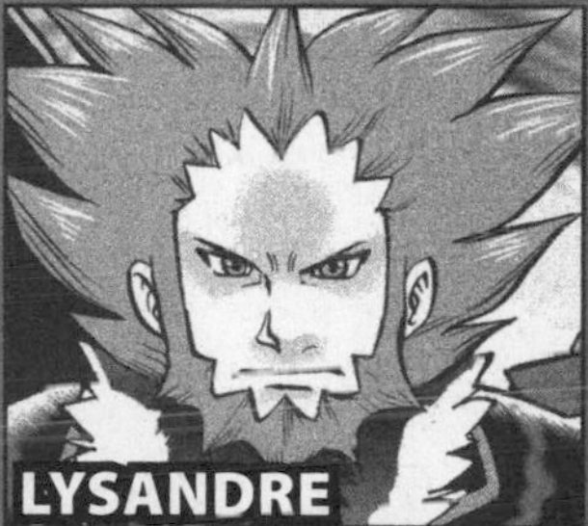

LYSANDRE
The developer of the Holo Caster. He has a reputation for charitable acts but is secretly the boss of Team Flare. He plans to destroy the world and rebuild it from scratch.

Loyalty
Trust
Support
Reports on his research

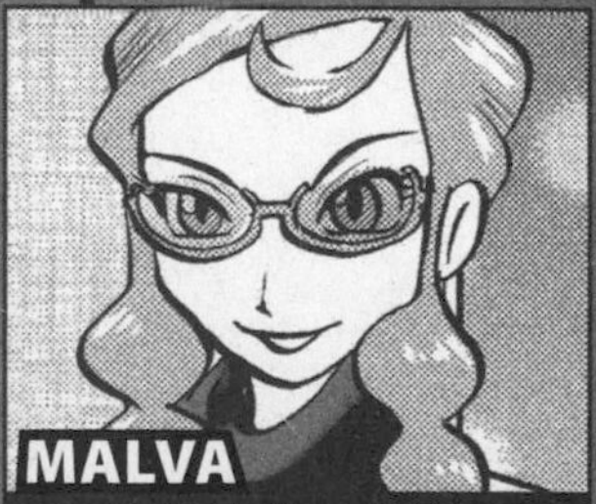

MALVA
A member of the Kalos Elite Four and also secretly a member of Team Flare. Often works as a news reporter and manipulates the media to the benefit of Team Flare.

Proposes plans, assists others

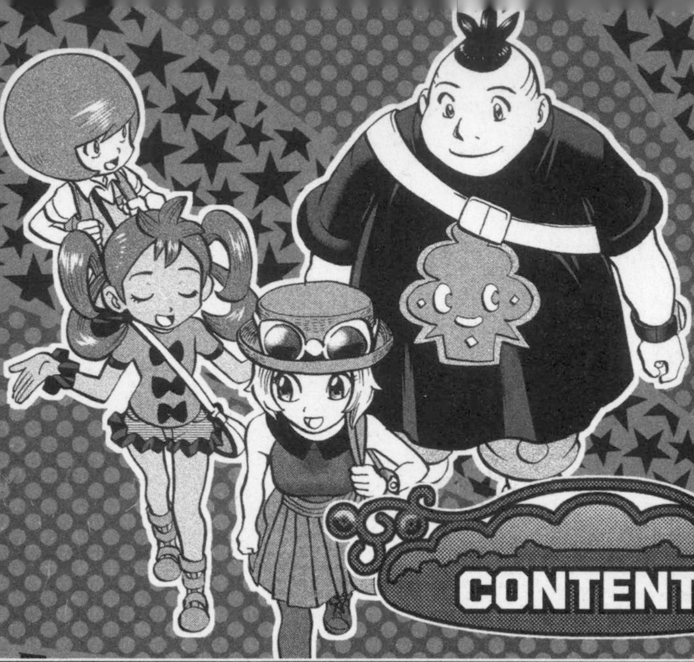

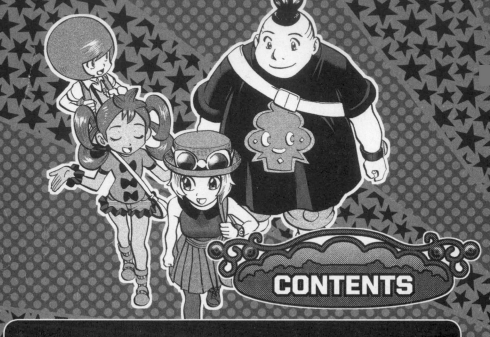

CONTENTS

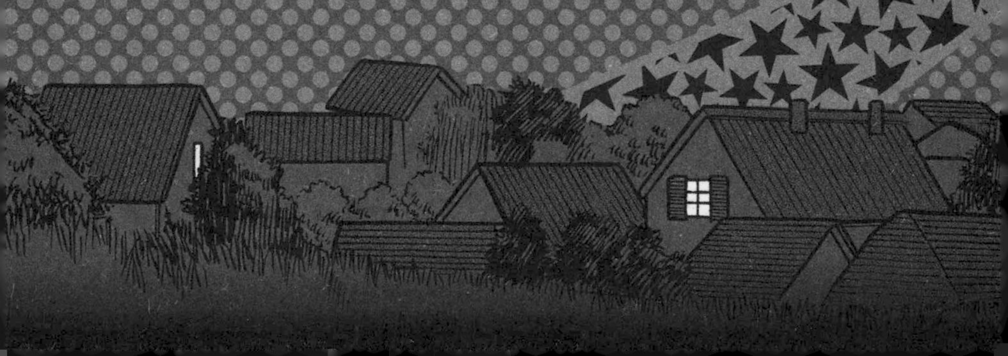

Adventure 37 Zygarde Agitated

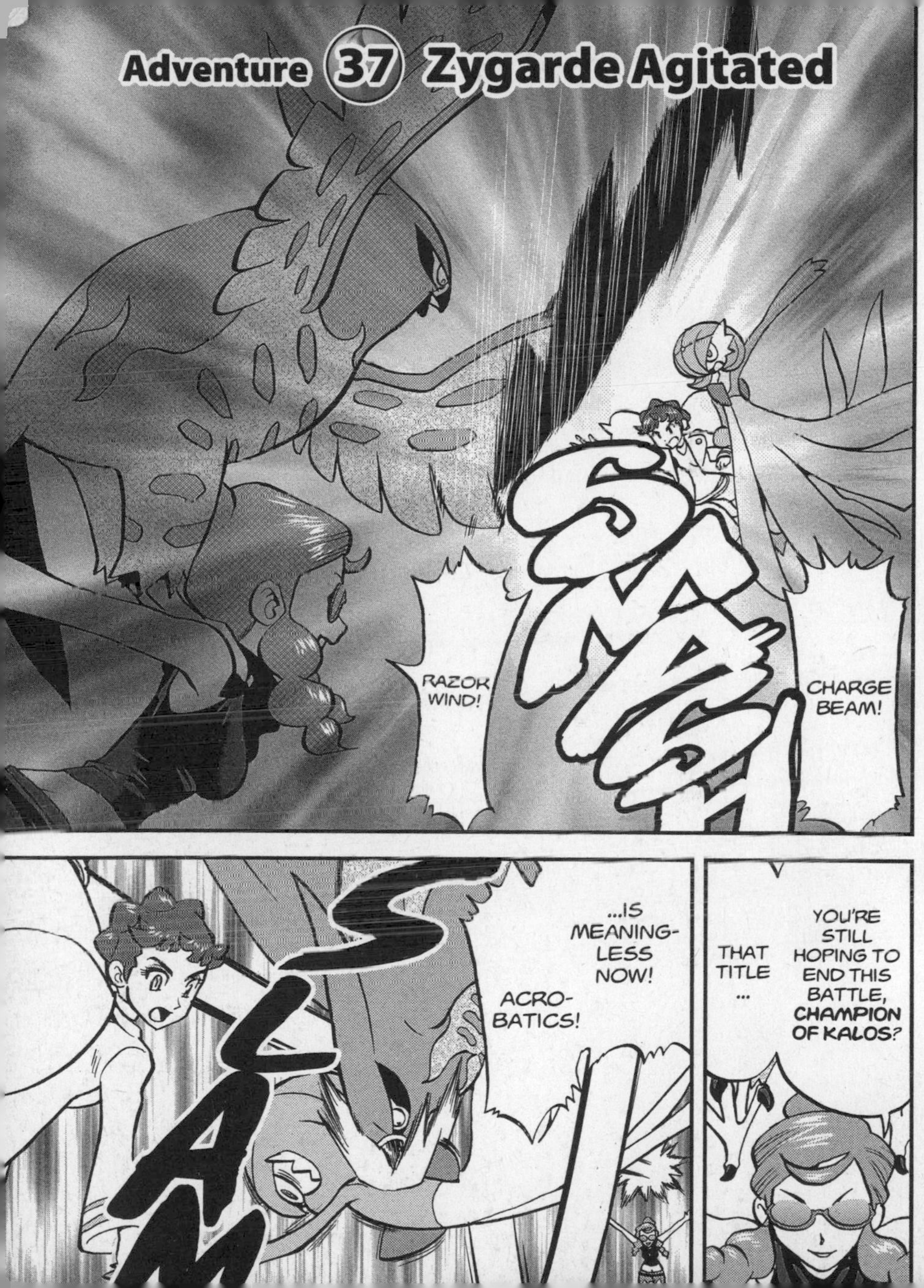
CHARGE BEAM!
SMASH
RAZOR WIND!
YOU'RE STILL HOPING TO END THIS BATTLE, **CHAMPION OF KALOS?**
THAT TITLE...
...IS MEANING-LESS NOW!
ACRO-BATICS!
SLAM

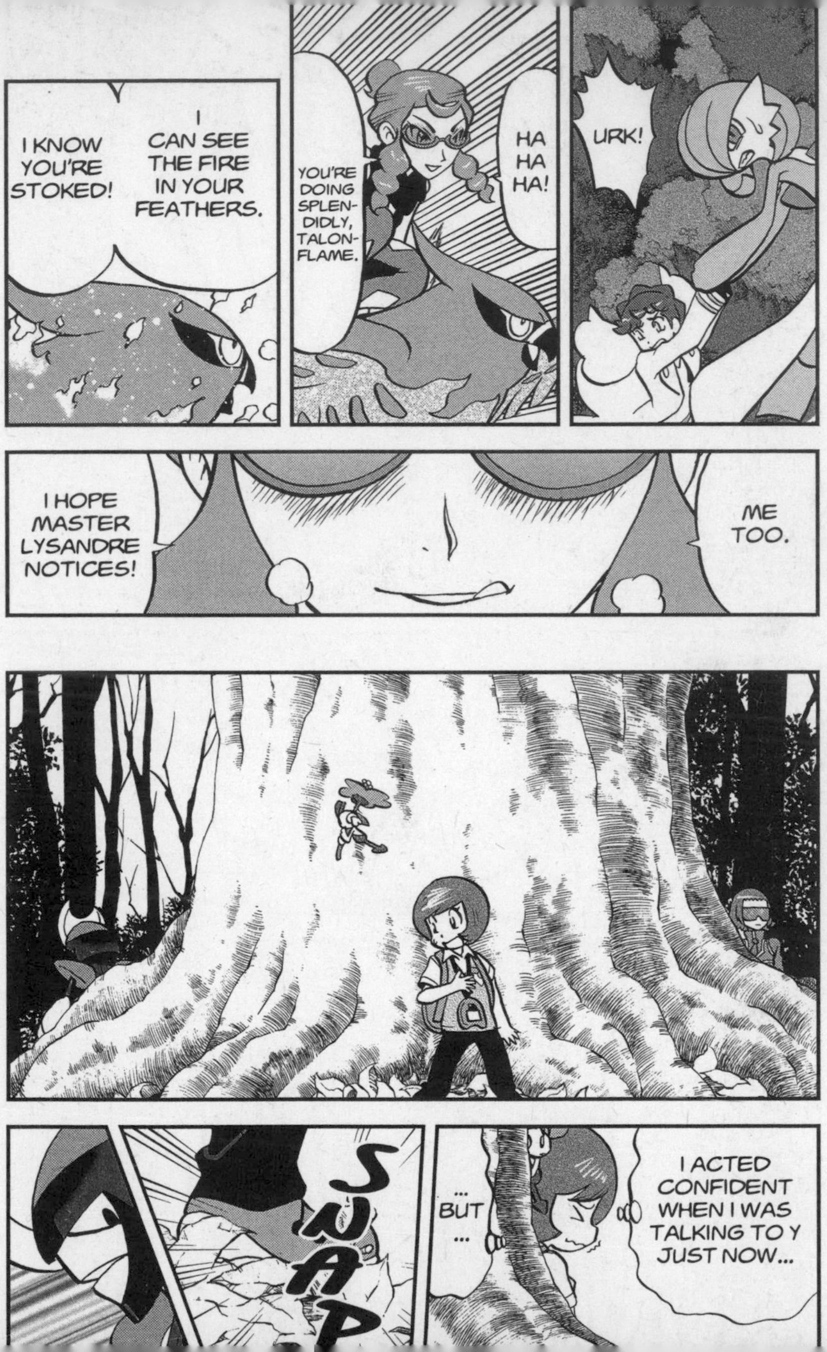
URK!
HA HA HA!
YOU'RE DOING SPLENDIDLY, TALONFLAME.
I CAN SEE THE FIRE IN YOUR FEATHERS.
I KNOW YOU'RE STOKED!
I HOPE MASTER LYSANDRE NOTICES!
ME TOO.
I ACTED CONFIDENT WHEN I WAS TALKING TO Y JUST NOW...
... BUT ...
SWAP

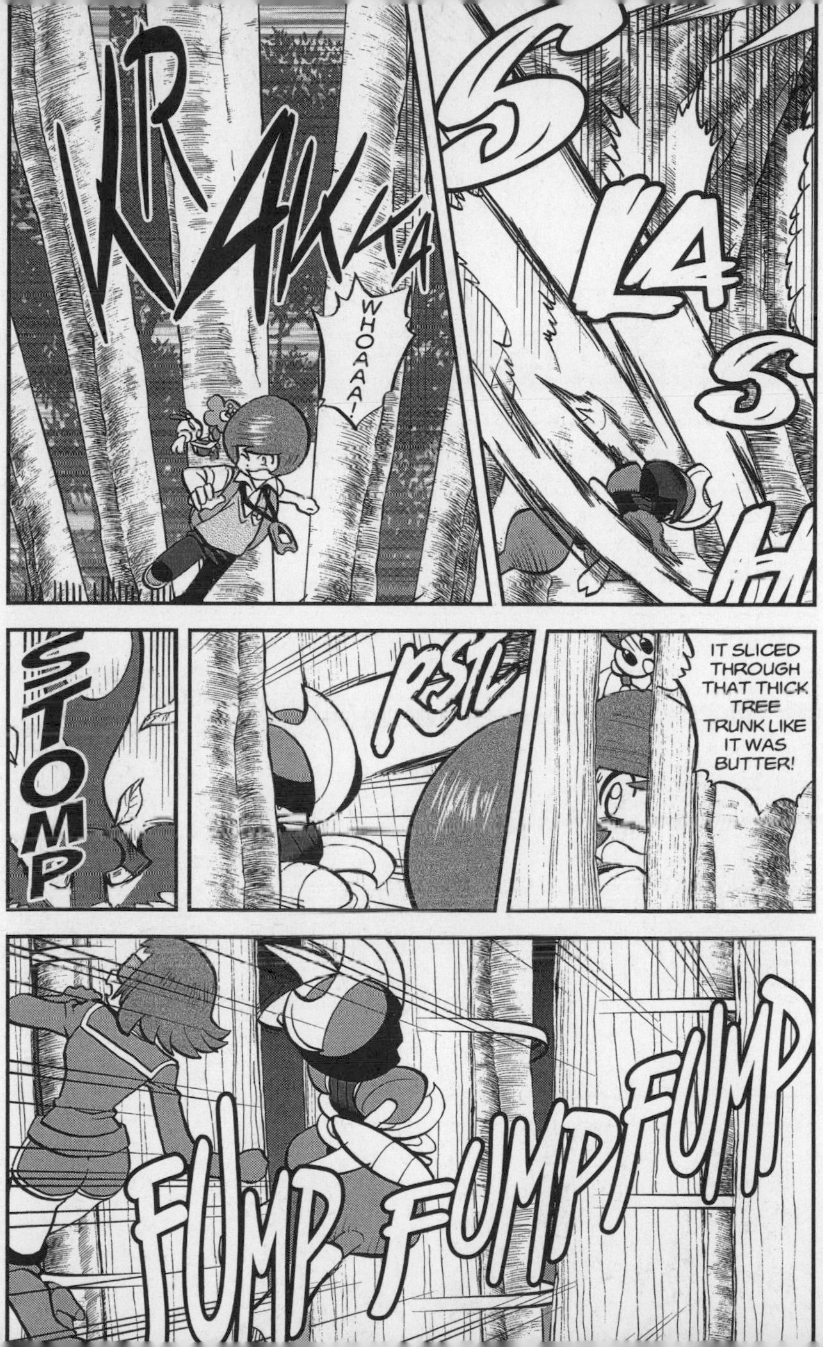
SLASH
WRAKKA
WHOAAAA!
IT SLICED THROUGH THAT THICK TREE TRUNK LIKE IT WAS BUTTER!
RSTL
STOMP
FUMP FUMP FUMP FUMP

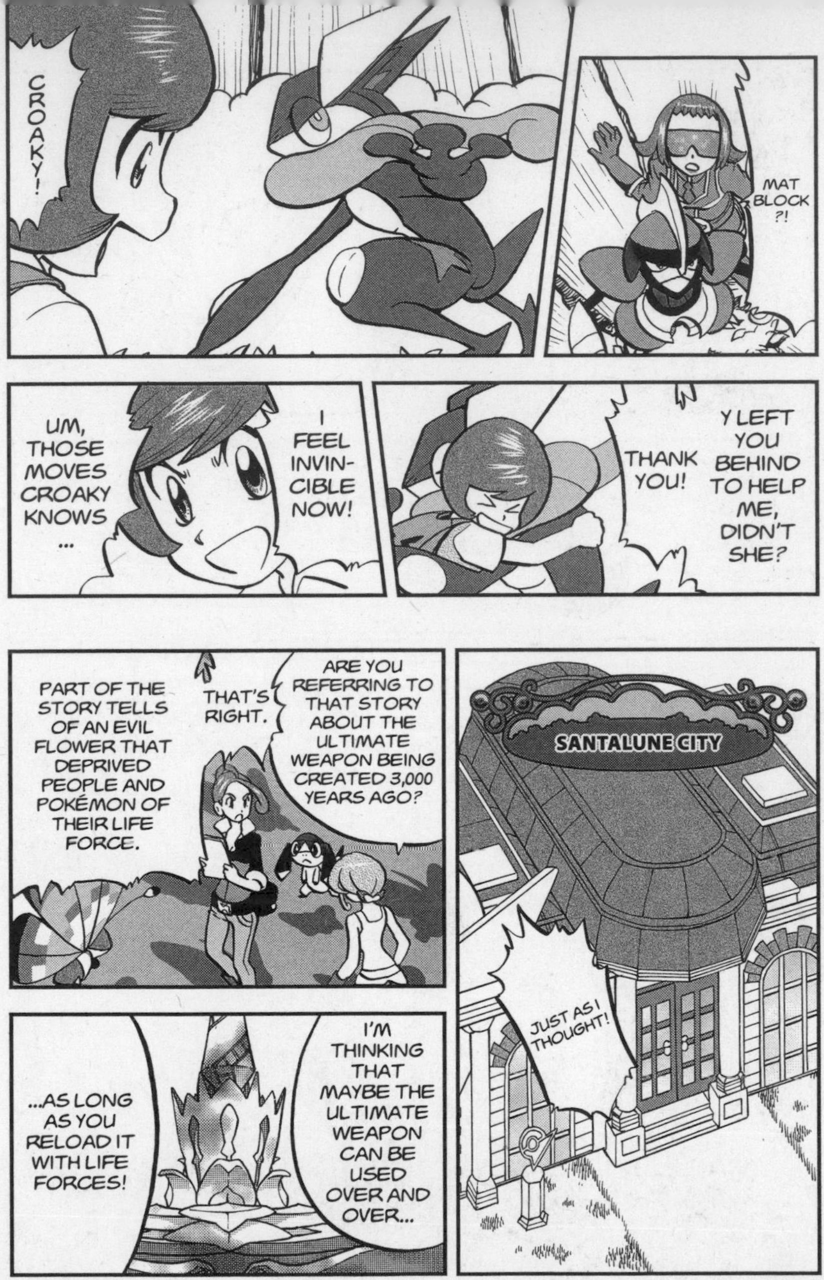
MAT BLOCK ?!
CROAKY!
Y LEFT YOU BEHIND TO HELP ME, DIDN'T SHE?
THANK YOU!
I FEEL INVIN-CIBLE NOW!
UM, THOSE MOVES CROAKY KNOWS ...
SANTALUNE CITY
JUST AS I THOUGHT!
ARE YOU REFERRING TO THAT STORY ABOUT THE ULTIMATE WEAPON BEING CREATED 3,000 YEARS AGO?
THAT'S RIGHT.
PART OF THE STORY TELLS OF AN EVIL FLOWER THAT DEPRIVED PEOPLE AND POKÉMON OF THEIR LIFE FORCE.
I'M THINKING THAT MAYBE THE ULTIMATE WEAPON CAN BE USED OVER AND OVER...
...AS LONG AS YOU RELOAD IT WITH LIFE FORCES!

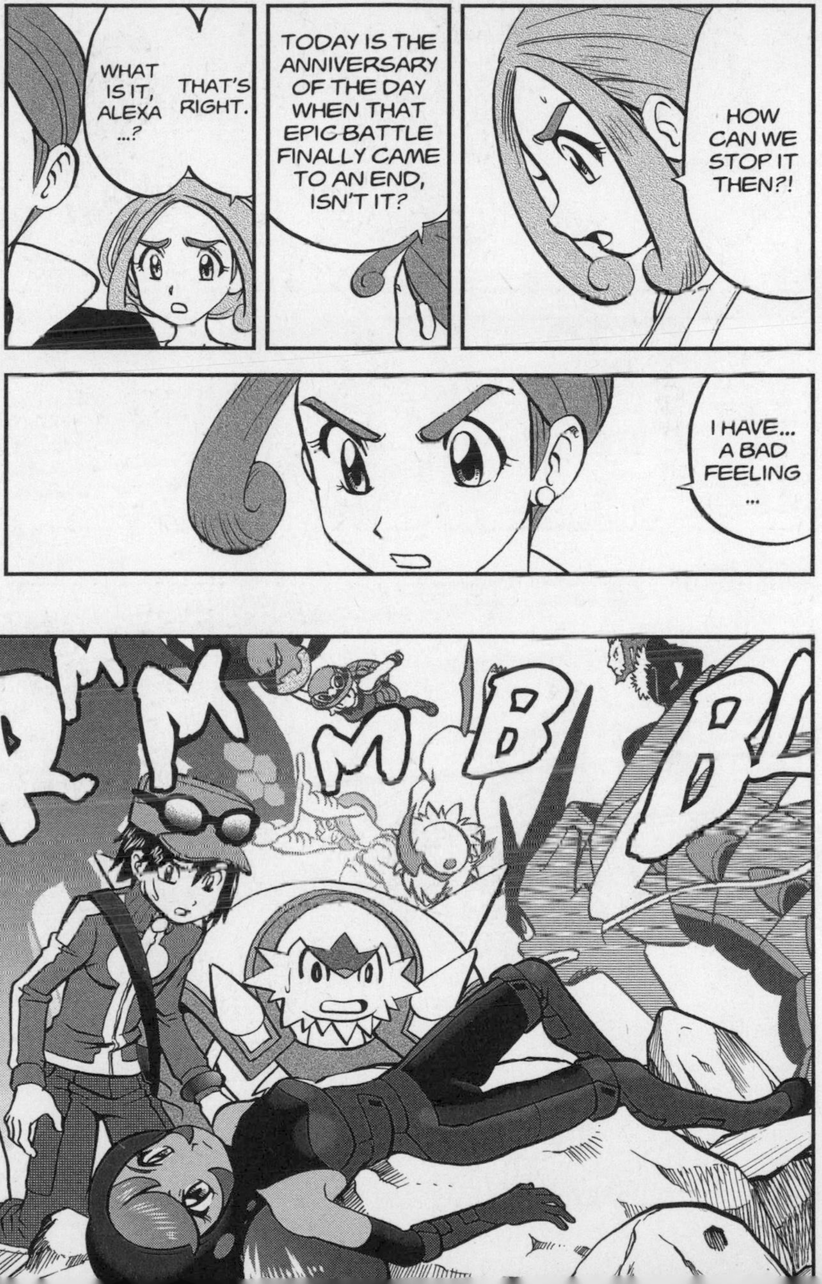
HOW CAN WE STOP IT THEN?!
TODAY IS THE ANNIVERSARY OF THE DAY WHEN THAT EPIC BATTLE FINALLY CAME TO AN END, ISN'T IT?
THAT'S RIGHT.
WHAT IS IT, ALEXA ...?
I HAVE... A BAD FEELING ...

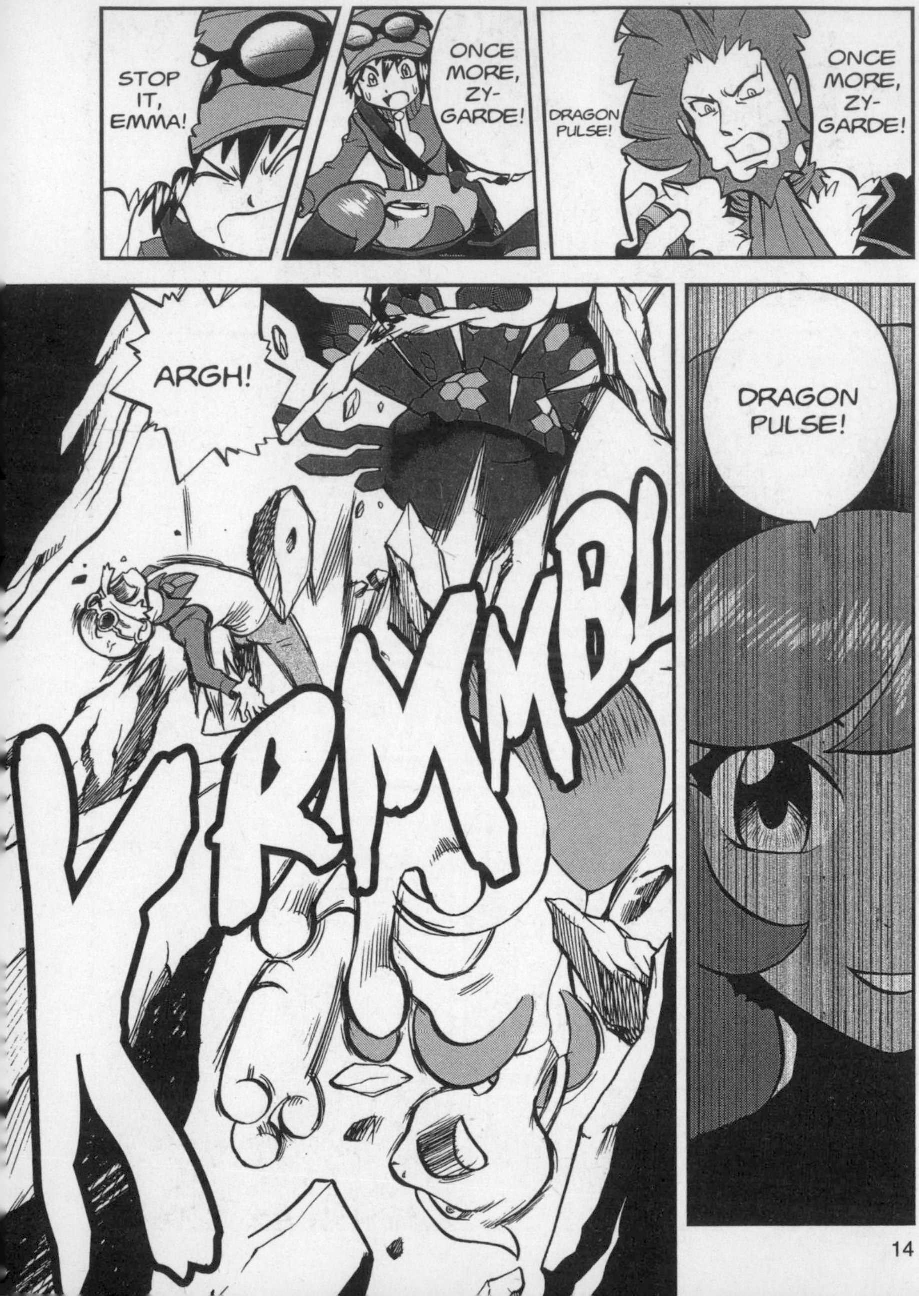
ONCE MORE, ZY-GARDE!
DRAGON PULSE!
ONCE MORE, ZY-GARDE!
STOP IT, EMMA!
DRAGON PULSE!
ARGH!
KRMMBL

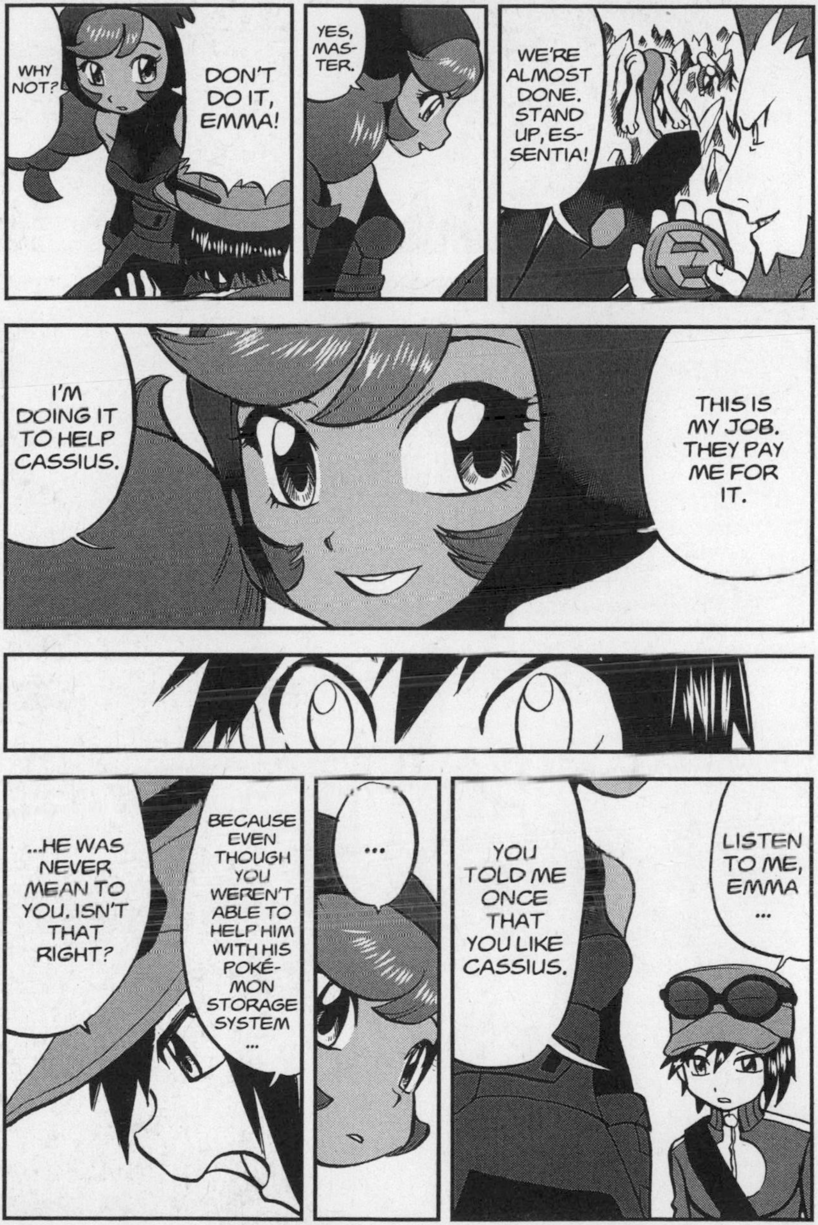
WE'RE ALMOST DONE. STAND UP, ES-SENTIA!
YES, MAS-TER.
DON'T DO IT, EMMA!
WHY NOT?
THIS IS MY JOB. THEY PAY ME FOR IT.
I'M DOING IT TO HELP CASSIUS.
LISTEN TO ME, EMMA ...
YOU TOLD ME ONCE THAT YOU LIKE CASSIUS.
...
BECAUSE EVEN THOUGH YOU WEREN'T ABLE TO HELP HIM WITH HIS POKÉ-MON STORAGE SYSTEM ...
...HE WAS NEVER MEAN TO YOU. ISN'T THAT RIGHT?

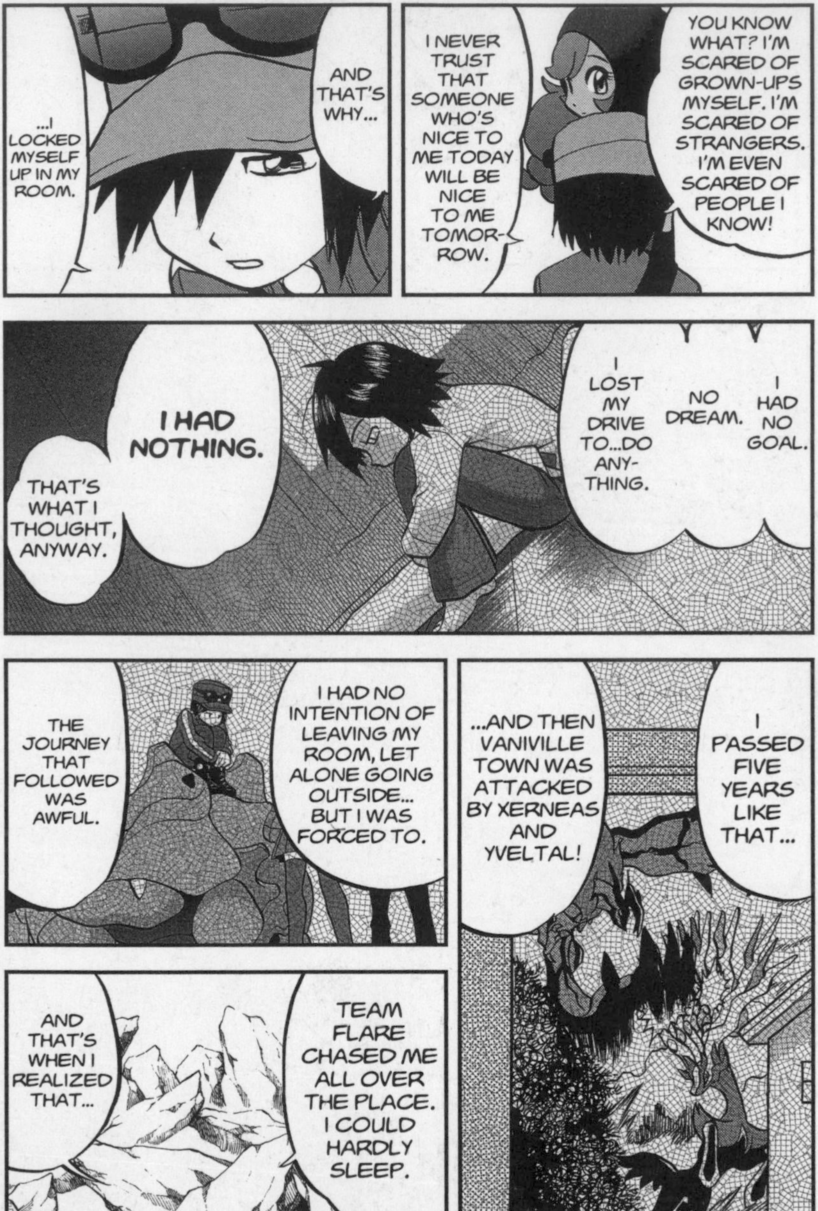
YOU KNOW WHAT? I'M SCARED OF GROWN-UPS MYSELF. I'M SCARED OF STRANGERS. I'M EVEN SCARED OF PEOPLE I KNOW!
I NEVER TRUST THAT SOMEONE WHO'S NICE TO ME TODAY WILL BE NICE TO ME TOMOR-ROW.
AND THAT'S WHY...
...I LOCKED MYSELF UP IN MY ROOM.
I HAD NO GOAL.
NO DREAM.
I LOST MY DRIVE TO...DO ANY-THING.
I HAD NOTHING.
THAT'S WHAT I THOUGHT, ANYWAY.
I PASSED FIVE YEARS LIKE THAT...
...AND THEN VANIVILLE TOWN WAS ATTACKED BY XERNEAS AND YVELTAL!
I HAD NO INTENTION OF LEAVING MY ROOM, LET ALONE GOING OUTSIDE... BUT I WAS FORCED TO.
THE JOURNEY THAT FOLLOWED WAS AWFUL.
TEAM FLARE CHASED ME ALL OVER THE PLACE. I COULD HARDLY SLEEP.
AND THAT'S WHEN I REALIZED THAT...

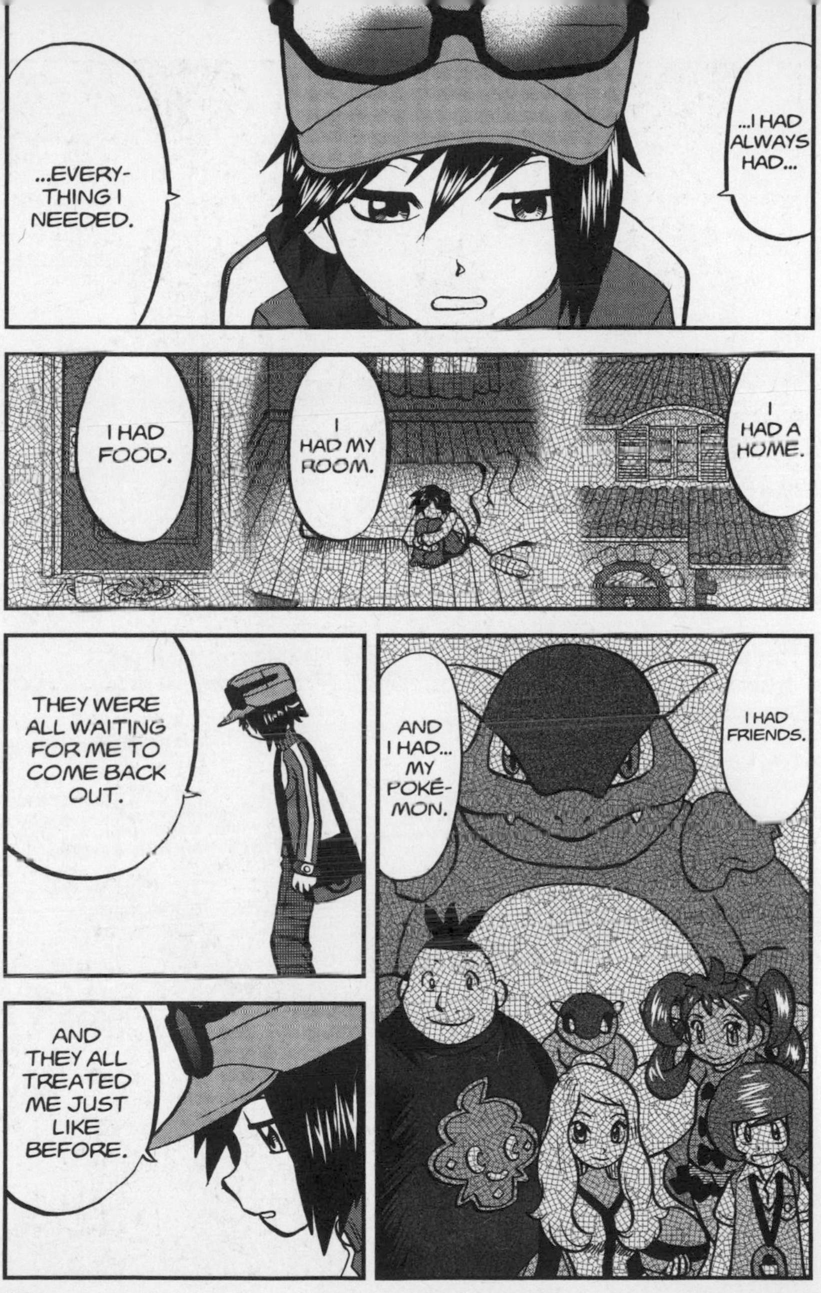
...I HAD ALWAYS HAD...
...EVERY-THING I NEEDED.
I HAD A HOME.
I HAD MY ROOM.
I HAD FOOD.
I HAD FRIENDS.
AND I HAD... MY POKÉ-MON.
THEY WERE ALL WAITING FOR ME TO COME BACK OUT.
AND THEY ALL TREATED ME JUST LIKE BEFORE.

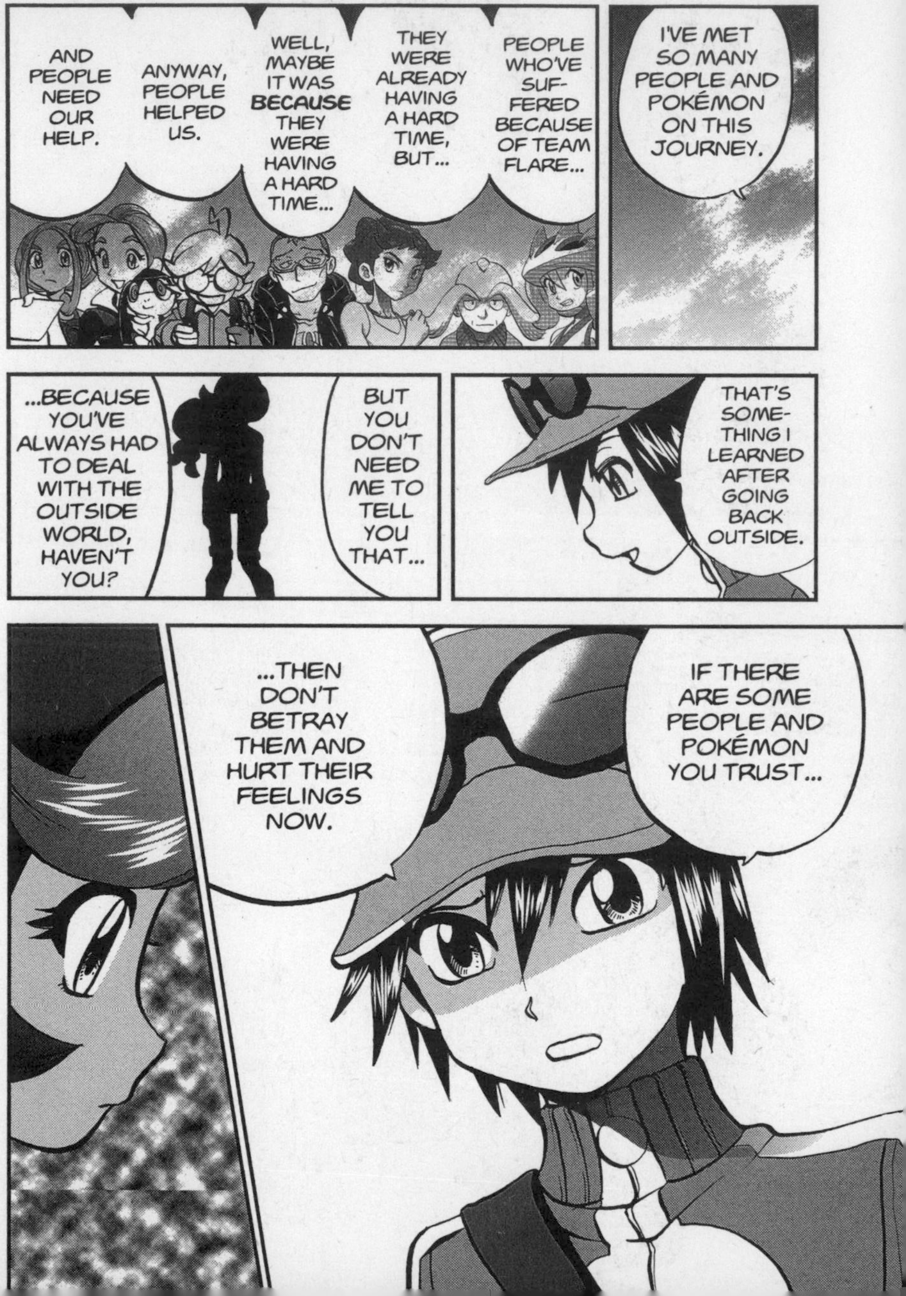
I'VE MET SO MANY PEOPLE AND POKÉMON ON THIS JOURNEY.
PEOPLE WHO'VE SUF-FERED BECAUSE OF TEAM FLARE...
THEY WERE ALREADY HAVING A HARD TIME, BUT...
WELL, MAYBE IT WAS **BECAUSE** THEY WERE HAVING A HARD TIME...
ANYWAY, PEOPLE HELPED US.
AND PEOPLE NEED OUR HELP.
THAT'S SOME-THING I LEARNED AFTER GOING BACK OUTSIDE.
BUT YOU DON'T NEED ME TO TELL YOU THAT...
...BECAUSE YOU'VE ALWAYS HAD TO DEAL WITH THE OUTSIDE WORLD, HAVEN'T YOU?
IF THERE ARE SOME PEOPLE AND POKÉMON YOU TRUST...
...THEN DON'T BETRAY THEM AND HURT THEIR FEELINGS NOW.

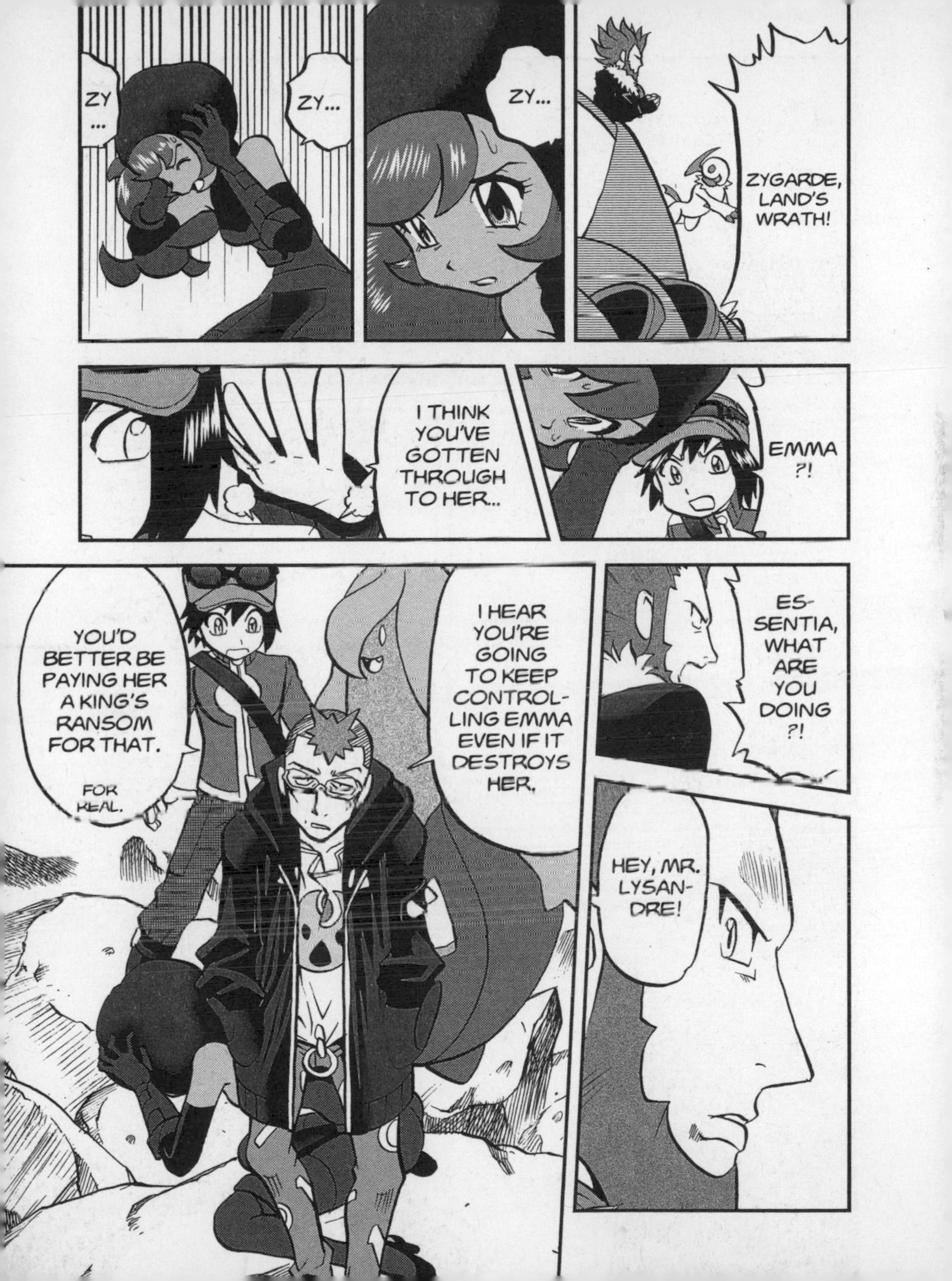
ZYGARDE, LAND'S WRATH!
ZY...
ZY...
ZY ...
EMMA ?!
I THINK YOU'VE GOTTEN THROUGH TO HER...
ES-SENTIA, WHAT ARE YOU DOING ?!
HEY, MR. LYSAN-DRE!
I HEAR YOU'RE GOING TO KEEP CONTROL-LING EMMA EVEN IF IT DESTROYS HER.
YOU'D BETTER BE PAYING HER A KING'S RANSOM FOR THAT.
FOR REAL.

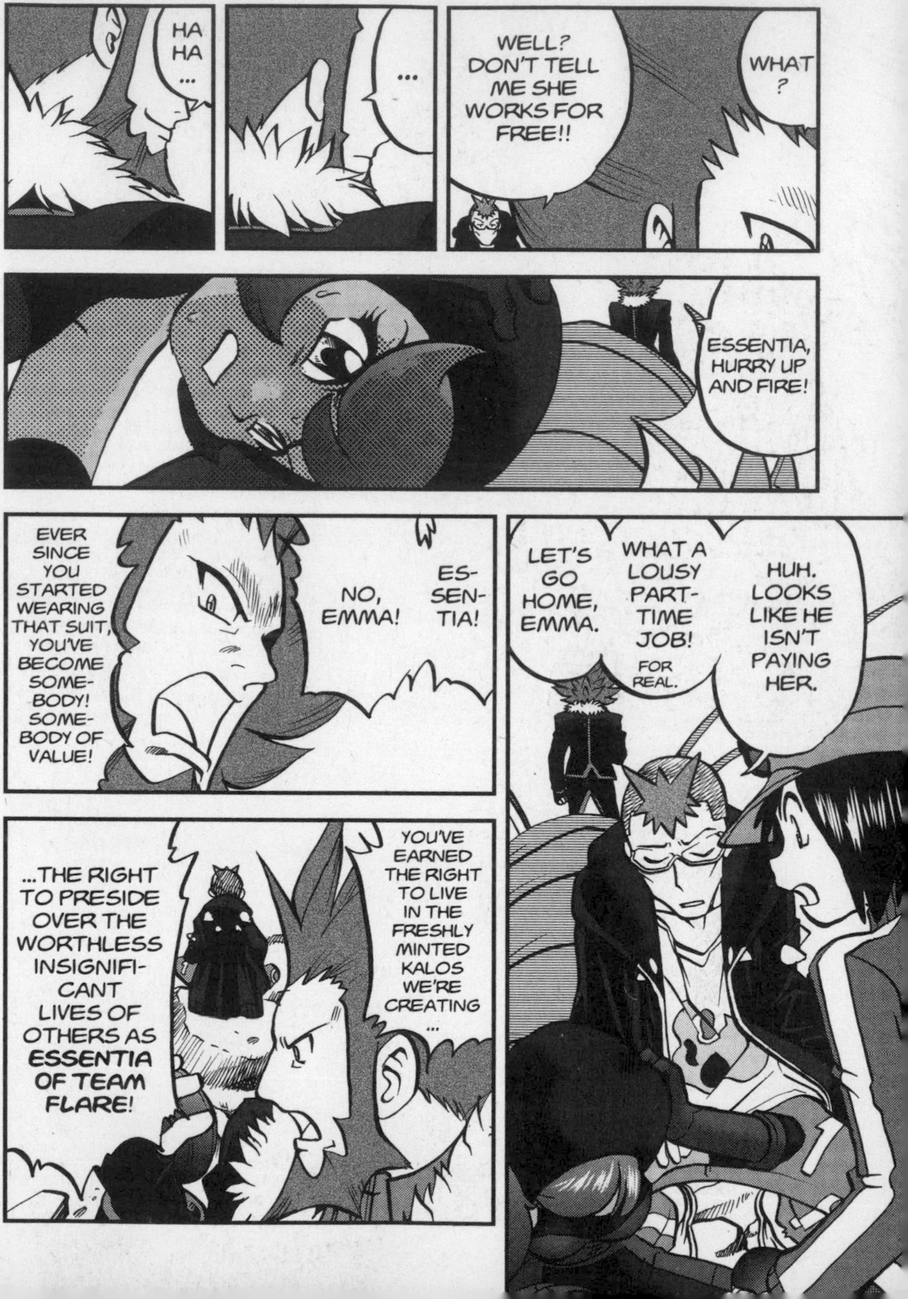
WHAT ?
WELL? DON'T TELL ME SHE WORKS FOR FREE!!
...
HA HA ...
ESSENTIA, HURRY UP AND FIRE!
HUH. LOOKS LIKE HE ISN'T PAYING HER.
WHAT A LOUSY PART-TIME JOB!
FOR REAL.
LET'S GO HOME, EMMA.
ES-SEN-TIA!
NO, EMMA!
EVER SINCE YOU STARTED WEARING THAT SUIT, YOU'VE BECOME SOME-BODY! SOME-BODY OF VALUE!
YOU'VE EARNED THE RIGHT TO LIVE IN THE FRESHLY MINTED KALOS WE'RE CREATING ...
...THE RIGHT TO PRESIDE OVER THE WORTHLESS INSIGNIFI-CANT LIVES OF OTHERS AS **ESSENTIA OF TEAM FLARE**!

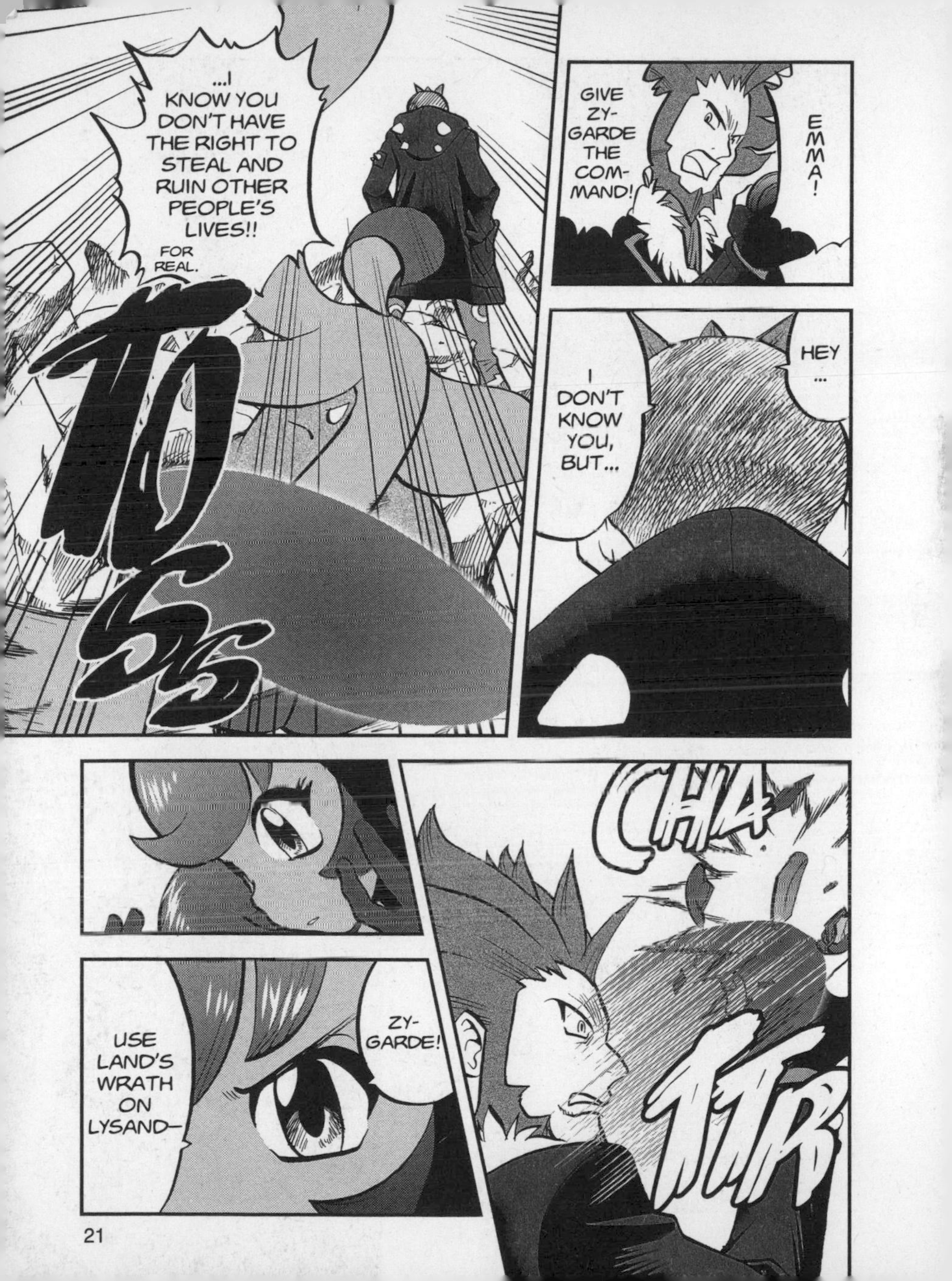
EMMA!
GIVE ZYGARDE THE COMMAND!
HEY...
I DON'T KNOW YOU, BUT...
...I KNOW YOU DON'T HAVE THE RIGHT TO STEAL AND RUIN OTHER PEOPLE'S LIVES!!
FOR REAL.
CHA
ZYGARDE!
USE LAND'S WRATH ON LYSAND—

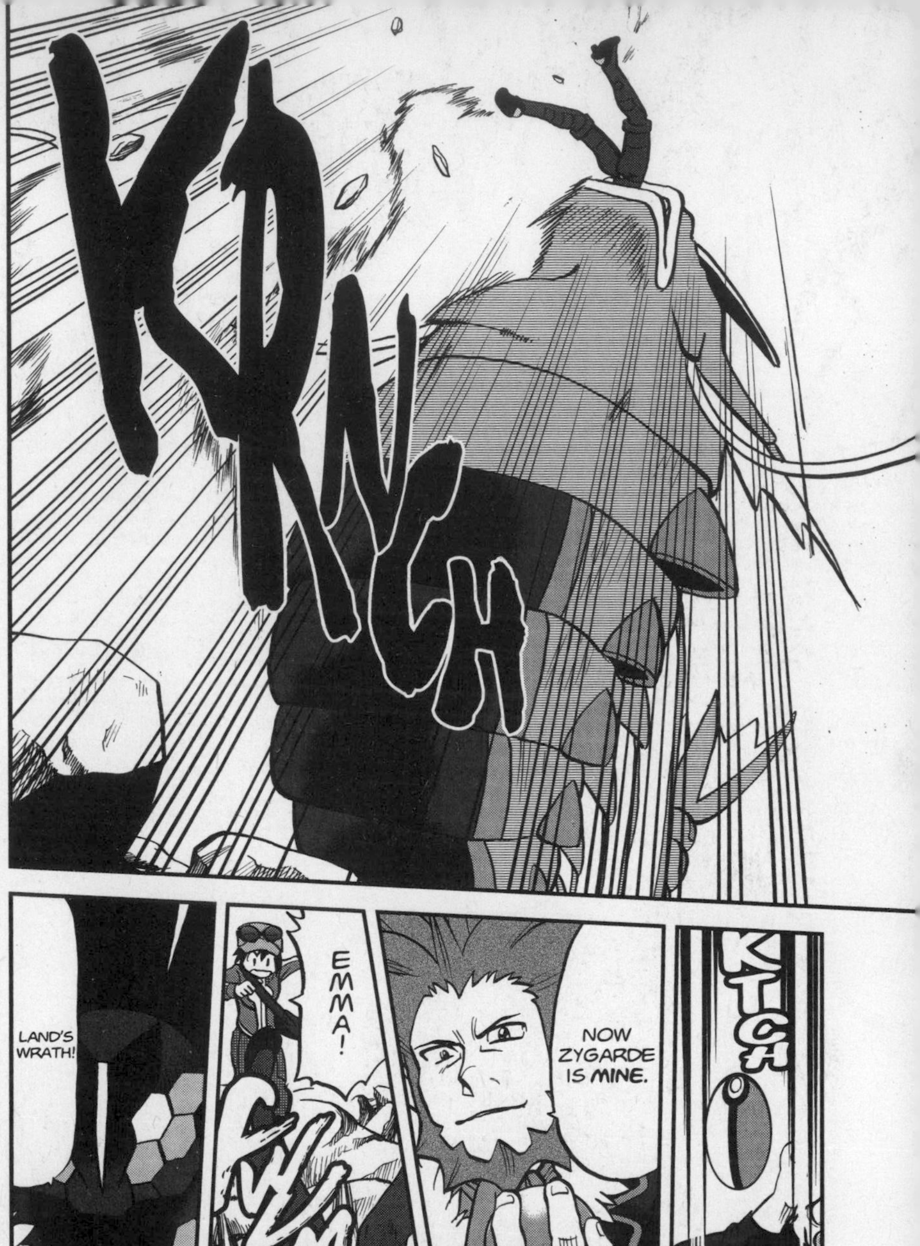
KRNCH
KTCH
NOW ZYGARDE IS MINE.
EMMA!
LAND'S WRATH!

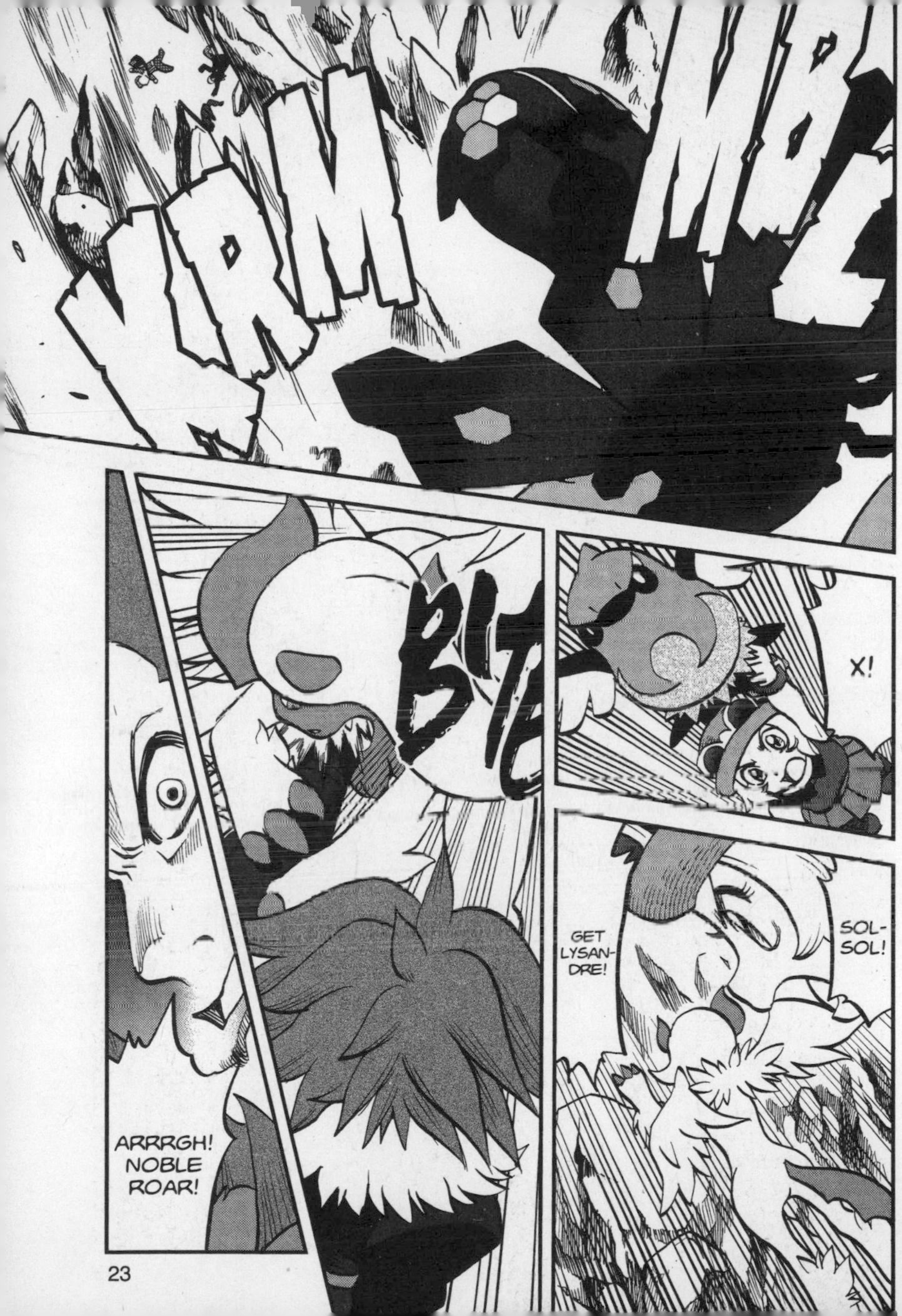
X!
SOL-SOL!
GET LYSANDRE!
ARRRGH! NOBLE ROAR!

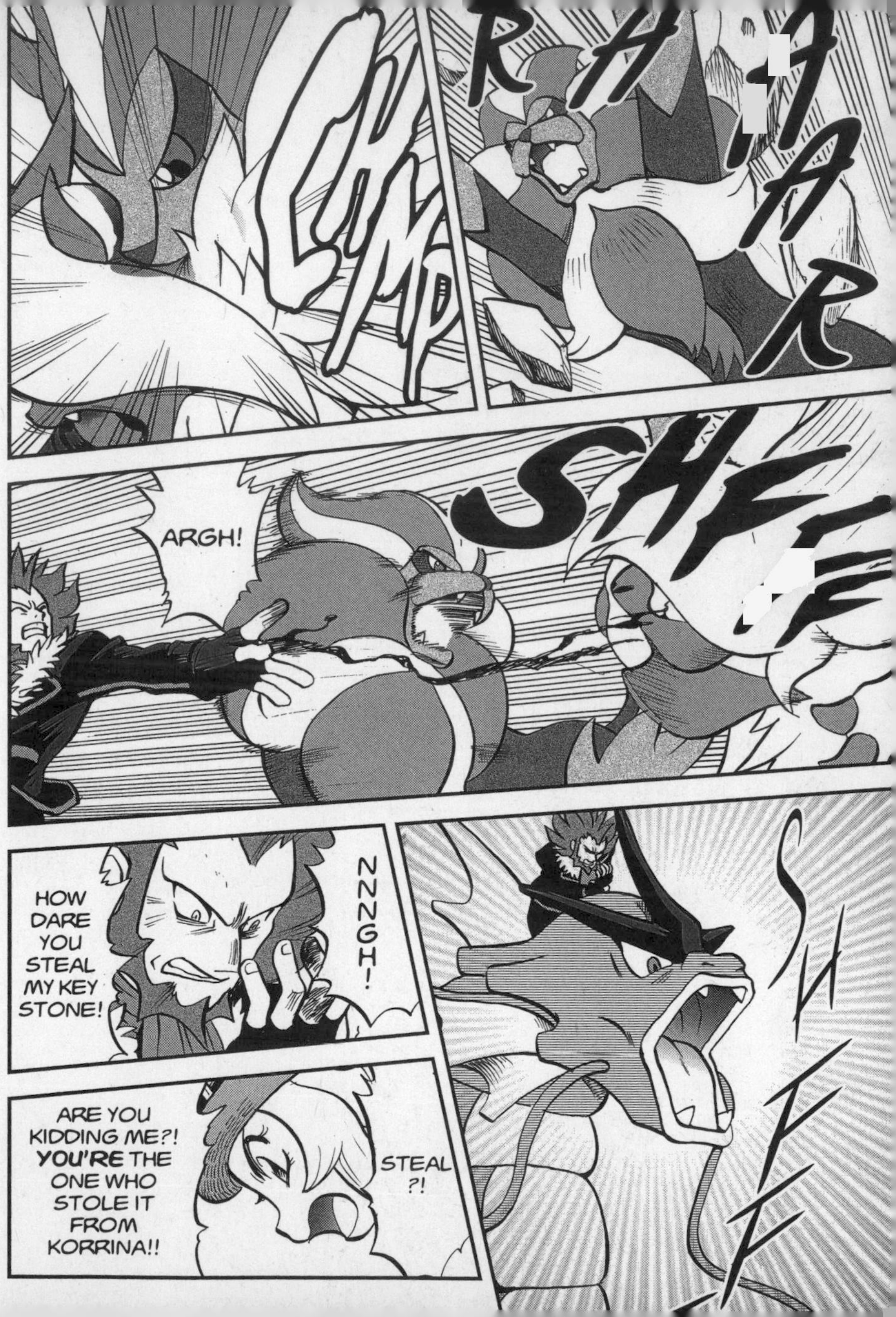
RHAAR
CHOMP
SHFF
ARGH!
SHFF
NNNGH!
HOW DARE YOU STEAL MY KEY STONE!
STEAL ?!
ARE YOU KIDDING ME?! **YOU'RE** THE ONE WHO STOLE IT FROM KORRINA!!

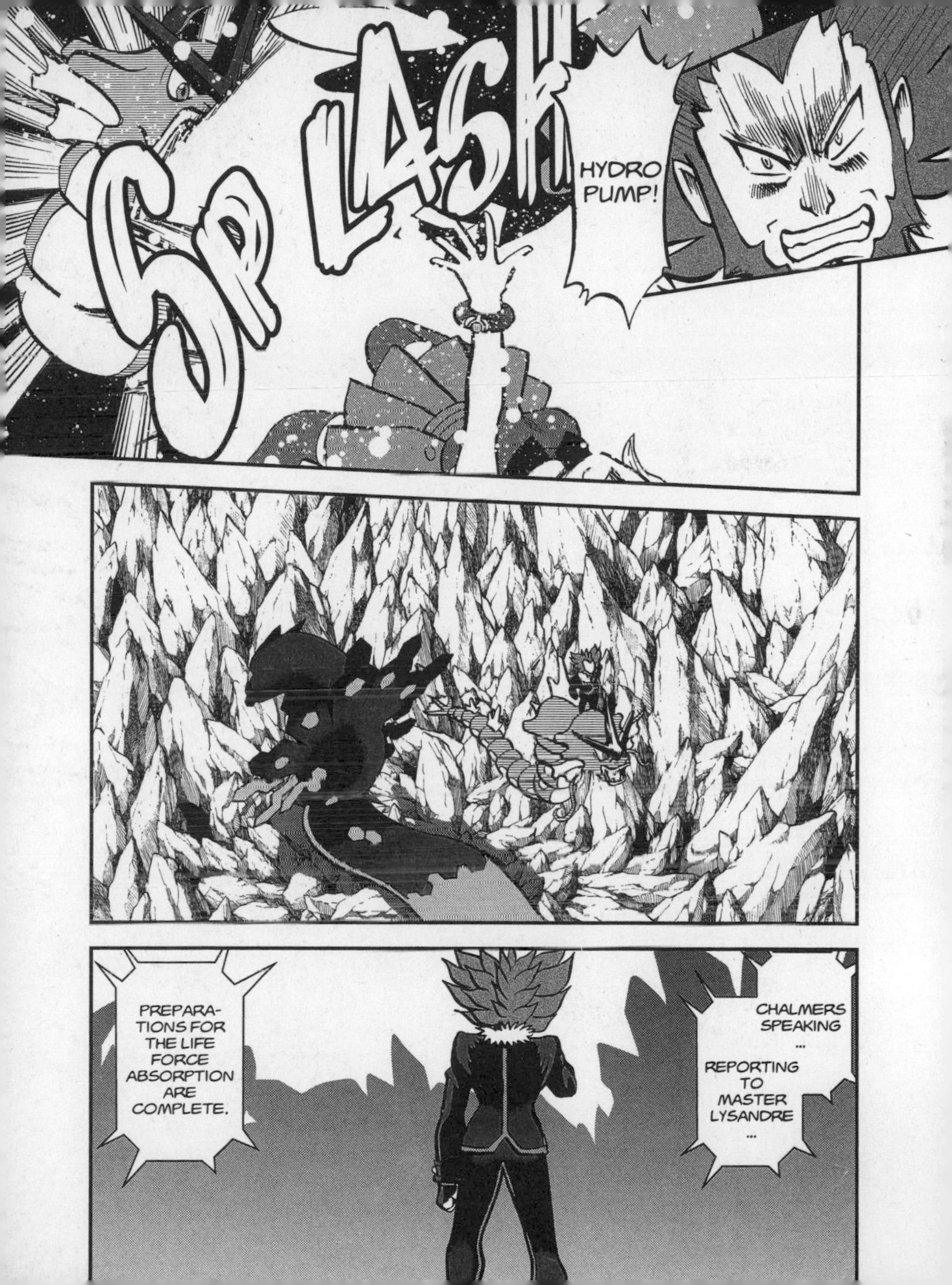
HYDRO PUMP!
SPLASH
CHALMERS SPEAKING ... REPORTING TO MASTER LYSANDRE ...
PREPARATIONS FOR THE LIFE FORCE ABSORPTION ARE COMPLETE.

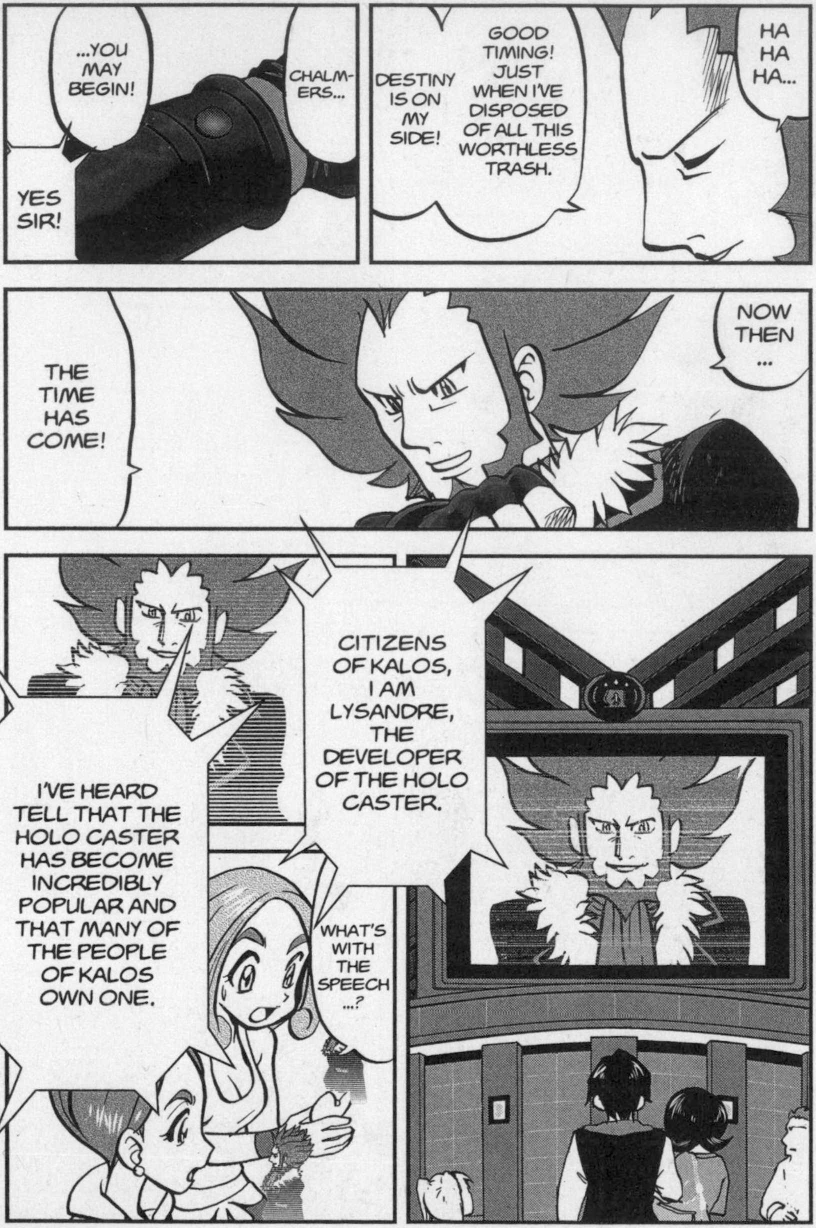
HA HA HA...
GOOD TIMING! JUST WHEN I'VE DISPOSED OF ALL THIS WORTHLESS TRASH.
DESTINY IS ON MY SIDE!
CHALM-ERS...
...YOU MAY BEGIN!
YES SIR!
NOW THEN ...
THE TIME HAS COME!
CITIZENS OF KALOS, I AM LYSANDRE, THE DEVELOPER OF THE HOLO CASTER.
I'VE HEARD TELL THAT THE HOLO CASTER HAS BECOME INCREDIBLY POPULAR AND THAT MANY OF THE PEOPLE OF KALOS OWN ONE.
WHAT'S WITH THE SPEECH ...?

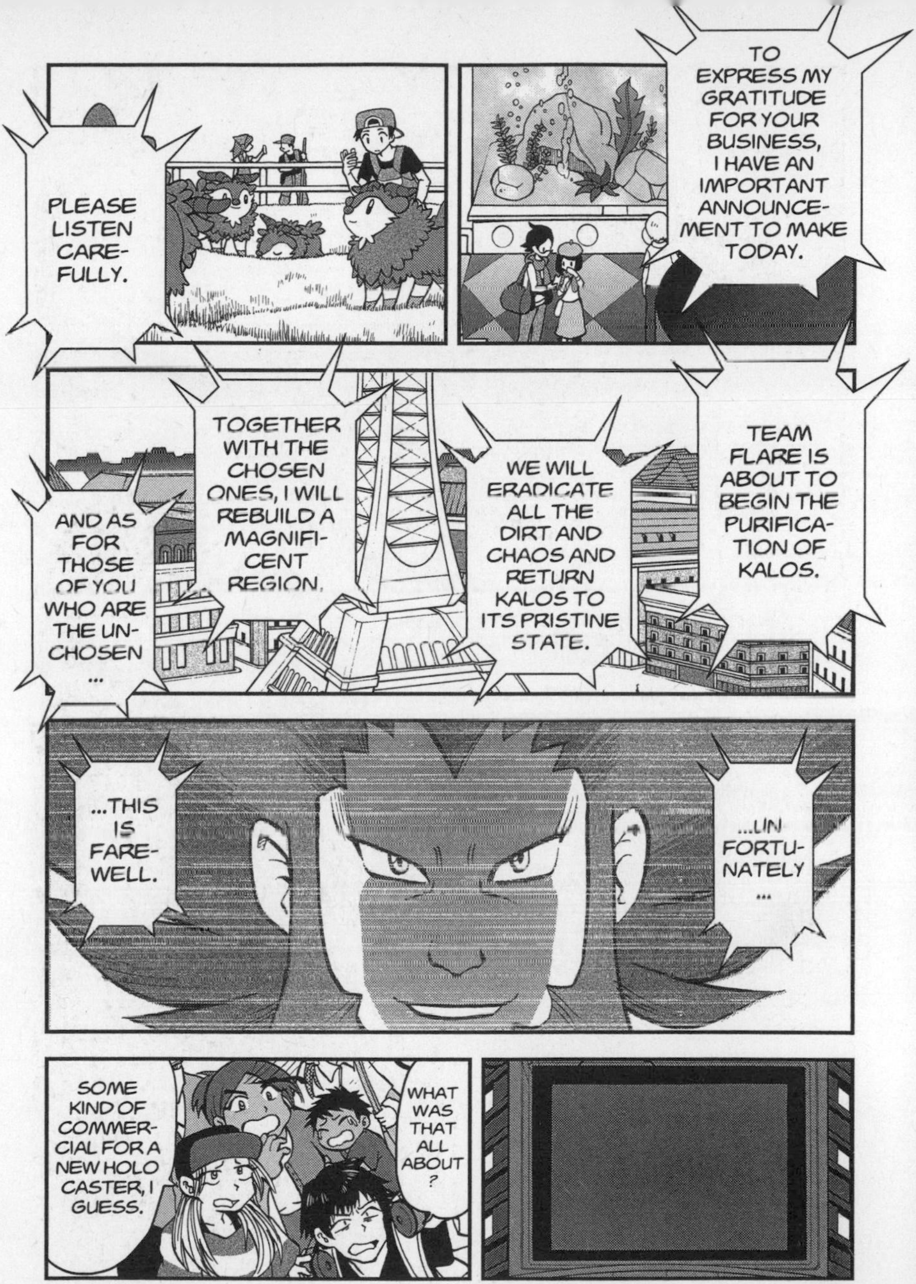
TO EXPRESS MY GRATITUDE FOR YOUR BUSINESS, I HAVE AN IMPORTANT ANNOUNCEMENT TO MAKE TODAY.
PLEASE LISTEN CAREFULLY.
TEAM FLARE IS ABOUT TO BEGIN THE PURIFICATION OF KALOS.
WE WILL ERADICATE ALL THE DIRT AND CHAOS AND RETURN KALOS TO ITS PRISTINE STATE.
TOGETHER WITH THE CHOSEN ONES, I WILL REBUILD A MAGNIFICENT REGION.
AND AS FOR THOSE OF YOU WHO ARE THE UNCHOSEN ...
...UNFORTUNATELY ...
...THIS IS FAREWELL.
WHAT WAS THAT ALL ABOUT?
SOME KIND OF COMMERCIAL FOR A NEW HOLO CASTER, I GUESS.

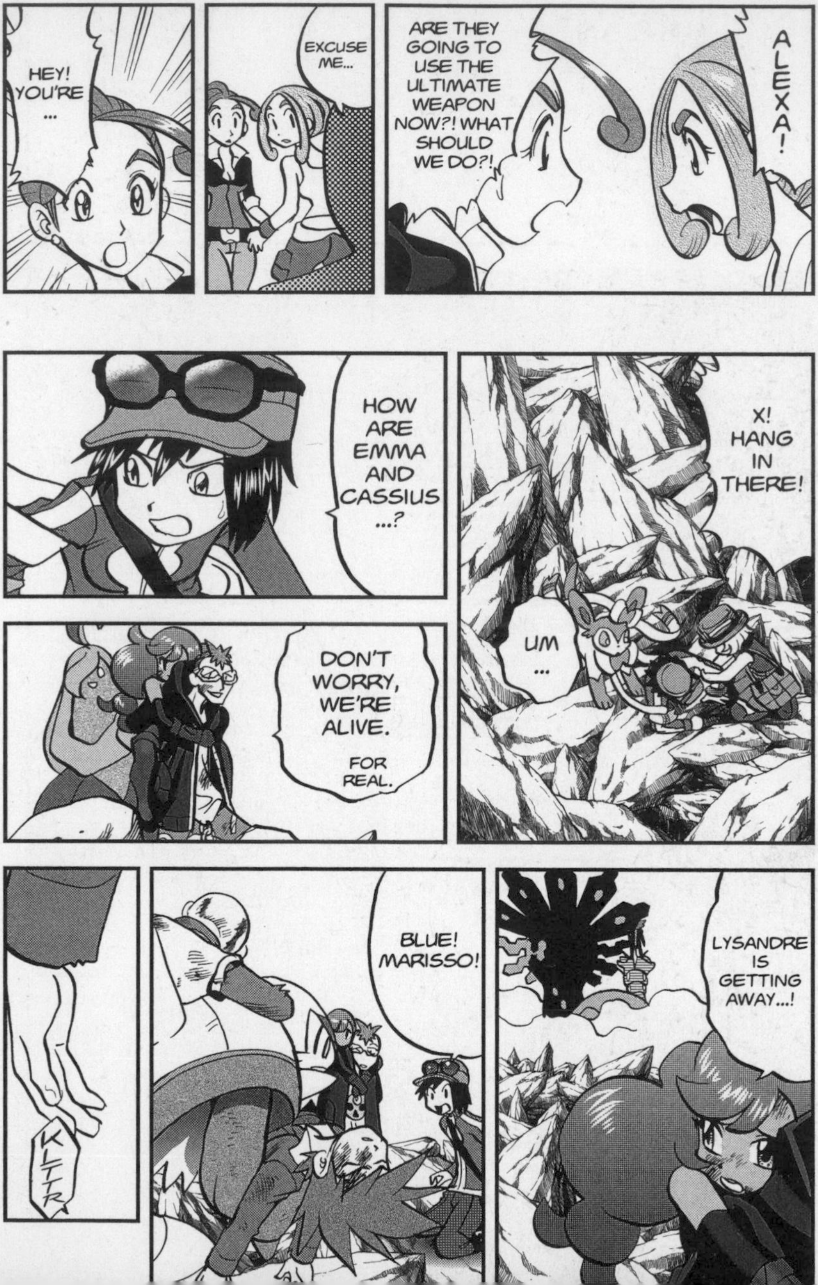
ALEXA!
ARE THEY GOING TO USE THE ULTIMATE WEAPON NOW?! WHAT SHOULD WE DO?!
EXCUSE ME...
HEY! YOU'RE ...
X! HANG IN THERE!
UM ...
HOW ARE EMMA AND CASSIUS ...?
DON'T WORRY, WE'RE ALIVE.
FOR REAL.
LYSANDRE IS GETTING AWAY...!
BLUE! MARISSO!
KLTTR

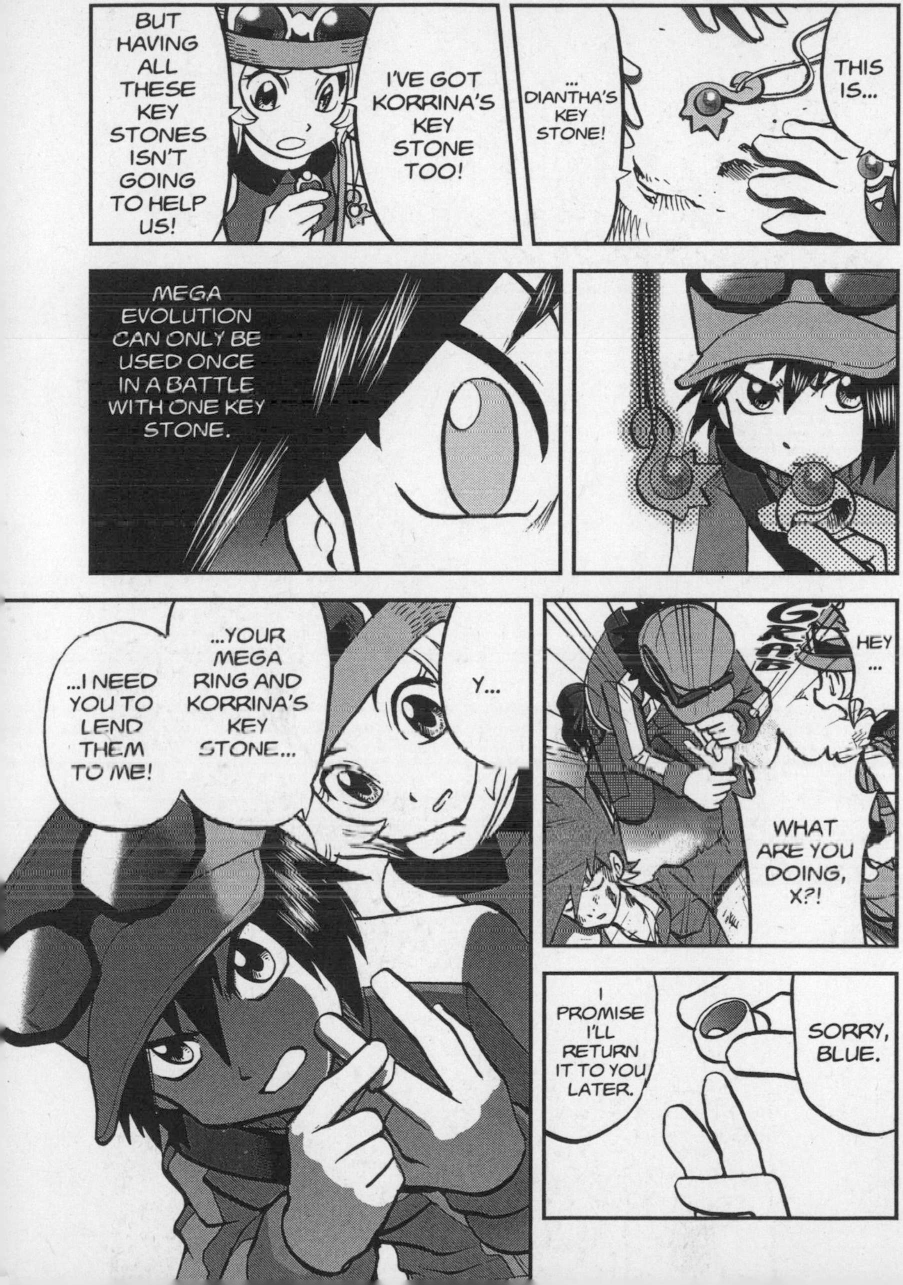
THIS IS...
...DIANTHA'S KEY STONE!
I'VE GOT KORRINA'S KEY STONE TOO!
BUT HAVING ALL THESE KEY STONES ISN'T GOING TO HELP US!
MEGA EVOLUTION CAN ONLY BE USED ONCE IN A BATTLE WITH ONE KEY STONE.
GRAB
HEY...
WHAT ARE YOU DOING, X?!
SORRY, BLUE.
I PROMISE I'LL RETURN IT TO YOU LATER.
Y...
...YOUR MEGA RING AND KORRINA'S KEY STONE...
...I NEED YOU TO LEND THEM TO ME!

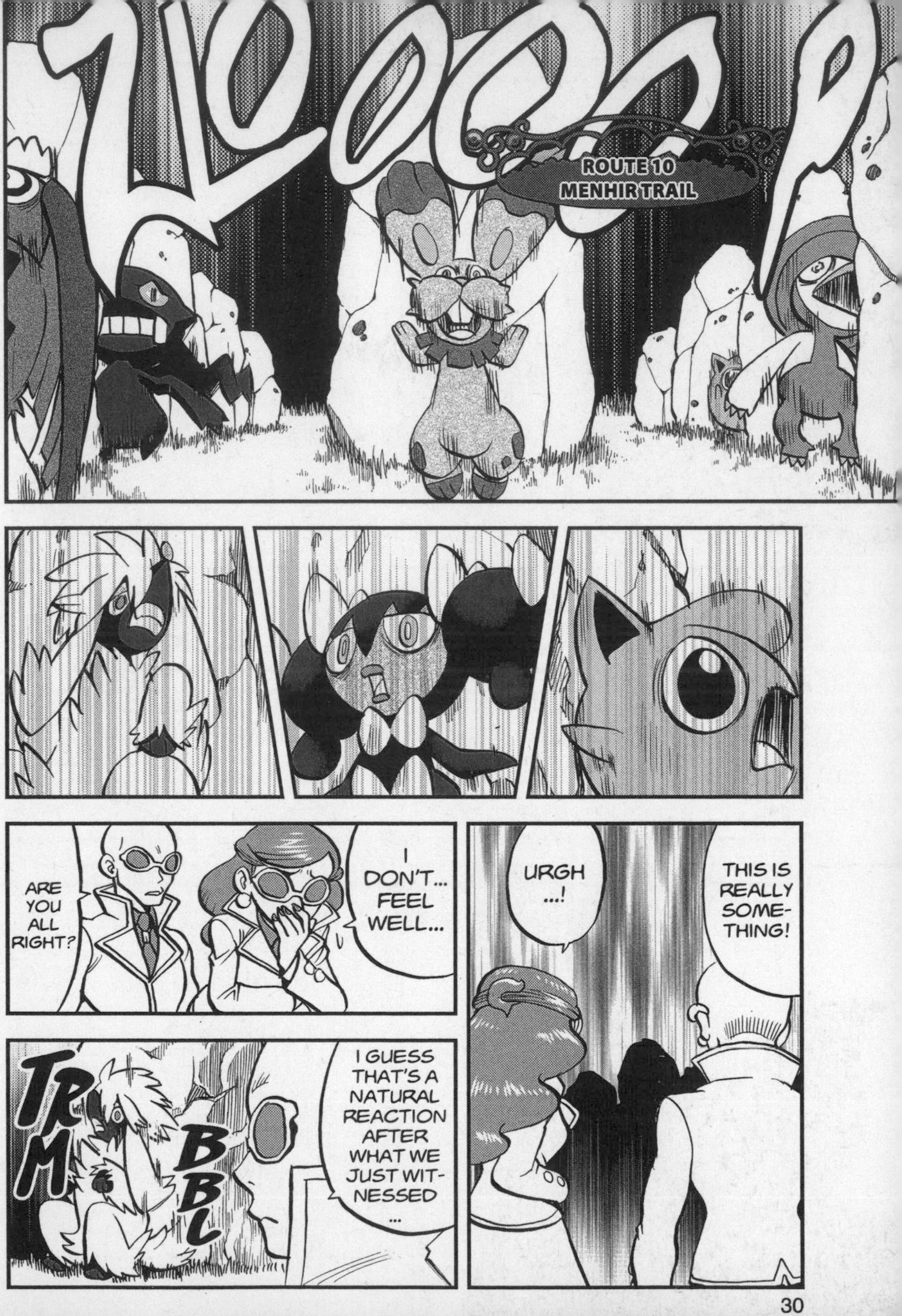
ROUTE 10
MENHIR TRAIL
THIS IS REALLY SOMETHING!
URGH...!
I DON'T... FEEL WELL...
ARE YOU ALL RIGHT?
I GUESS THAT'S A NATURAL REACTION AFTER WHAT WE JUST WITNESSED...
TRMBBL

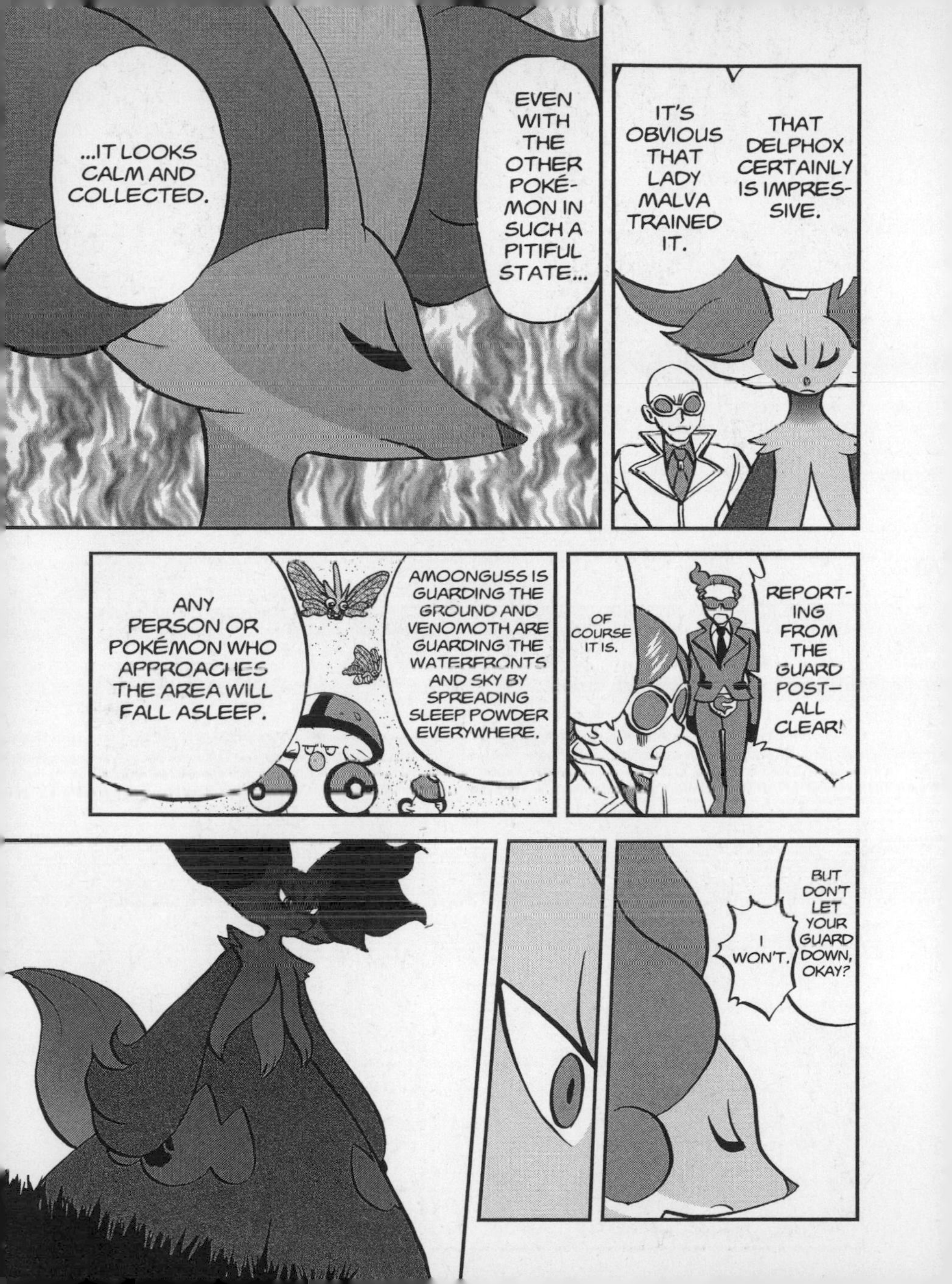
THAT DELPHOX CERTAINLY IS IMPRESSIVE.
IT'S OBVIOUS THAT LADY MALVA TRAINED IT.
EVEN WITH THE OTHER POKÉMON IN SUCH A PITIFUL STATE...
...IT LOOKS CALM AND COLLECTED.
REPORTING FROM THE GUARD POST—ALL CLEAR!
OF COURSE IT IS.
AMOONGUSS IS GUARDING THE GROUND AND VENOMOTH ARE GUARDING THE WATERFRONTS AND SKY BY SPREADING SLEEP POWDER EVERYWHERE.
ANY PERSON OR POKÉMON WHO APPROACHES THE AREA WILL FALL ASLEEP.
BUT DON'T LET YOUR GUARD DOWN, OKAY?
I WON'T.

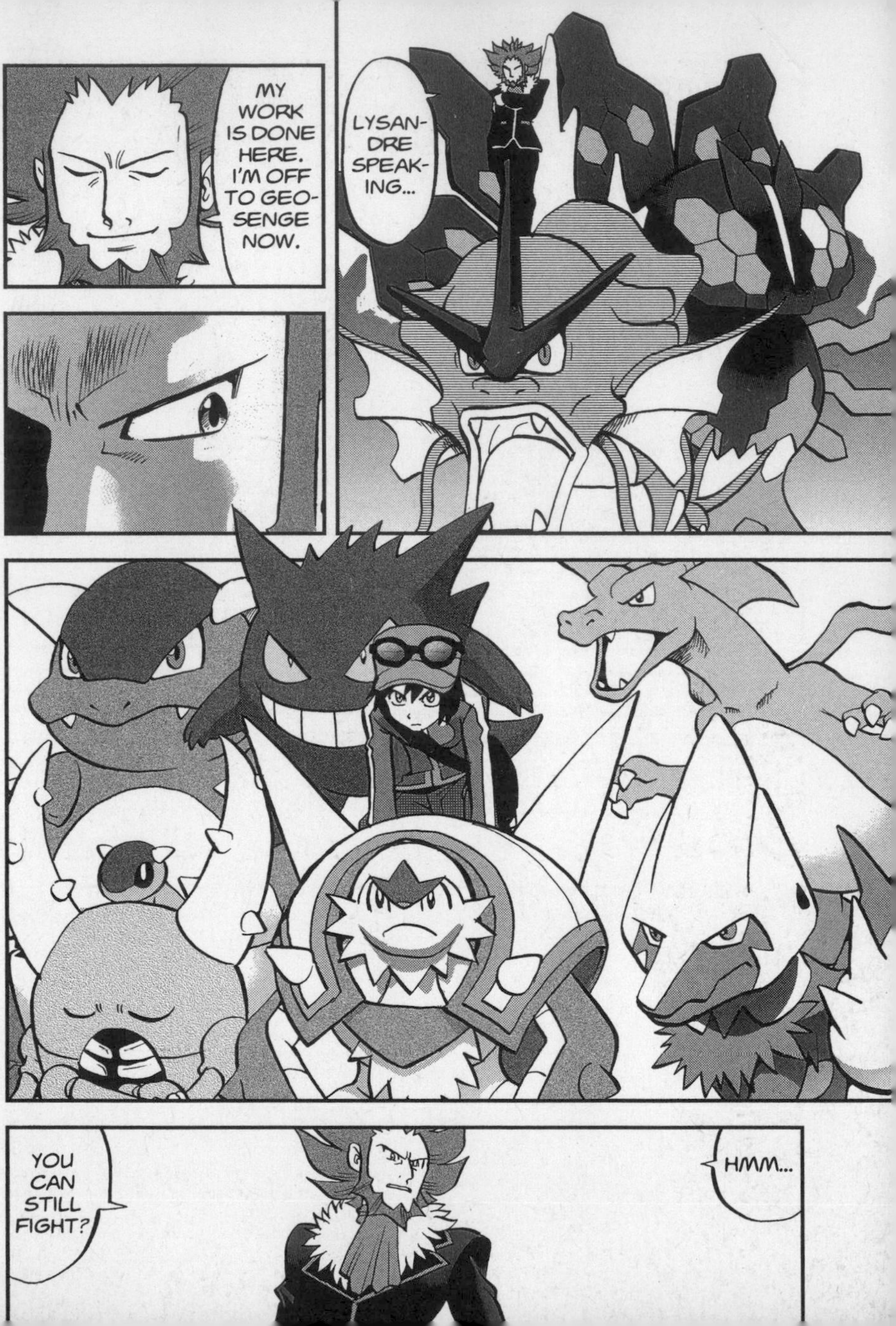
LYSANDRE SPEAKING...
MY WORK IS DONE HERE. I'M OFF TO GEOSENGE NOW.
HMM...
YOU CAN STILL FIGHT?

Y.

BLUE.

DIANTHA.

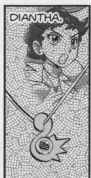

KORRINA.

...AND THE LIGHT OF THE FIVE MEGA STONES SHALL MERGE!

THE LIGHT OF THE FIVE KEY STONES...

GO!

MEGA EVOLU-TION!

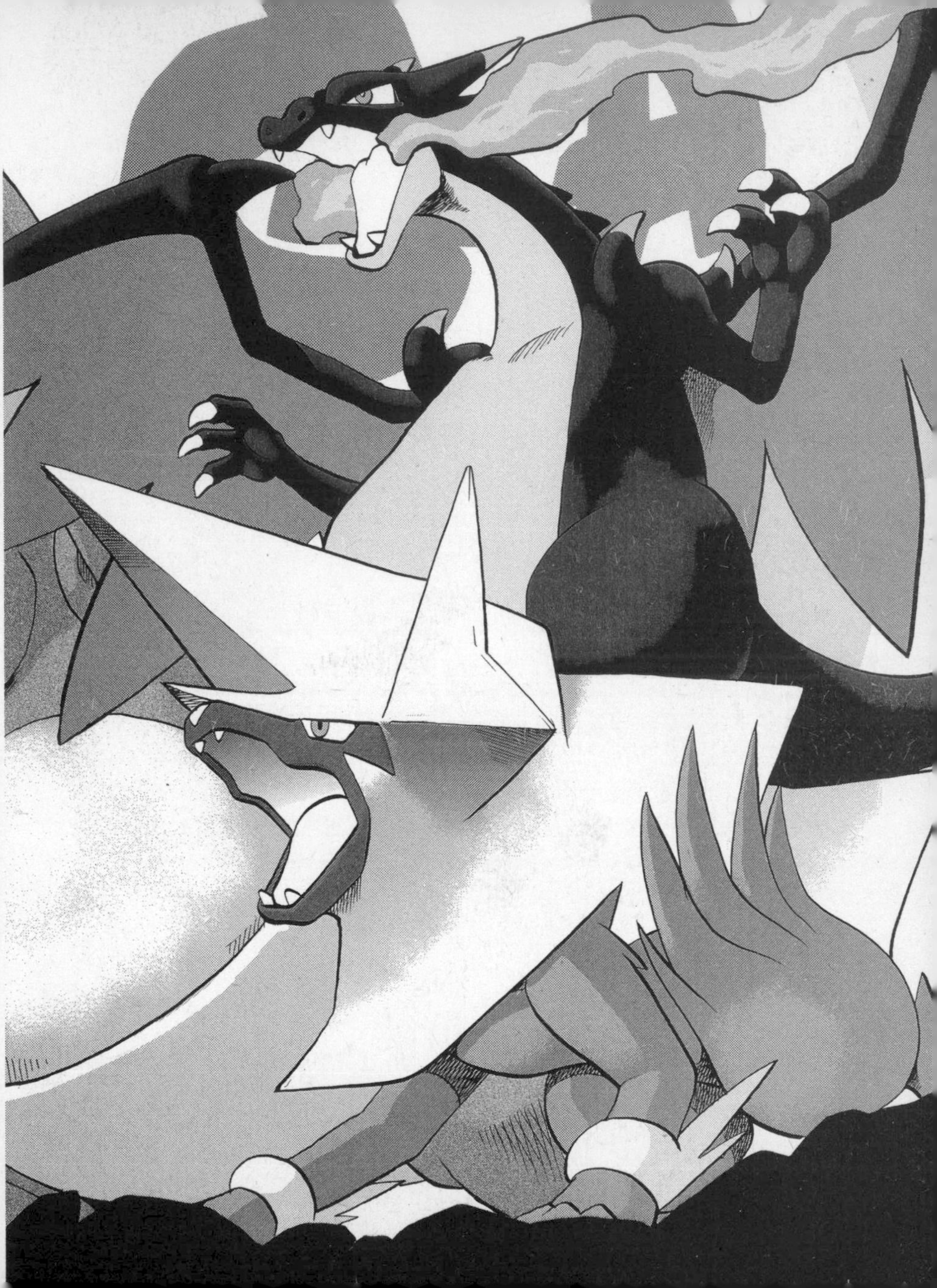

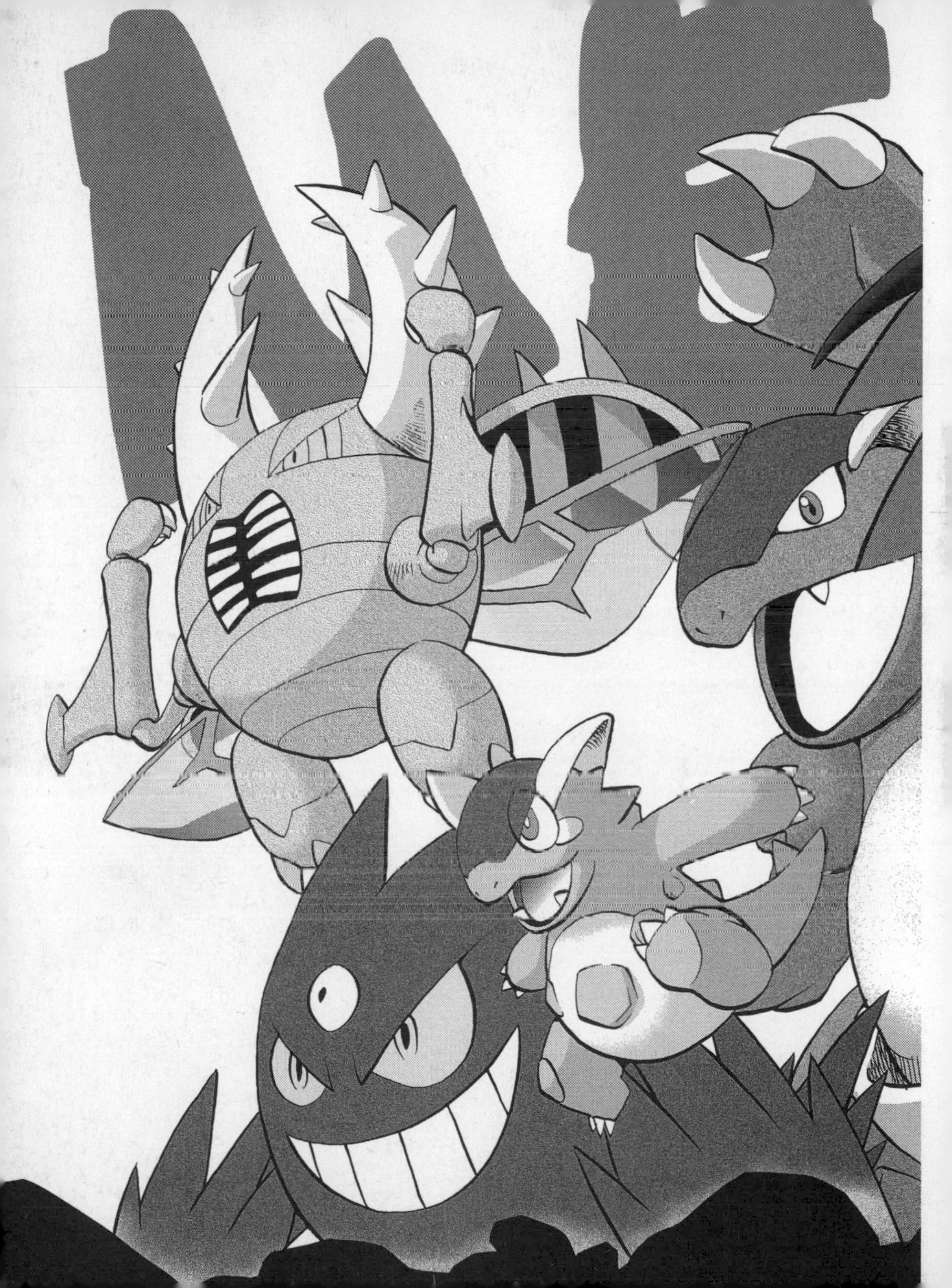

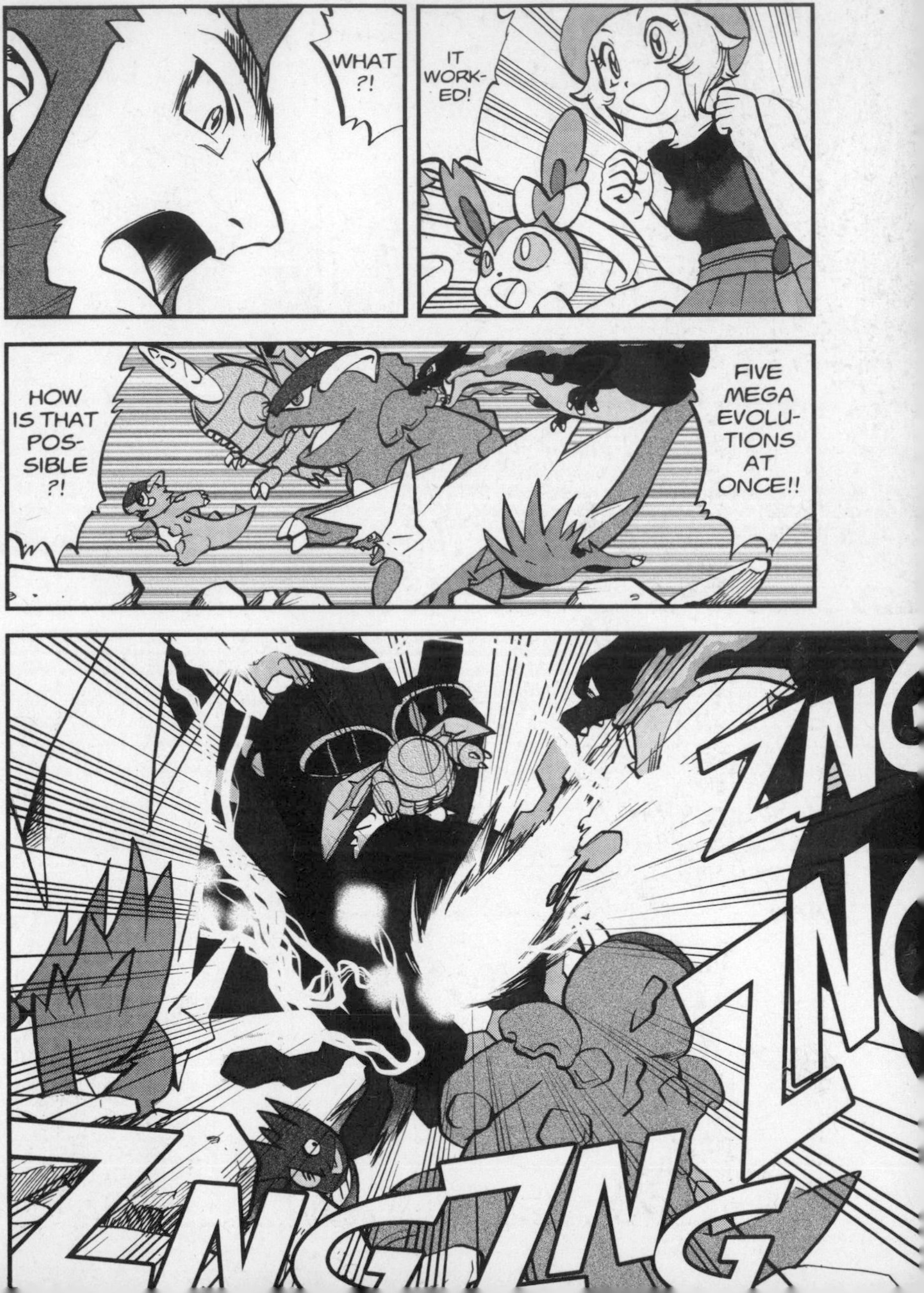
IT WORK-ED!
WHAT ?!
FIVE MEGA EVOLU-TIONS AT ONCE!!
HOW IS THAT POS-SIBLE ?!
ZNG ZNG

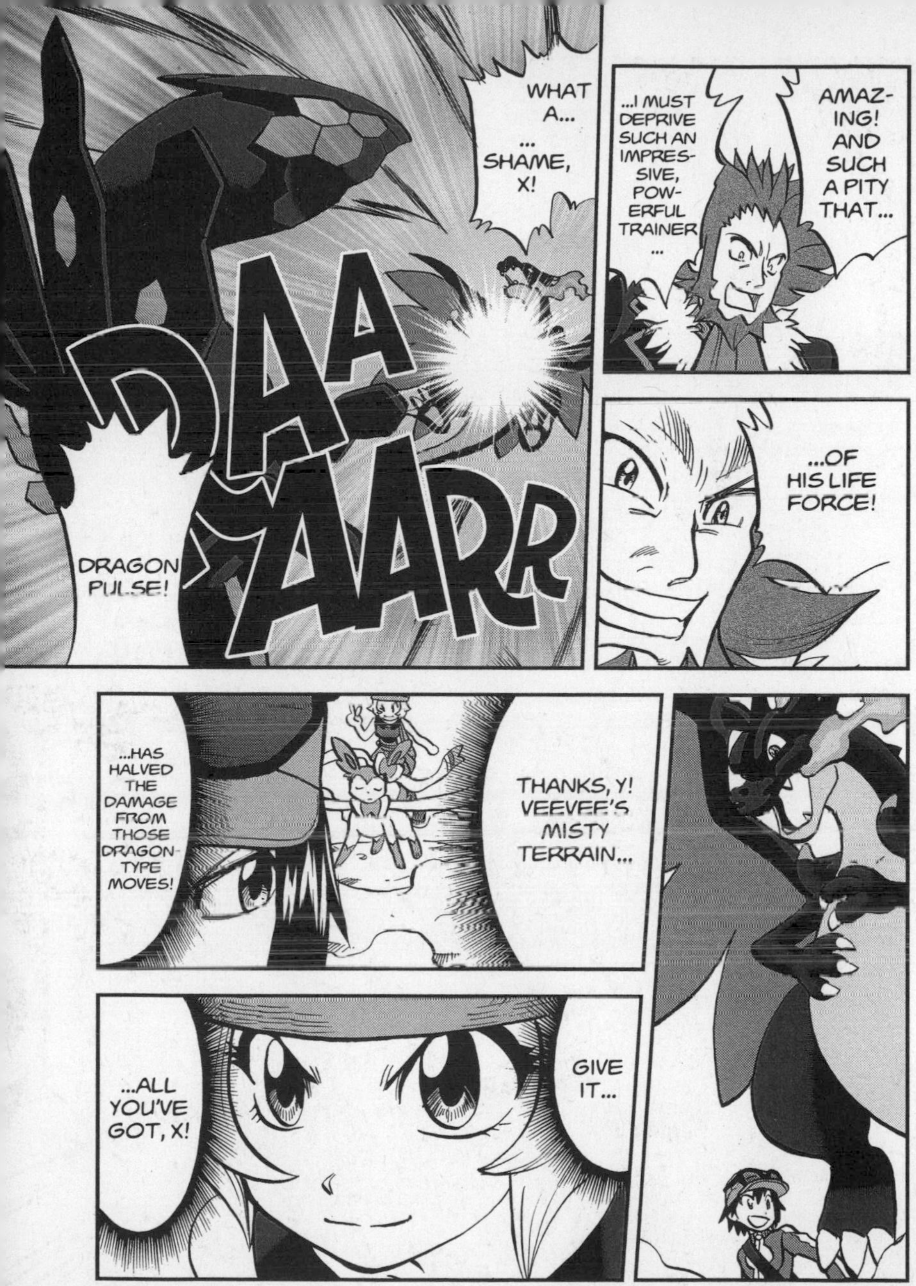
AMAZ-ING! AND SUCH A PITY THAT...
...I MUST DEPRIVE SUCH AN IMPRES-SIVE, POW-ERFUL TRAINER...
...OF HIS LIFE FORCE!
WHAT A... ... SHAME, X!
DAAAARR
DRAGON PULSE!
THANKS, Y! VEEVEE'S MISTY TERRAIN...
...HAS HALVED THE DAMAGE FROM THOSE DRAGON-TYPE MOVES!
GIVE IT...
...ALL YOU'VE GOT, X!

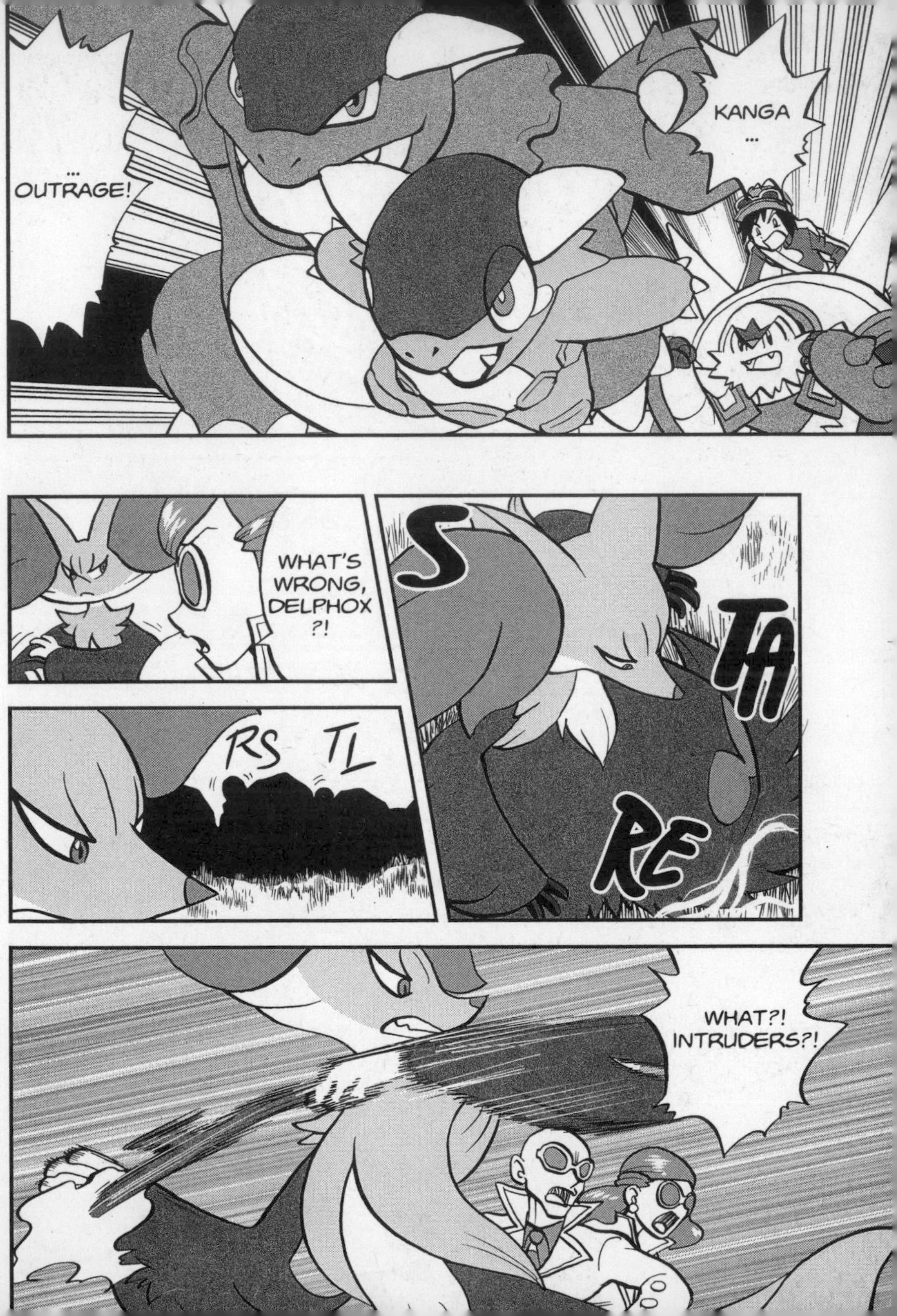
KANGA ...
... OUTRAGE!
S TA RE
WHAT'S WRONG, DELPHOX?!
RS TL
WHAT?! INTRUDERS?!

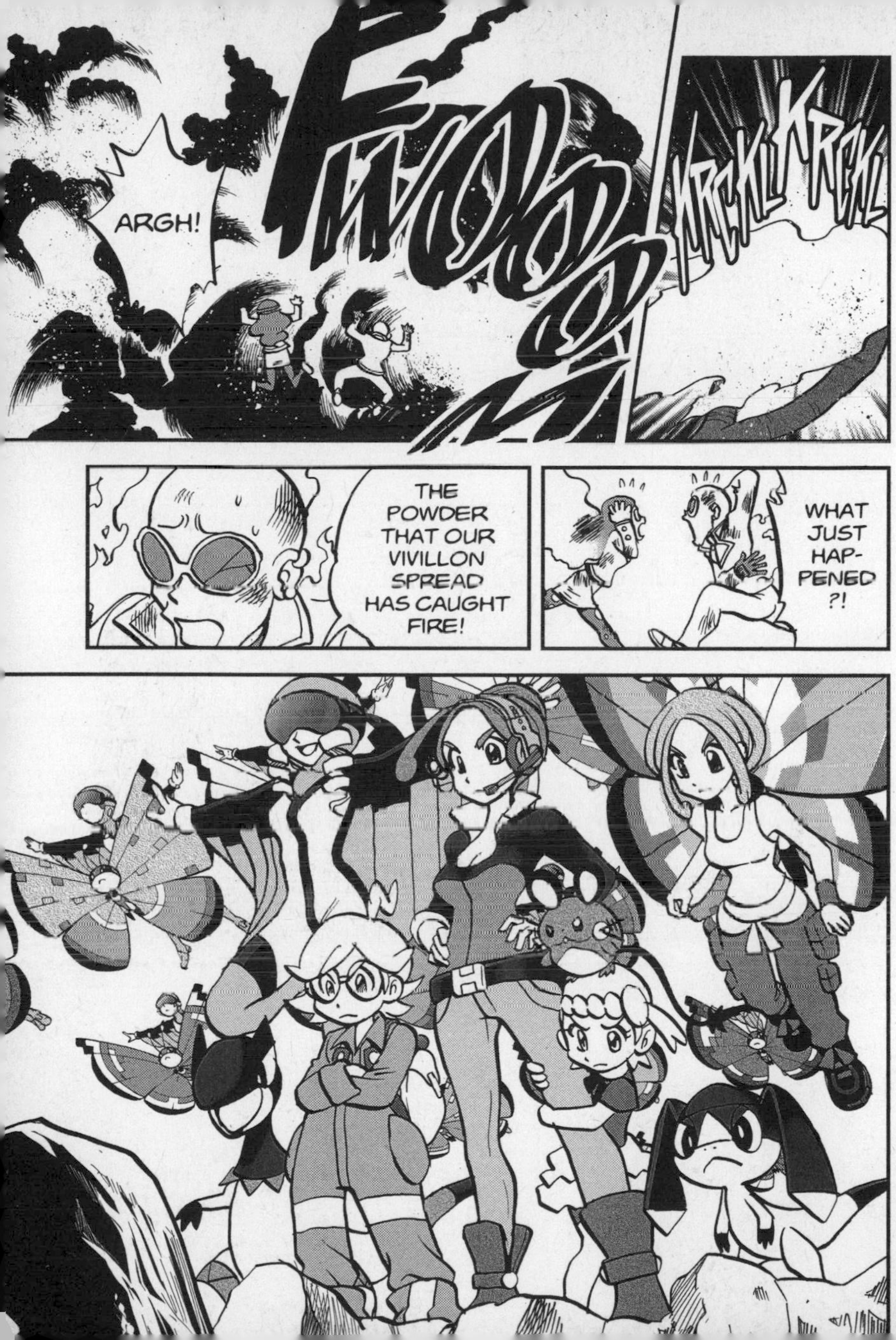
KRCKL KRCKL
ARGH!
WHAT JUST HAP-PENED?!
THE POWDER THAT OUR VIVILLON SPREAD HAS CAUGHT FIRE!

Current Location

Pokémon Village

Legends say a place exists where Pokémon live in hiding, but no one has ever found it.

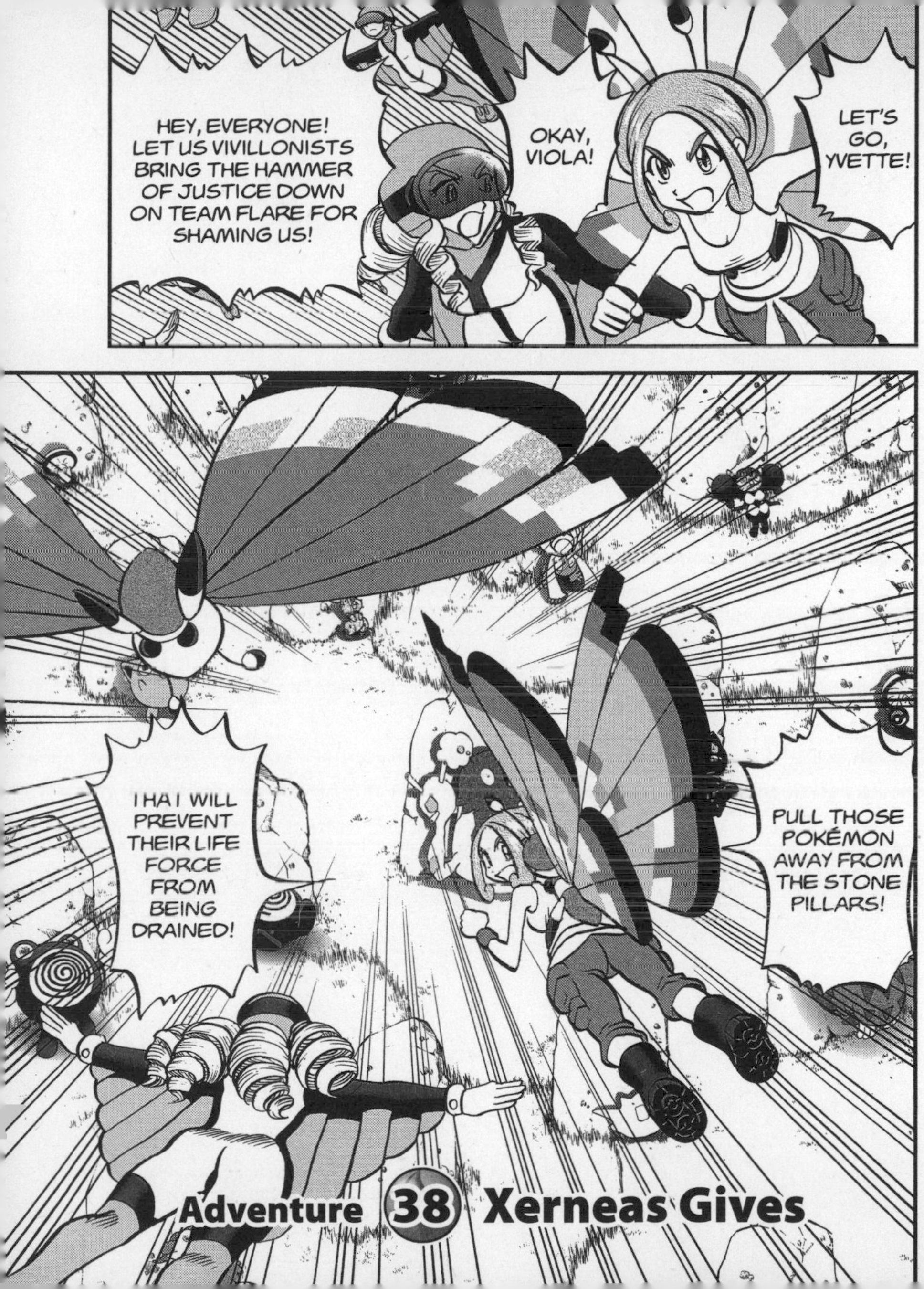
LET'S GO, YVETTE!
OKAY, VIOLA!
HEY, EVERYONE! LET US VIVILLONISTS BRING THE HAMMER OF JUSTICE DOWN ON TEAM FLARE FOR SHAMING US!
PULL THOSE POKÉMON AWAY FROM THE STONE PILLARS!
THAT WILL PREVENT THEIR LIFE FORCE FROM BEING DRAINED!

Adventure 38 Xerneas Gives

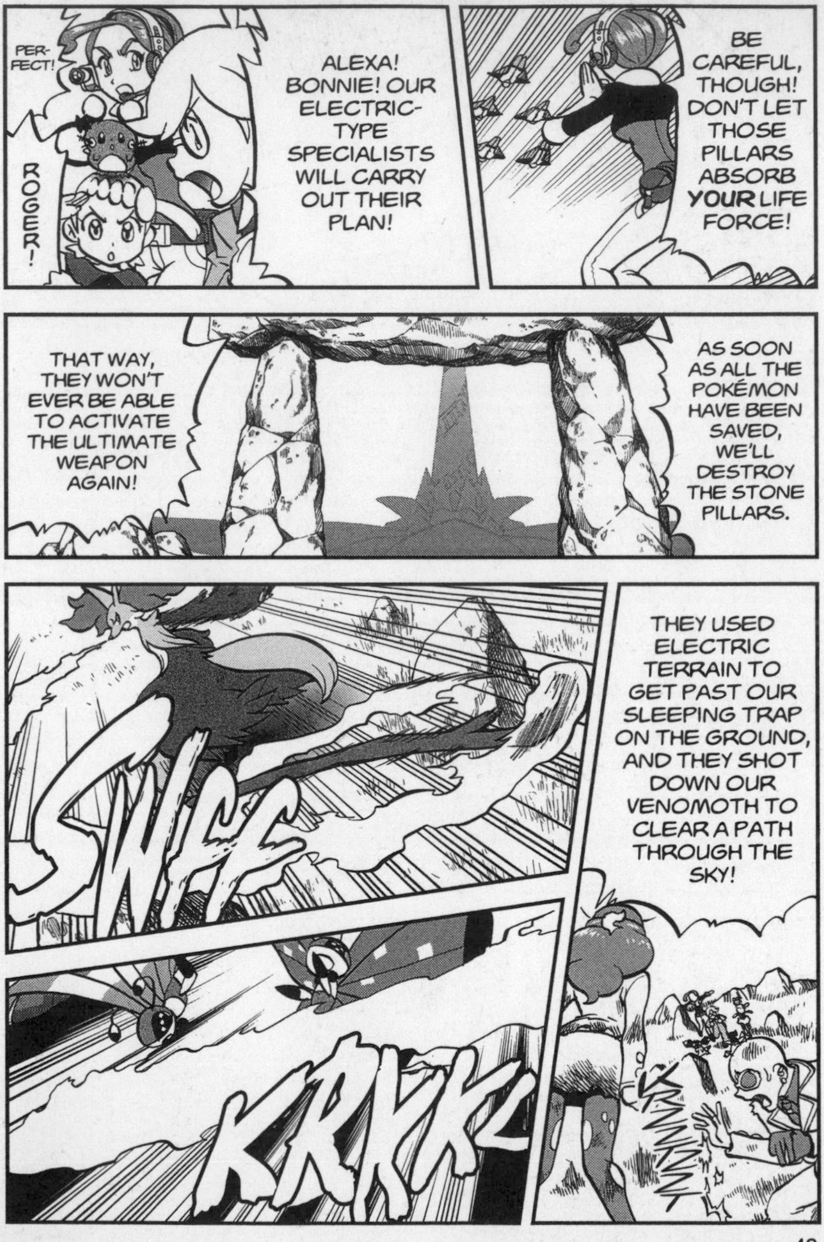
BE CAREFUL, THOUGH! DON'T LET THOSE PILLARS ABSORB **YOUR** LIFE FORCE!
ALEXA! BONNIE! OUR ELECTRIC-TYPE SPECIALISTS WILL CARRY OUT THEIR PLAN!
PER-FECT!
ROGER!
AS SOON AS ALL THE POKÉMON HAVE BEEN SAVED, WE'LL DESTROY THE STONE PILLARS.
THAT WAY, THEY WON'T EVER BE ABLE TO ACTIVATE THE ULTIMATE WEAPON AGAIN!
THEY USED ELECTRIC TERRAIN TO GET PAST OUR SLEEPING TRAP ON THE GROUND, AND THEY SHOT DOWN OUR VENOMOTH TO CLEAR A PATH THROUGH THE SKY!

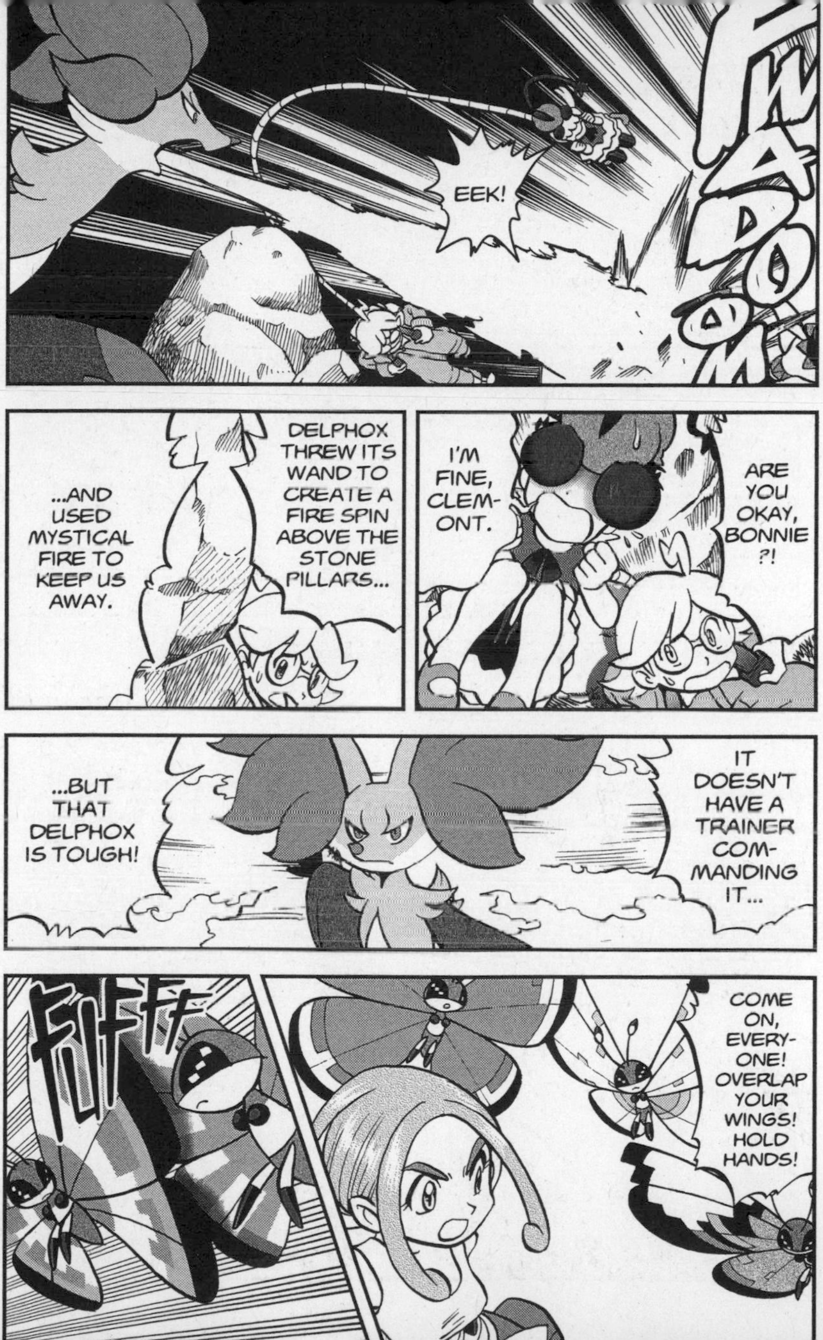
FWADOOM
EEK!
ARE YOU OKAY, BONNIE?!
I'M FINE, CLEMONT.
DELPHOX THREW ITS WAND TO CREATE A FIRE SPIN ABOVE THE STONE PILLARS...
...AND USED MYSTICAL FIRE TO KEEP US AWAY.
IT DOESN'T HAVE A TRAINER COM-MANDING IT...
...BUT THAT DELPHOX IS TOUGH!
COME ON, EVERY-ONE! OVERLAP YOUR WINGS! HOLD HANDS!

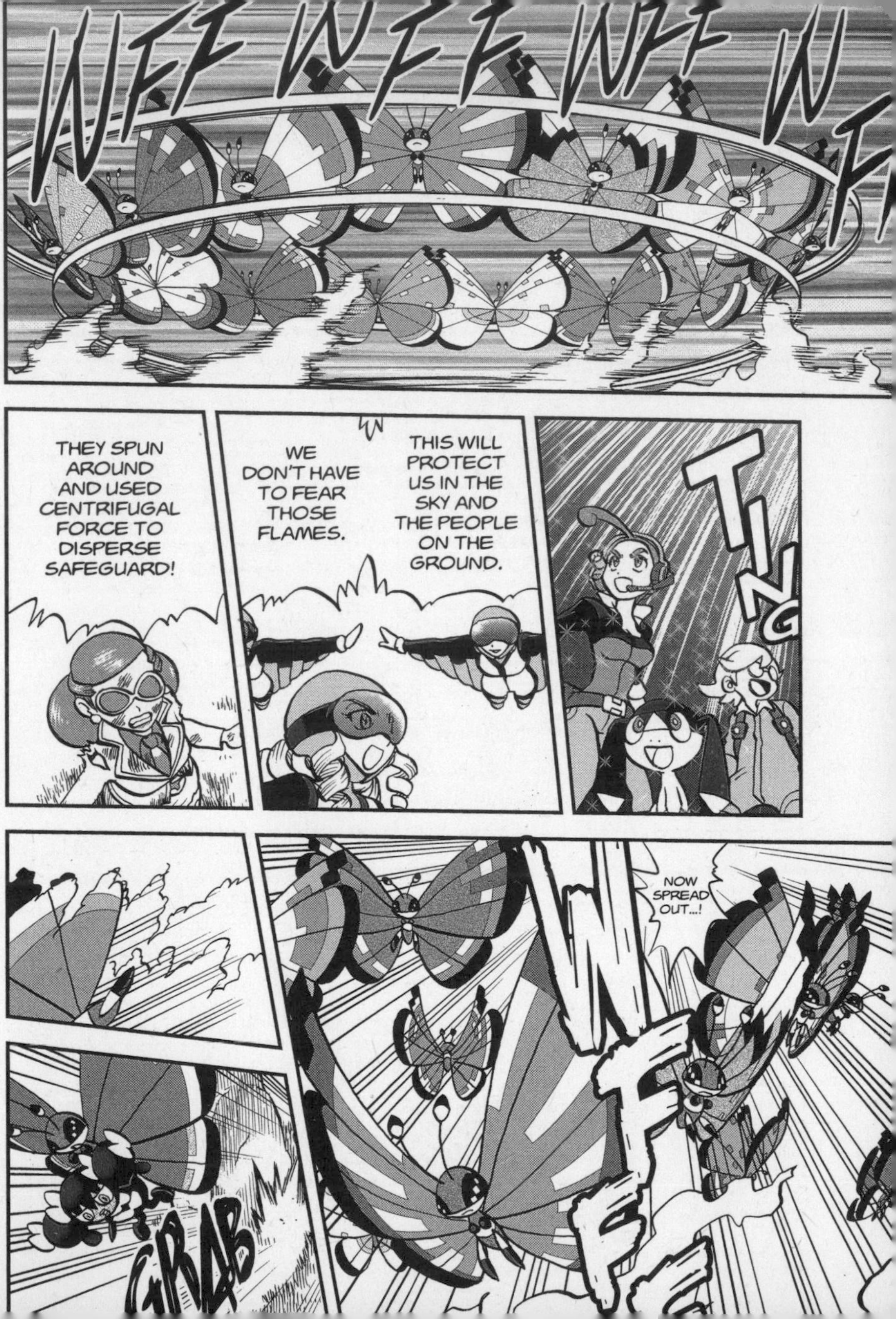
WFF WFF WFF WF
TING
THIS WILL PROTECT US IN THE SKY AND THE PEOPLE ON THE GROUND.
WE DON'T HAVE TO FEAR THOSE FLAMES.
THEY SPUN AROUND AND USED CENTRIFUGAL FORCE TO DISPERSE SAFEGUARD!
NOW SPREAD OUT...!
WFF
GRAB

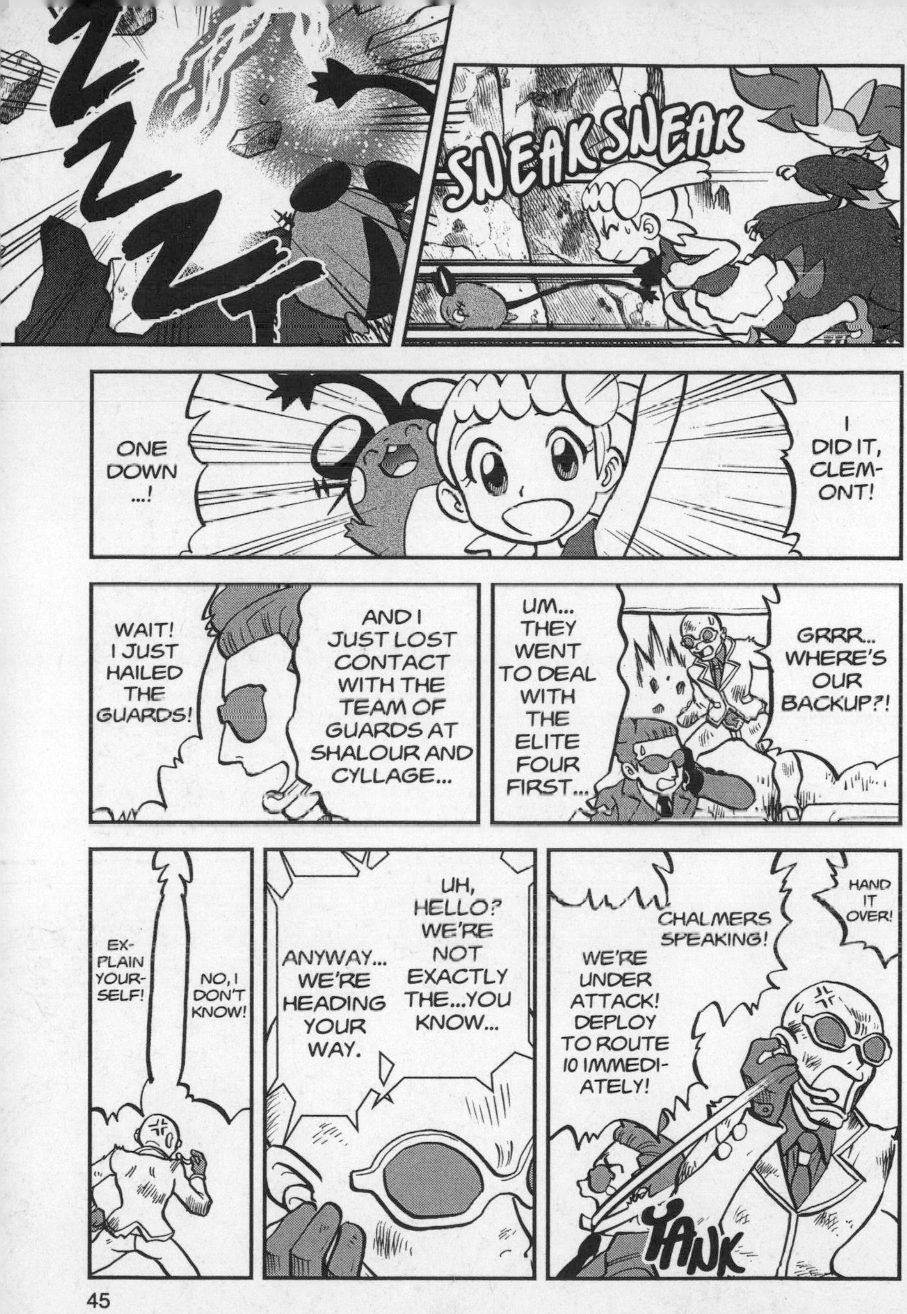
SNEAKSNEAK
I DID IT, CLEMONT!
ONE DOWN...!
GRRR... WHERE'S OUR BACKUP?!
UM... THEY WENT TO DEAL WITH THE ELITE FOUR FIRST...
AND I JUST LOST CONTACT WITH THE TEAM OF GUARDS AT SHALOUR AND CYLLAGE...
WAIT! I JUST HAILED THE GUARDS!
HAND IT OVER!
CHALMERS SPEAKING!
WE'RE UNDER ATTACK! DEPLOY TO ROUTE 10 IMMEDIATELY!
YANK
UH, HELLO? WE'RE NOT EXACTLY THE...YOU KNOW...
ANYWAY... WE'RE HEADING YOUR WAY.
NO, I DON'T KNOW!
EXPLAIN YOURSELF!

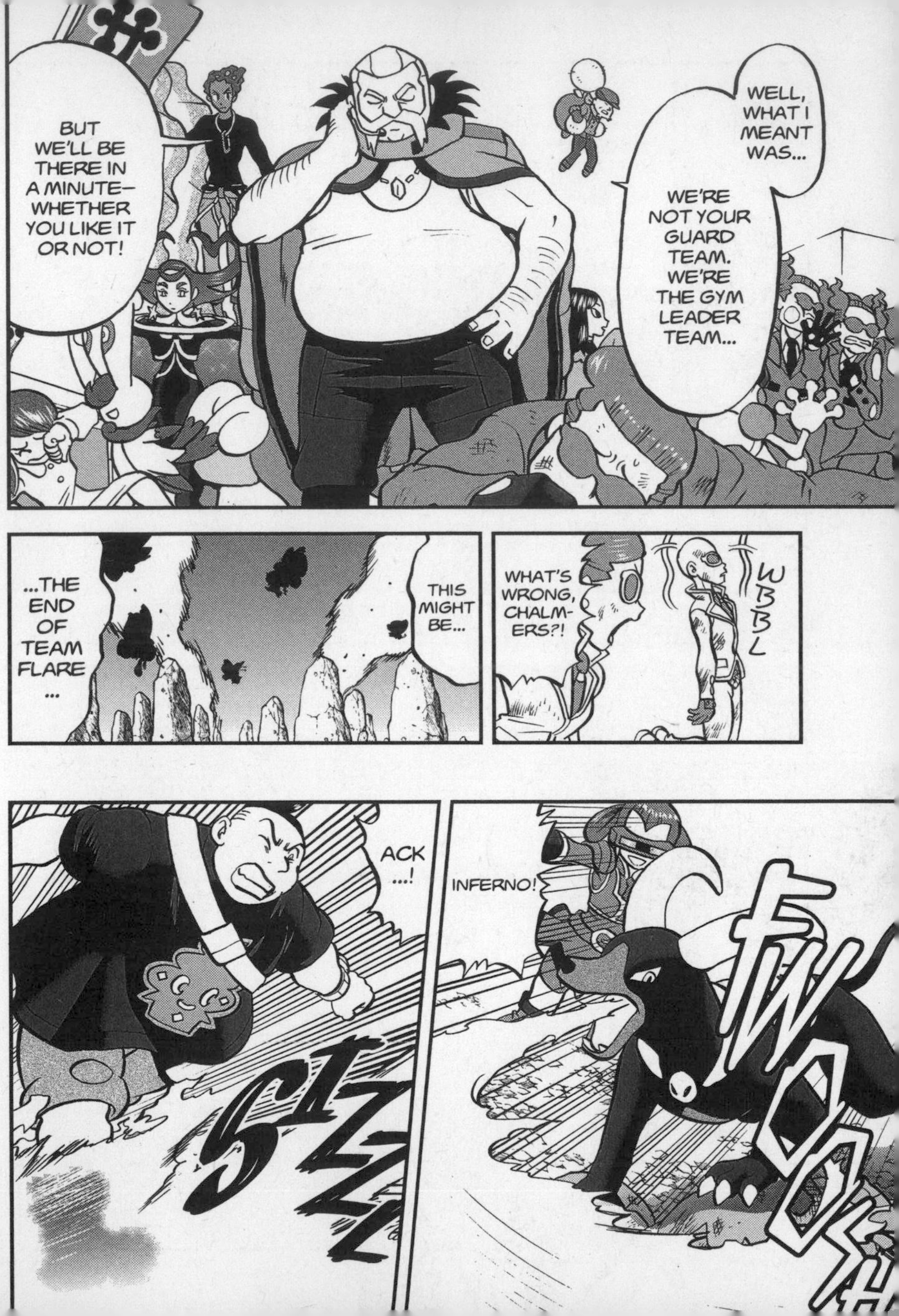
WELL, WHAT I MEANT WAS...
WE'RE NOT YOUR GUARD TEAM. WE'RE THE GYM LEADER TEAM...
BUT WE'LL BE THERE IN A MINUTE—WHETHER YOU LIKE IT OR NOT!
WBBL
WHAT'S WRONG, CHALMERS?!
THIS MIGHT BE...
...THE END OF TEAM FLARE...
FWOOSH
INFERNO!
ACK...!
SIZZ

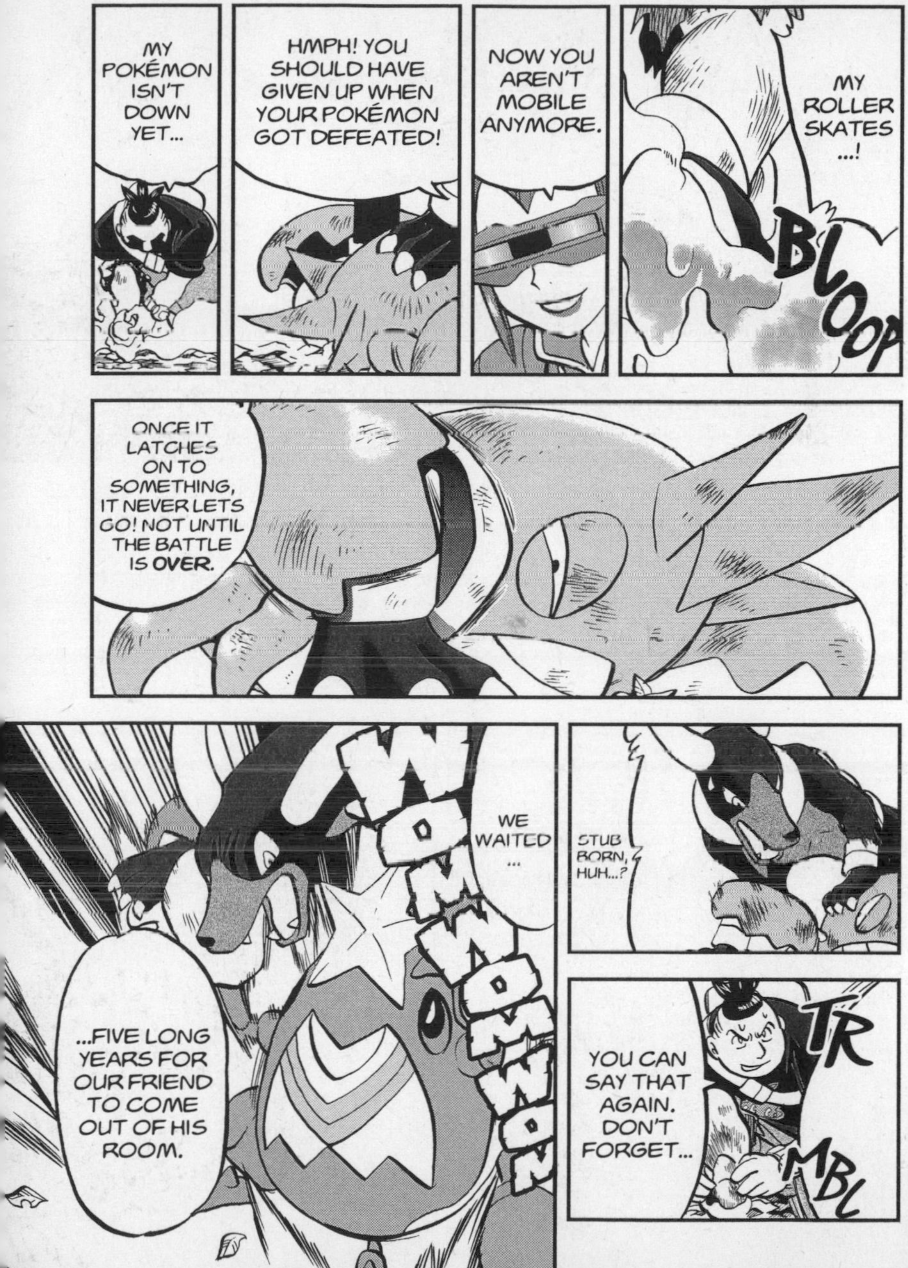
MY POKÉMON ISN'T DOWN YET...
HMPH! YOU SHOULD HAVE GIVEN UP WHEN YOUR POKÉMON GOT DEFEATED!
NOW YOU AREN'T MOBILE ANYMORE.
MY ROLLER SKATES ...!
BLOOP
ONCE IT LATCHES ON TO SOMETHING, IT NEVER LETS GO! NOT UNTIL THE BATTLE IS **OVER**.
WOMWOMWON
WE WAITED ...
...FIVE LONG YEARS FOR OUR FRIEND TO COME OUT OF HIS ROOM.
STUB BORN, HUH...?
TR
MBL
YOU CAN SAY THAT AGAIN. DON'T FORGET...

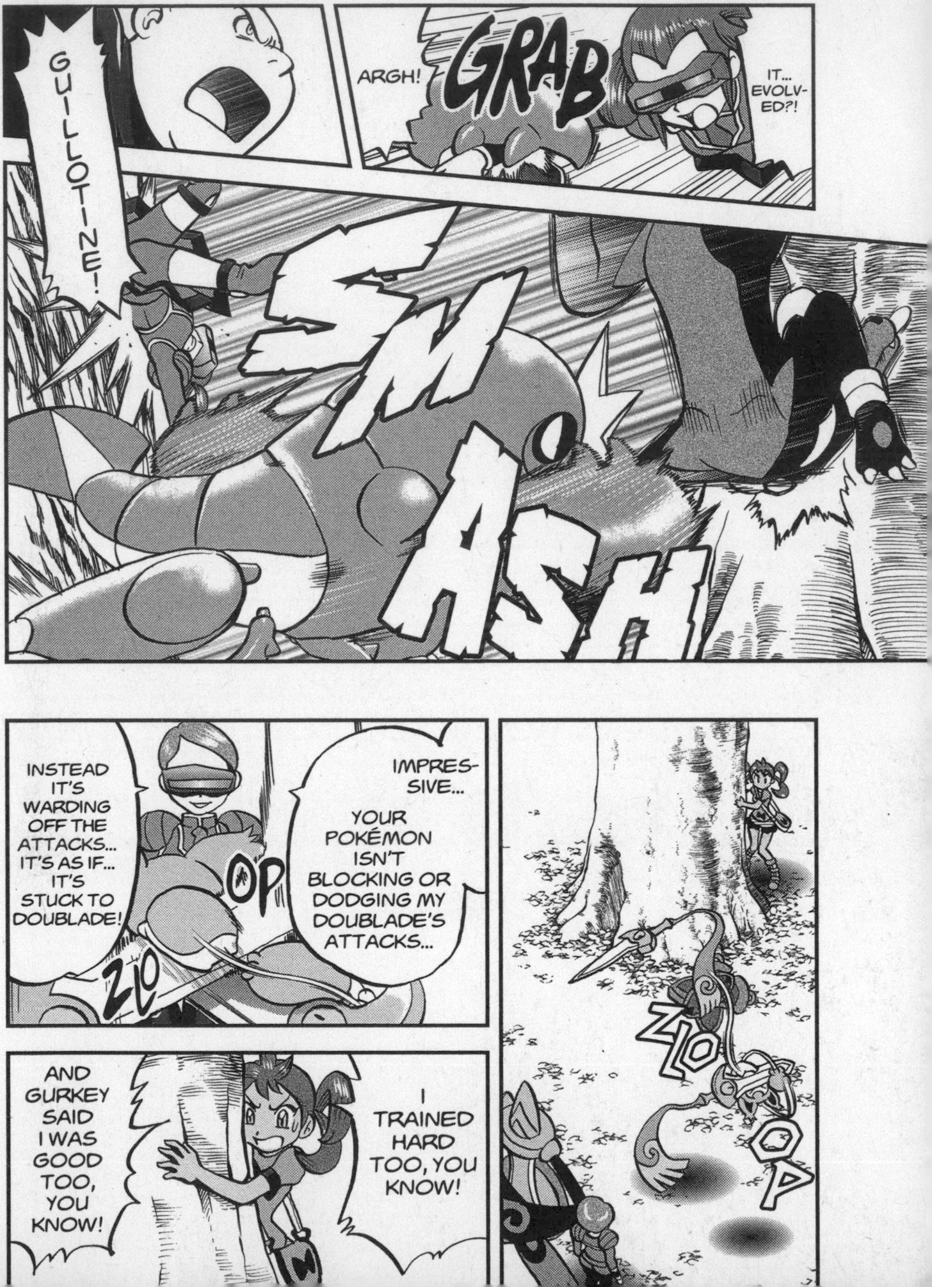
IT... EVOLVED?!
GRAB
ARGH!
GUILLOTINE!
SMASH
ZLOOP
IMPRESSIVE...
YOUR POKÉMON ISN'T BLOCKING OR DODGING MY DOUBLADE'S ATTACKS...
INSTEAD IT'S WARDING OFF THE ATTACKS... IT'S AS IF... IT'S STUCK TO DOUBLADE!
OP
ZLO
I TRAINED HARD TOO, YOU KNOW!
AND GURKEY SAID I WAS GOOD TOO, YOU KNOW!

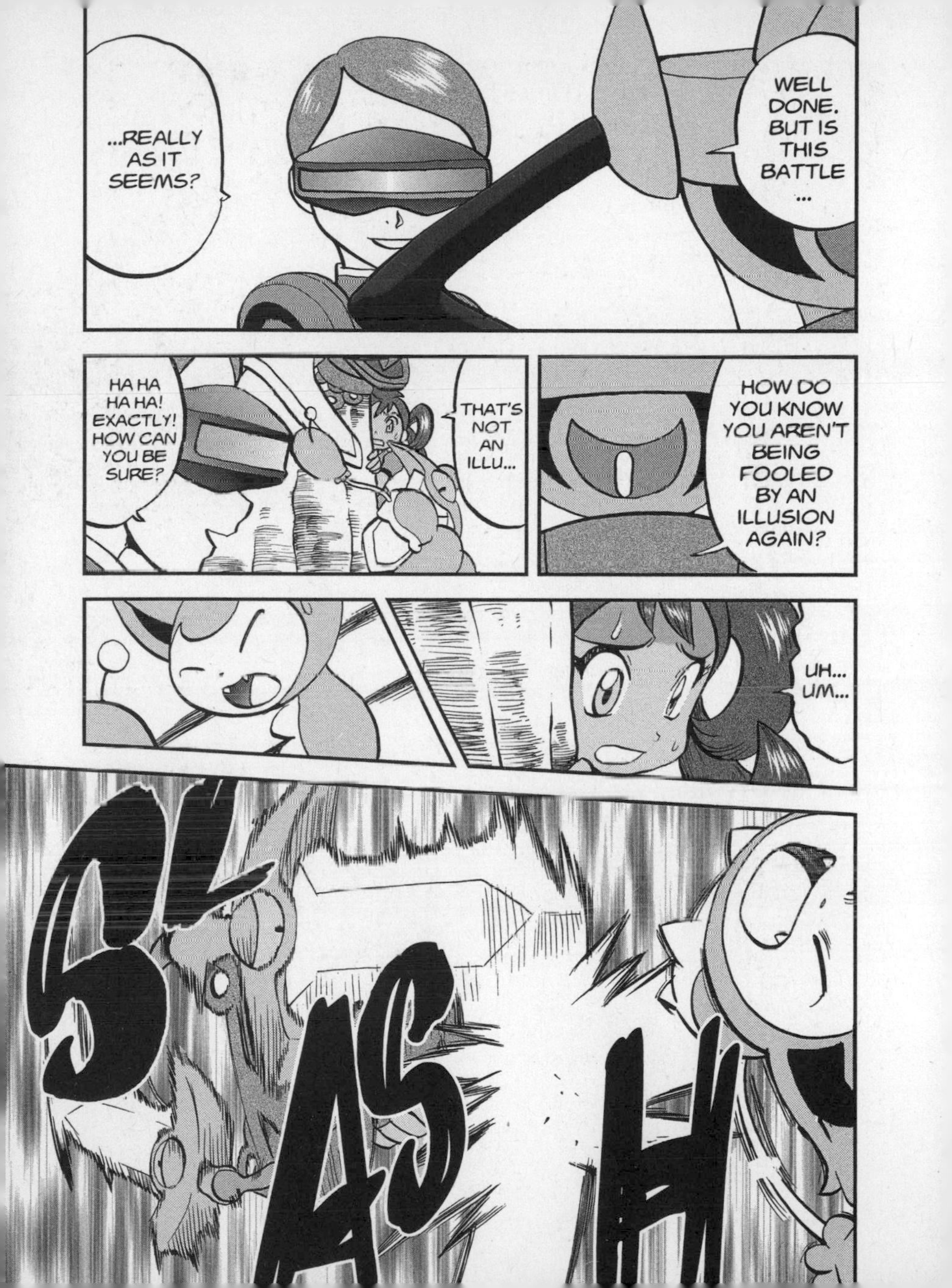
WELL DONE. BUT IS THIS BATTLE...
...REALLY AS IT SEEMS?
HOW DO YOU KNOW YOU AREN'T BEING FOOLED BY AN ILLUSION AGAIN?
THAT'S NOT AN ILLU...
HA HA HA HA! EXACTLY! HOW CAN YOU BE SURE?
UH... UM...
SLASH

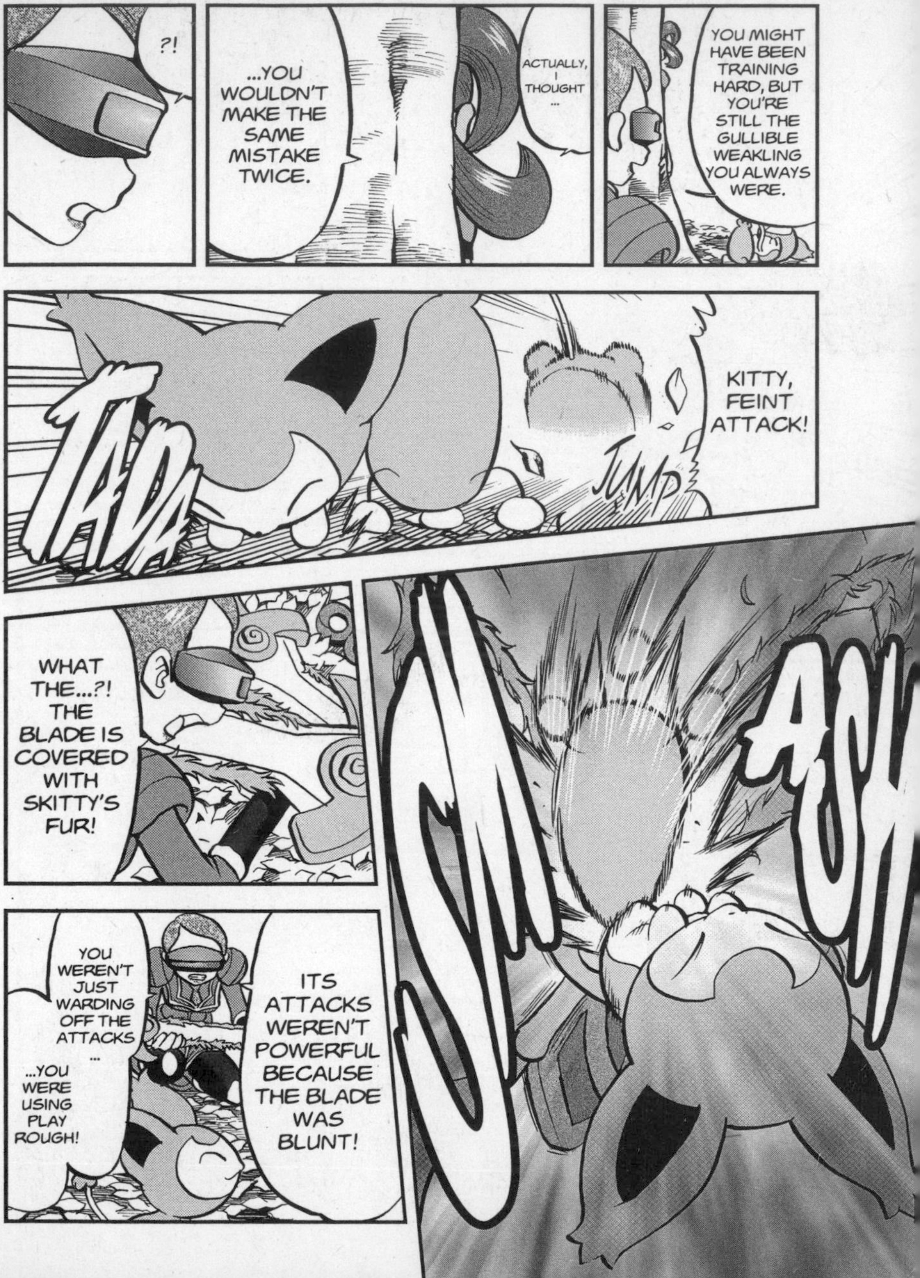
YOU MIGHT HAVE BEEN TRAINING HARD, BUT YOU'RE STILL THE GULLIBLE WEAKLING YOU ALWAYS WERE.
ACTUALLY, I THOUGHT ...
...YOU WOULDN'T MAKE THE SAME MISTAKE TWICE.
?!
KITTY, FEINT ATTACK!
JUMP
TADA
SMASH
WHAT THE...?! THE BLADE IS COVERED WITH SKITTY'S FUR!
ITS ATTACKS WEREN'T POWERFUL BECAUSE THE BLADE WAS BLUNT!
YOU WEREN'T JUST WARDING OFF THE ATTACKS ...
...YOU WERE USING PLAY ROUGH!

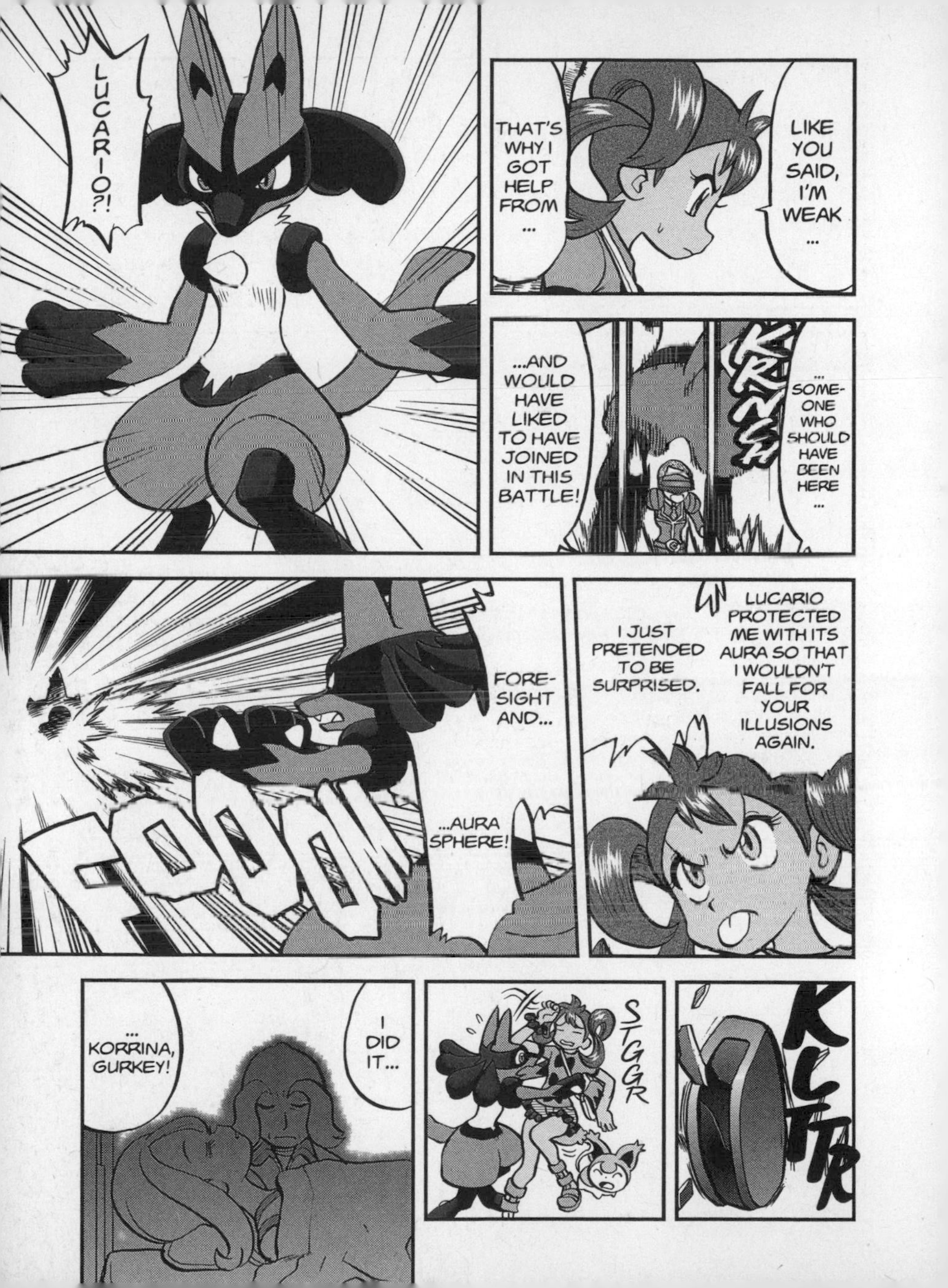
LIKE YOU SAID, I'M WEAK...
THAT'S WHY I GOT HELP FROM...
...SOME-ONE WHO SHOULD HAVE BEEN HERE...
KRNSH
...AND WOULD HAVE LIKED TO HAVE JOINED IN THIS BATTLE!
LUCARIO?!
LUCARIO PROTECTED ME WITH ITS AURA SO THAT I WOULDN'T FALL FOR YOUR ILLUSIONS AGAIN.
I JUST PRETENDED TO BE SURPRISED.
FORE-SIGHT AND...
...AURA SPHERE!
FOOOM
KLTTR
STGGR
I DID IT...
...KORRINA, GURKEY!

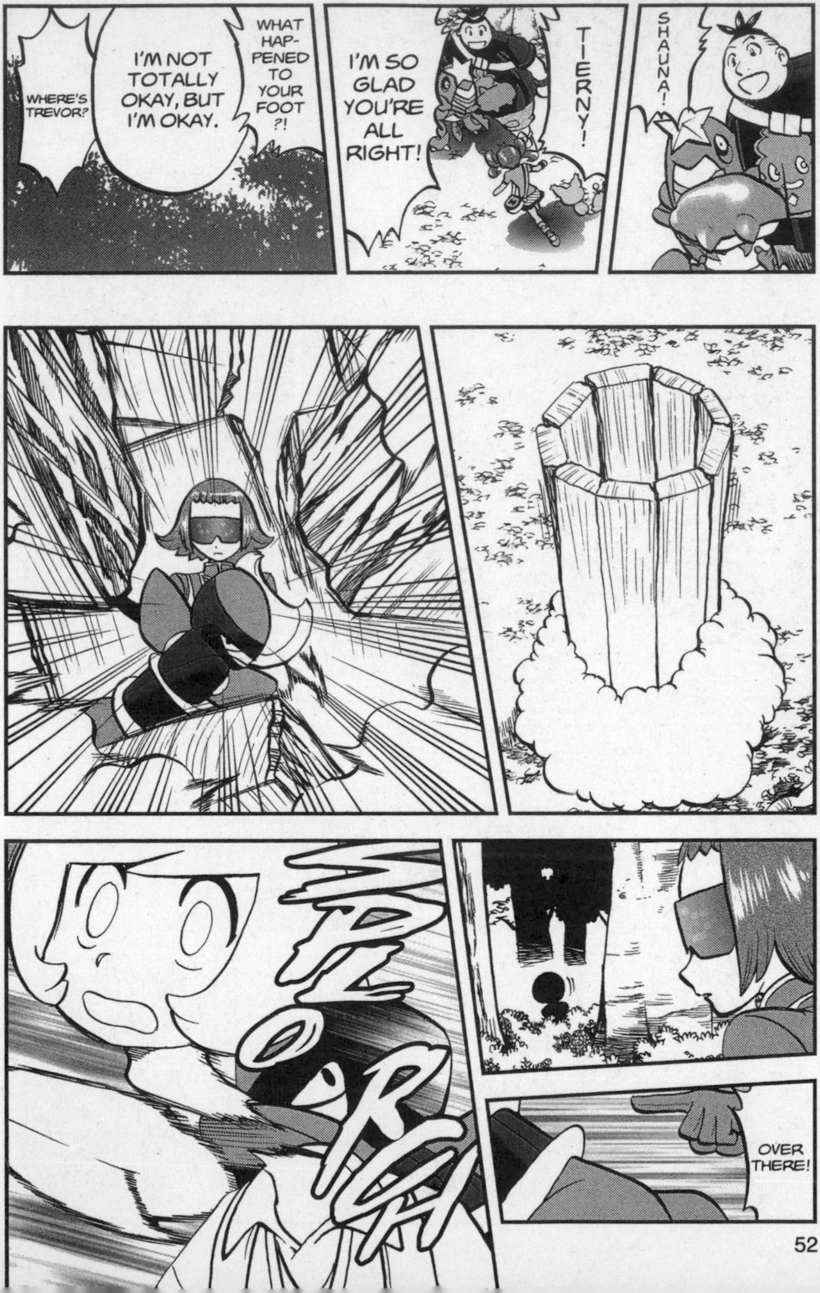
SHAUNA!
TIERNY!
I'M SO GLAD YOU'RE ALL RIGHT!
WHAT HAP-PENED TO YOUR FOOT?!
I'M NOT TOTALLY OKAY, BUT I'M OKAY.
WHERE'S TREVOR?
OVER THERE!

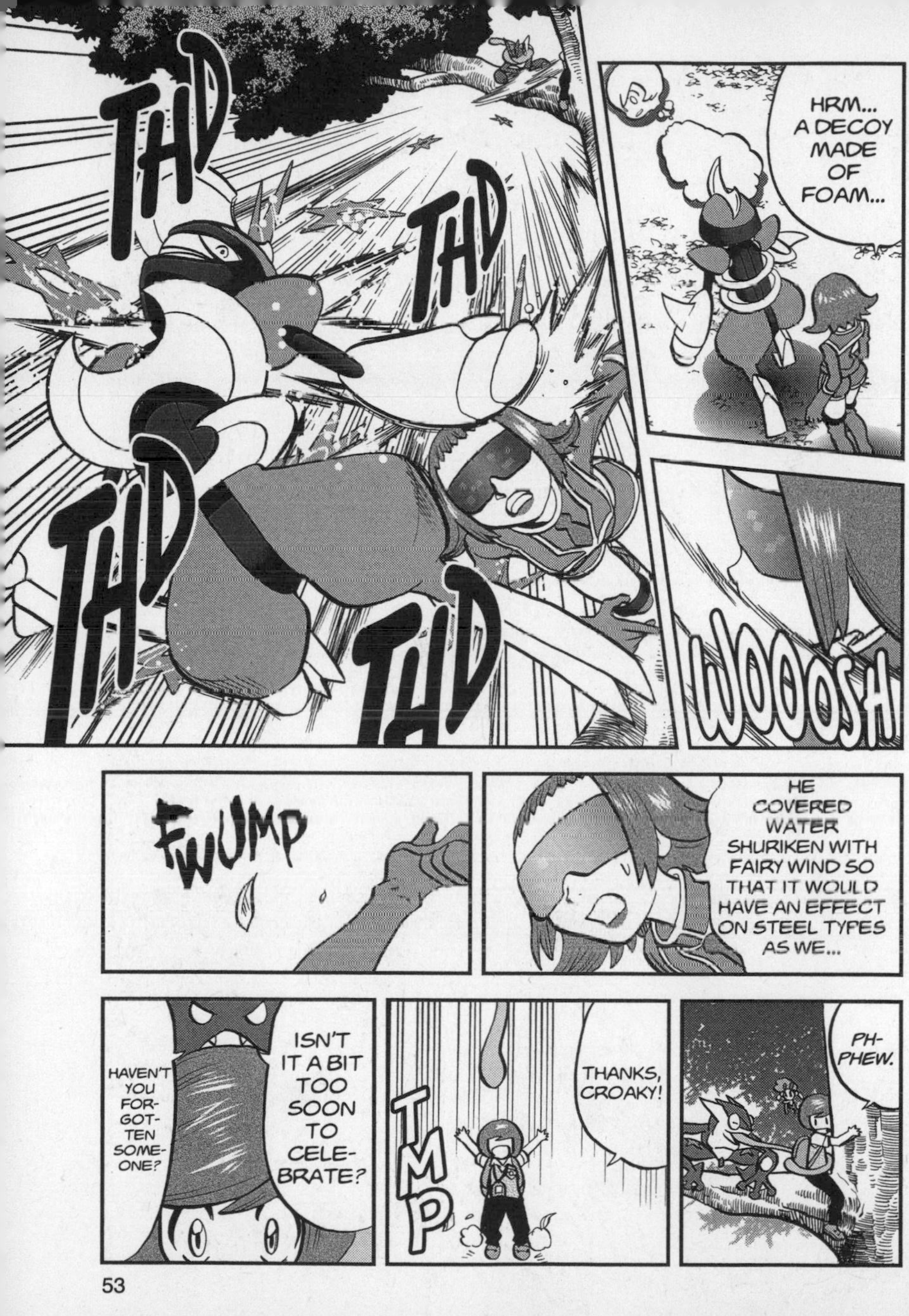
HRM... A DECOY MADE OF FOAM...
WOOOSH
THD
THD
THD
THD
HE COVERED WATER SHURIKEN WITH FAIRY WIND SO THAT IT WOULD HAVE AN EFFECT ON STEEL TYPES AS WE...
FWUMP
PH-PHEW.
THANKS, CROAKY!
TMP
ISN'T IT A BIT TOO SOON TO CELE-BRATE?
HAVEN'T YOU FOR-GOT-TEN SOME-ONE?

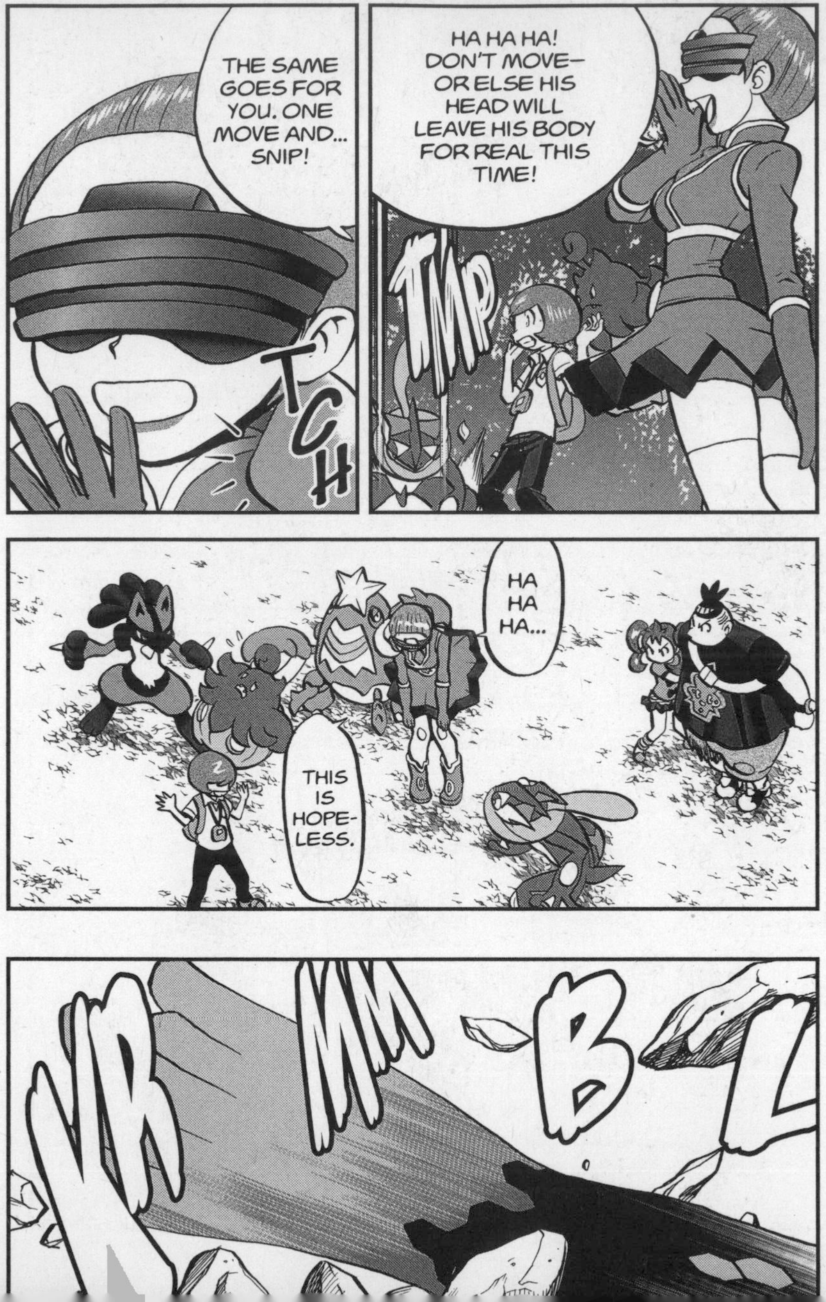
HA HA HA! DON'T MOVE—OR ELSE HIS HEAD WILL LEAVE HIS BODY FOR REAL THIS TIME!
TMP
THE SAME GOES FOR YOU. ONE MOVE AND... SNIP!
TCH
HA HA HA...
THIS IS HOPE-LESS.
VRMMBL

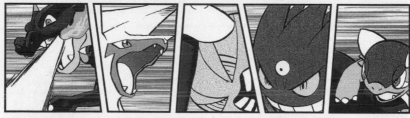

BE CAREFUL, X!

GO, PYROAR! GYARA-DOS!

ATTACK X!

X? X?! CAN YOU HEAR ME?!

HFF

HFF

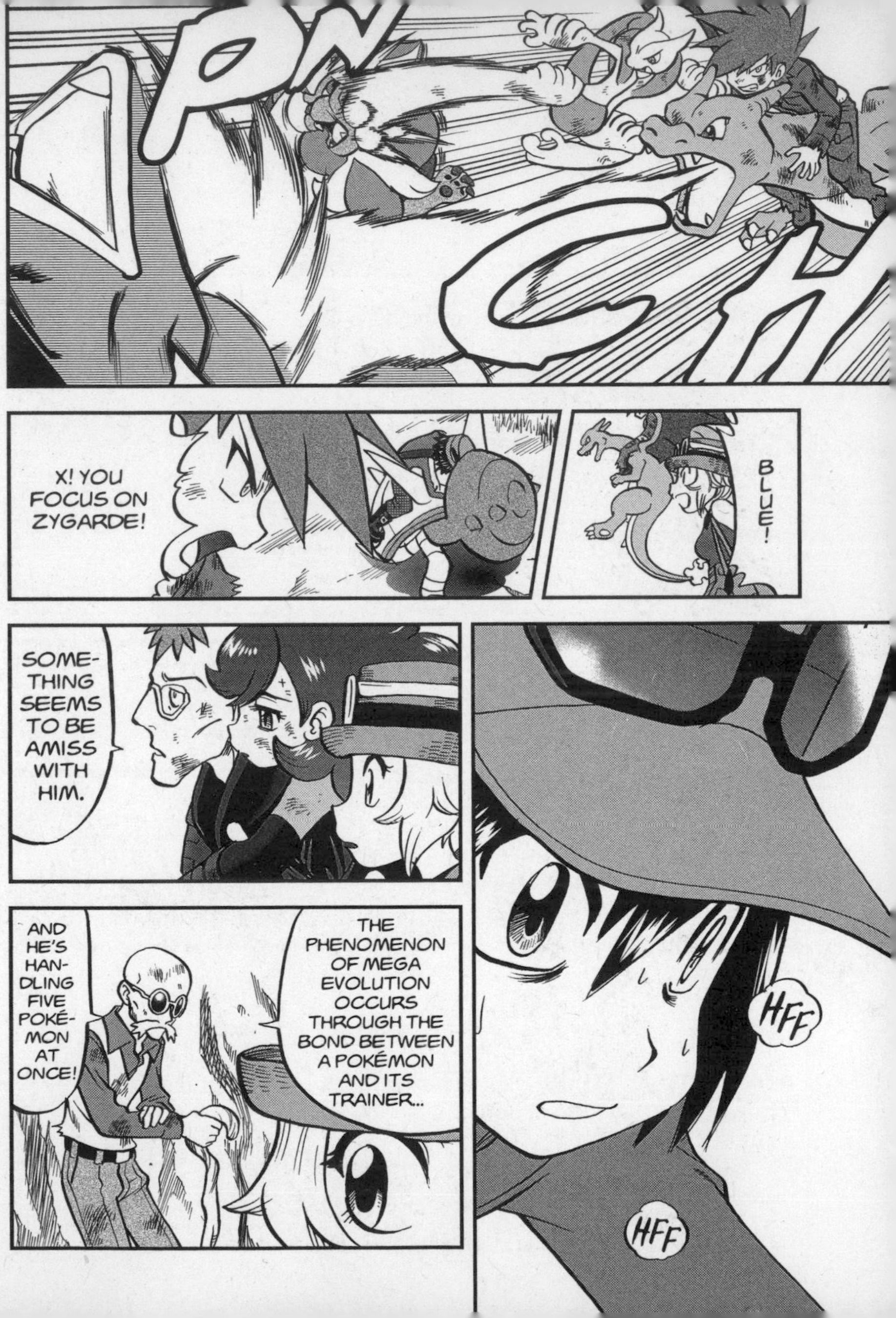
BLUE!
X! YOU FOCUS ON ZYGARDE!
HFF
HFF
SOME-THING SEEMS TO BE AMISS WITH HIM.
THE PHENOMENON OF MEGA EVOLUTION OCCURS THROUGH THE BOND BETWEEN A POKÉMON AND ITS TRAINER...
AND HE'S HAN-DLING FIVE POKÉ-MON AT ONCE!

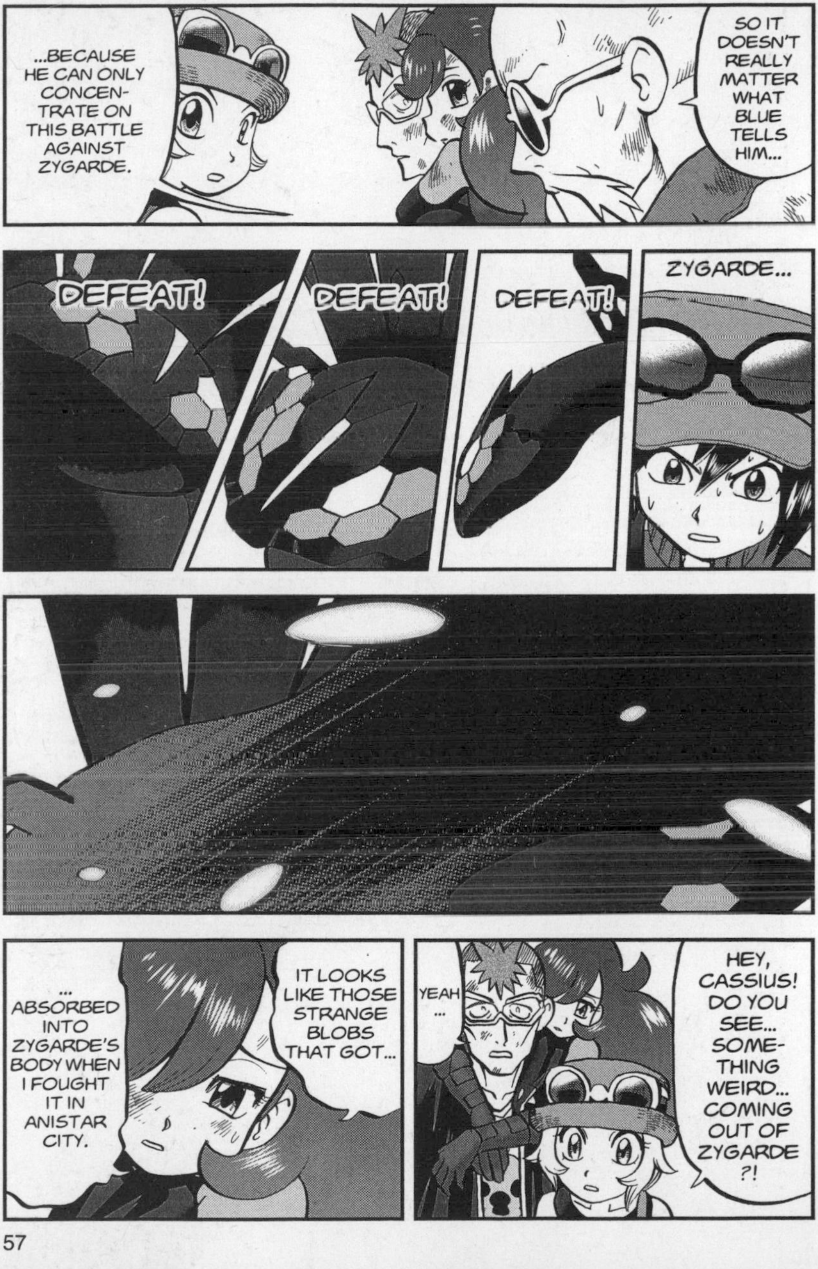
SO IT DOESN'T REALLY MATTER WHAT BLUE TELLS HIM...
...BECAUSE HE CAN ONLY CONCENTRATE ON THIS BATTLE AGAINST ZYGARDE.
ZYGARDE...
DEFEAT!
DEFEAT!
DEFEAT!
HEY, CASSIUS! DO YOU SEE... SOMETHING WEIRD... COMING OUT OF ZYGARDE?!
YEAH...
IT LOOKS LIKE THOSE STRANGE BLOBS THAT GOT...
...ABSORBED INTO ZYGARDE'S BODY WHEN I FOUGHT IT IN ANISTAR CITY.

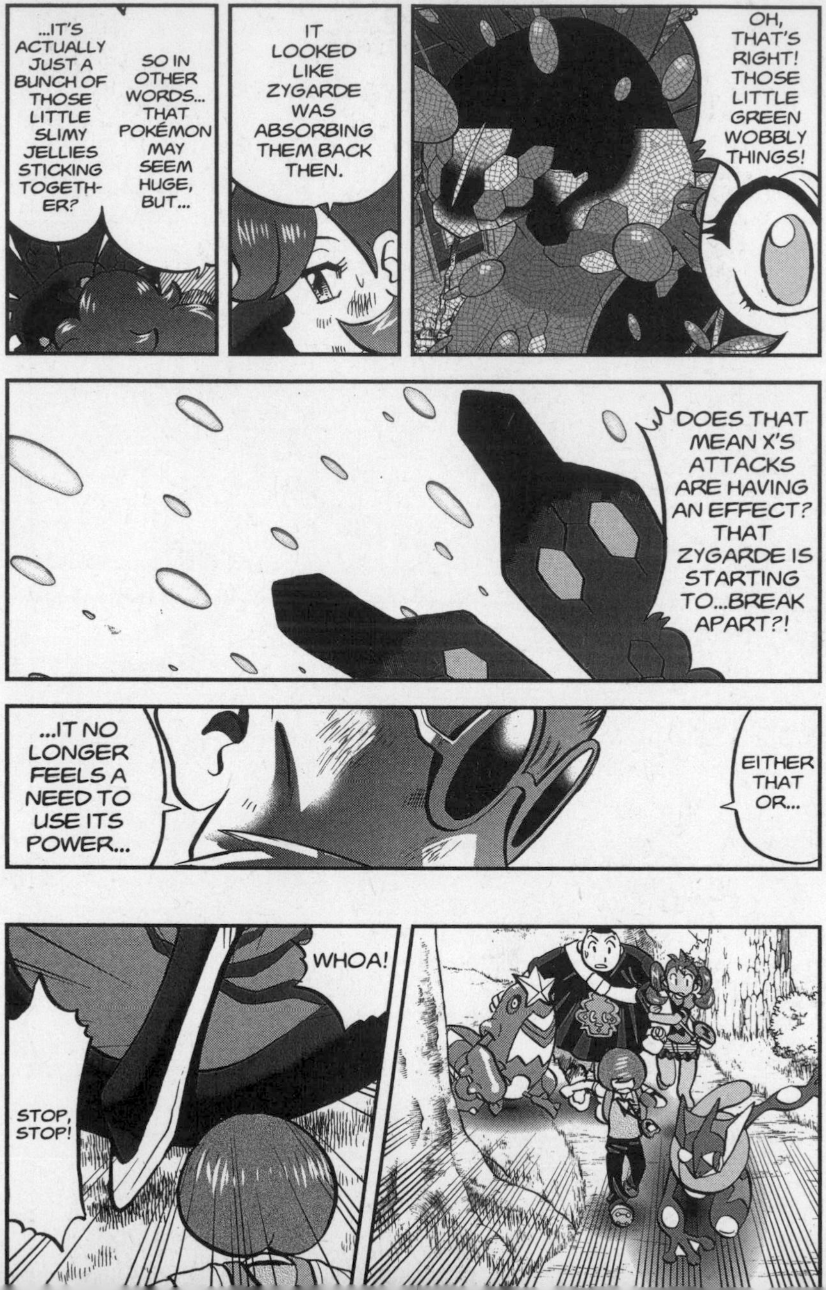
OH, THAT'S RIGHT! THOSE LITTLE GREEN WOBBLY THINGS!
IT LOOKED LIKE ZYGARDE WAS ABSORBING THEM BACK THEN.
SO IN OTHER WORDS... THAT POKÉMON MAY SEEM HUGE, BUT...
...IT'S ACTUALLY JUST A BUNCH OF THOSE LITTLE SLIMY JELLIES STICKING TOGETH-ER?
DOES THAT MEAN X'S ATTACKS ARE HAVING AN EFFECT? THAT ZYGARDE IS STARTING TO...BREAK APART?!
EITHER THAT OR...
...IT NO LONGER FEELS A NEED TO USE ITS POWER...
WHOA!
STOP, STOP!

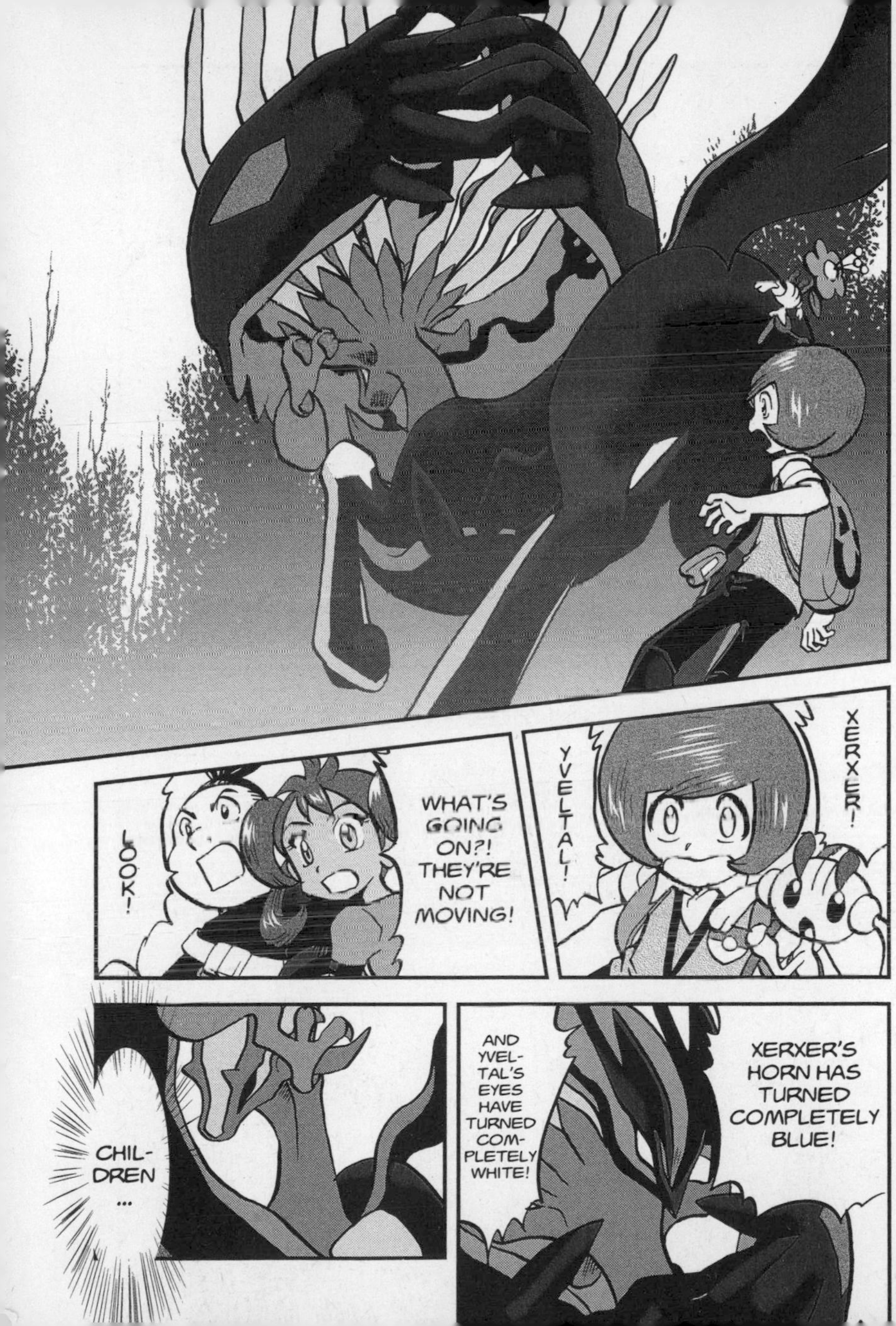
XERXER!
YVELTAL!
WHAT'S GOING ON?! THEY'RE NOT MOVING!
LOOK!
XERXER'S HORN HAS TURNED COMPLETELY BLUE!
AND YVEL-TAL'S EYES HAVE TURNED COM-PLETELY WHITE!
CHIL-DREN ...

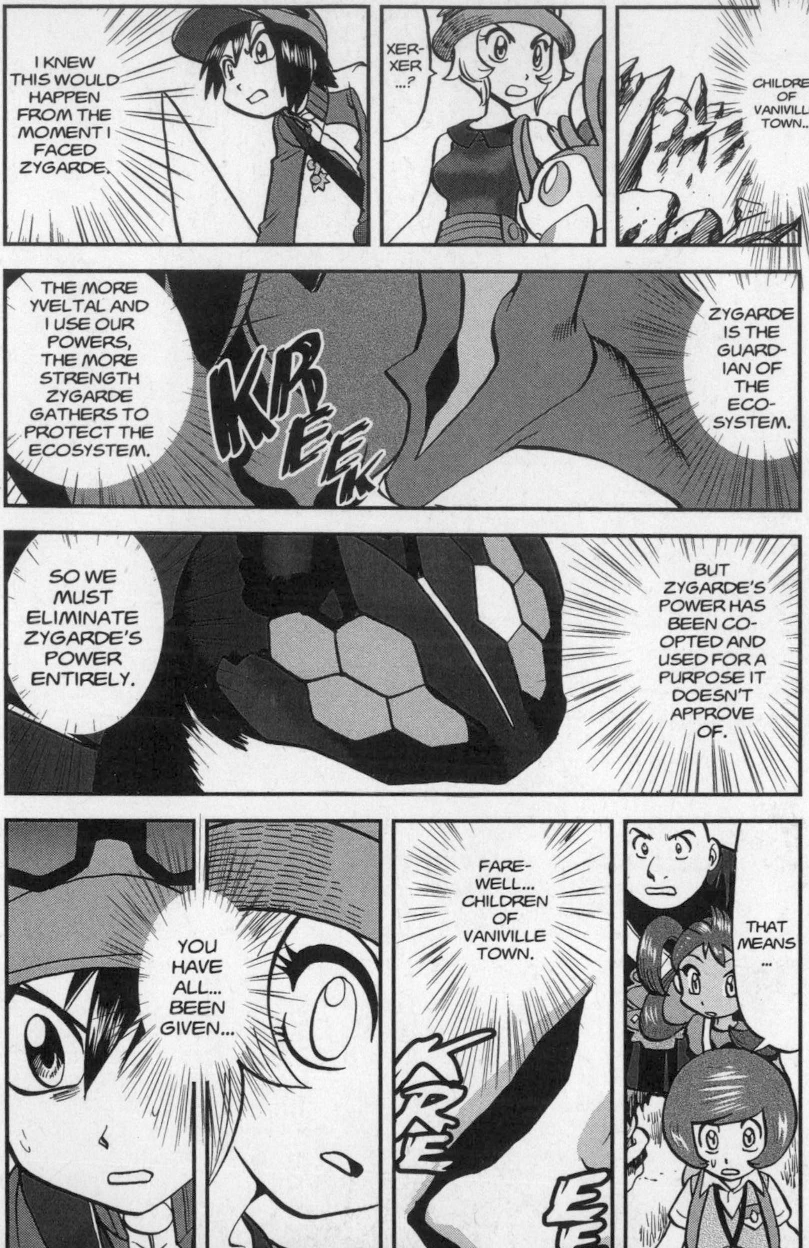

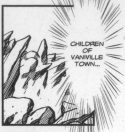

CHILDREN OF VANIVILLE TOWN...
XER-XER ...?
I KNEW THIS WOULD HAPPEN FROM THE MOMENT I FACED ZYGARDE.
ZYGARDE IS THE GUARDIAN OF THE ECOSYSTEM.
THE MORE YVELTAL AND I USE OUR POWERS, THE MORE STRENGTH ZYGARDE GATHERS TO PROTECT THE ECOSYSTEM.
KRREEK
BUT ZYGARDE'S POWER HAS BEEN CO-OPTED AND USED FOR A PURPOSE IT DOESN'T APPROVE OF.
SO WE MUST ELIMINATE ZYGARDE'S POWER ENTIRELY.
THAT MEANS...
FARE-WELL... CHILDREN OF VANIVILLE TOWN.
KREEEEK
YOU HAVE ALL... BEEN GIVEN...

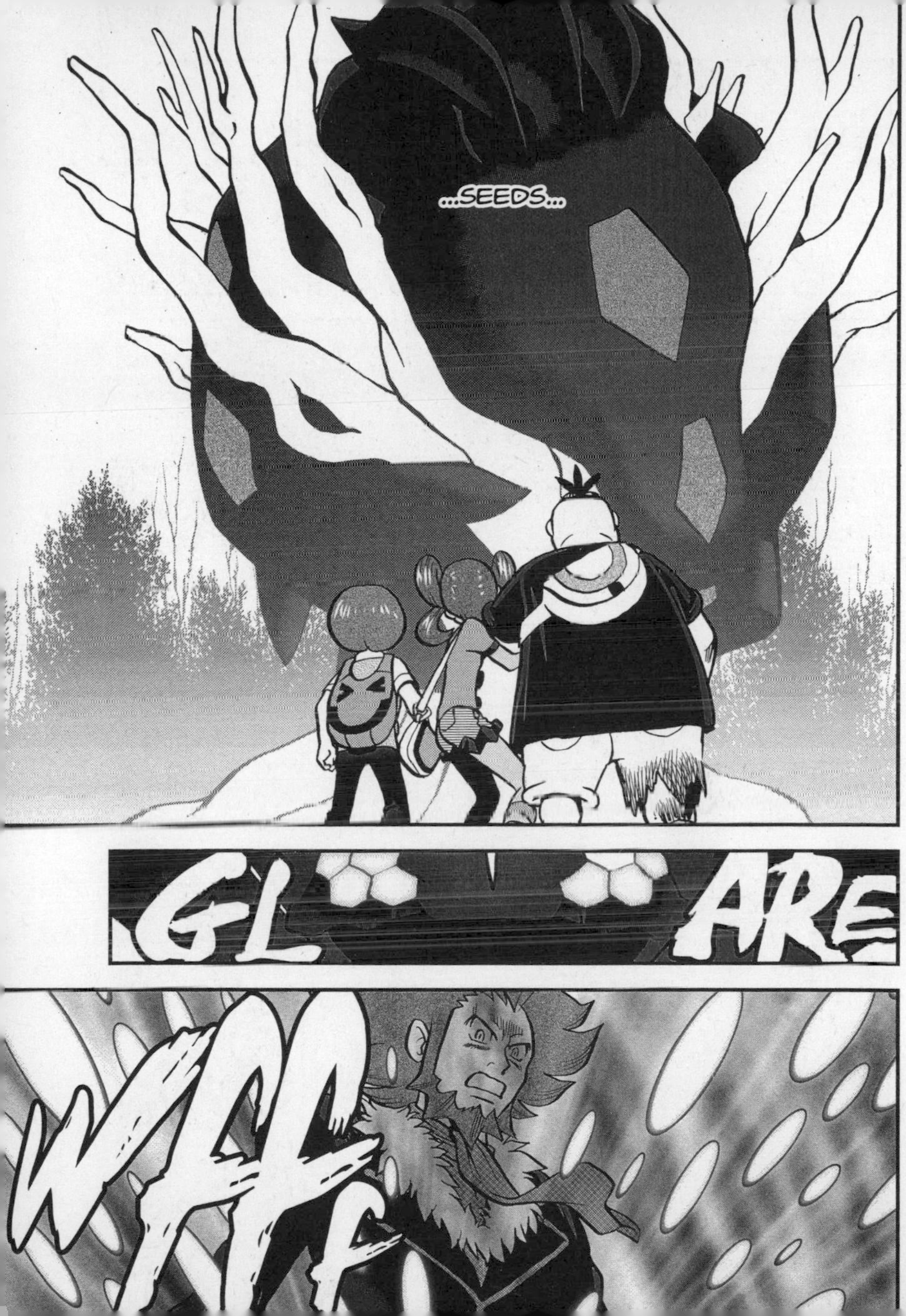
...SEEDS...
GLARE
WAH

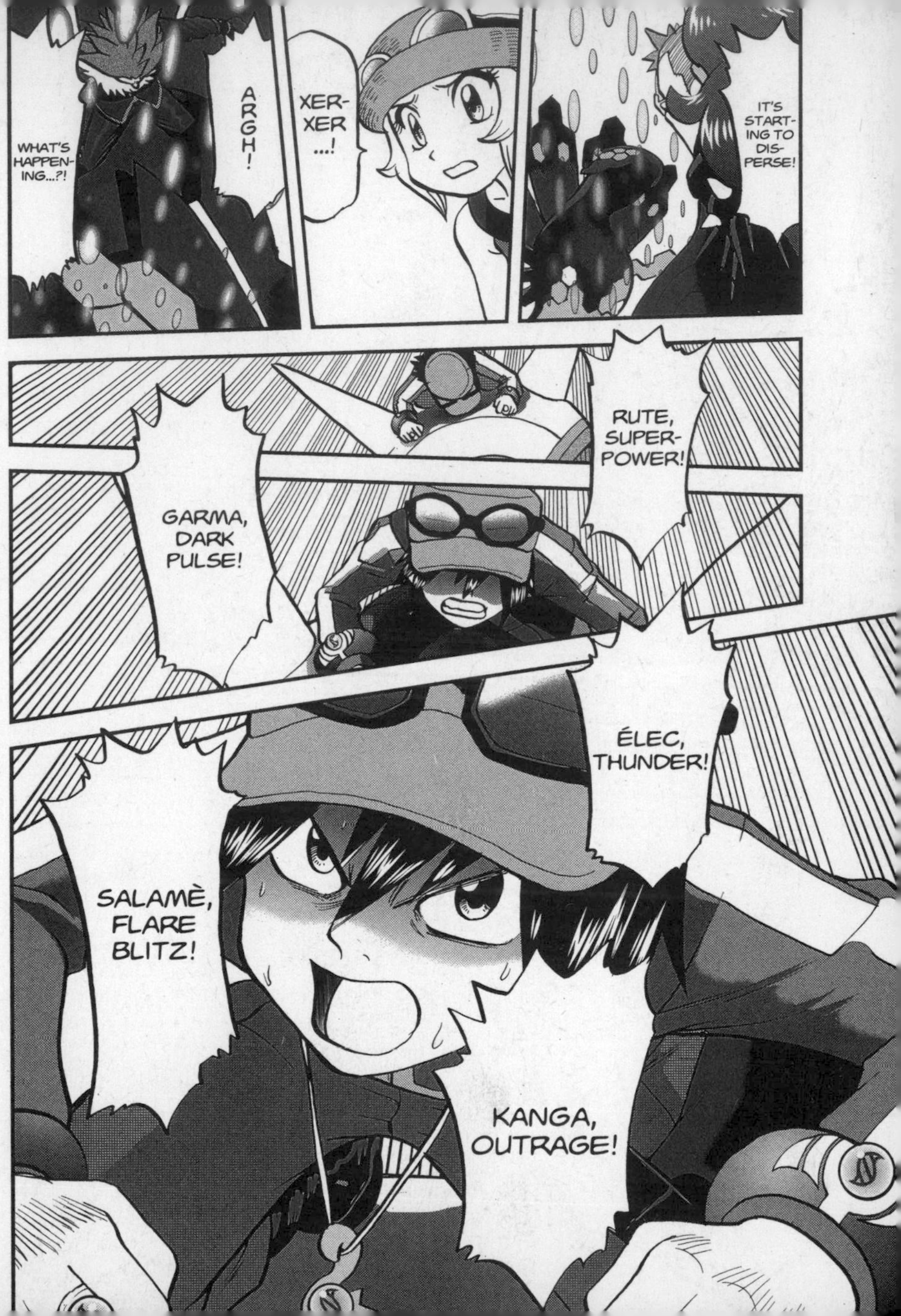
IT'S STARTING TO DISPERSE!
XER-XER...!
ARGH!
WHAT'S HAPPENING...?!
RUTE, SUPER-POWER!
GARMA, DARK PULSE!
ÉLEC, THUNDER!
SALAMÈ, FLARE BLITZ!
KANGA, OUTRAGE!

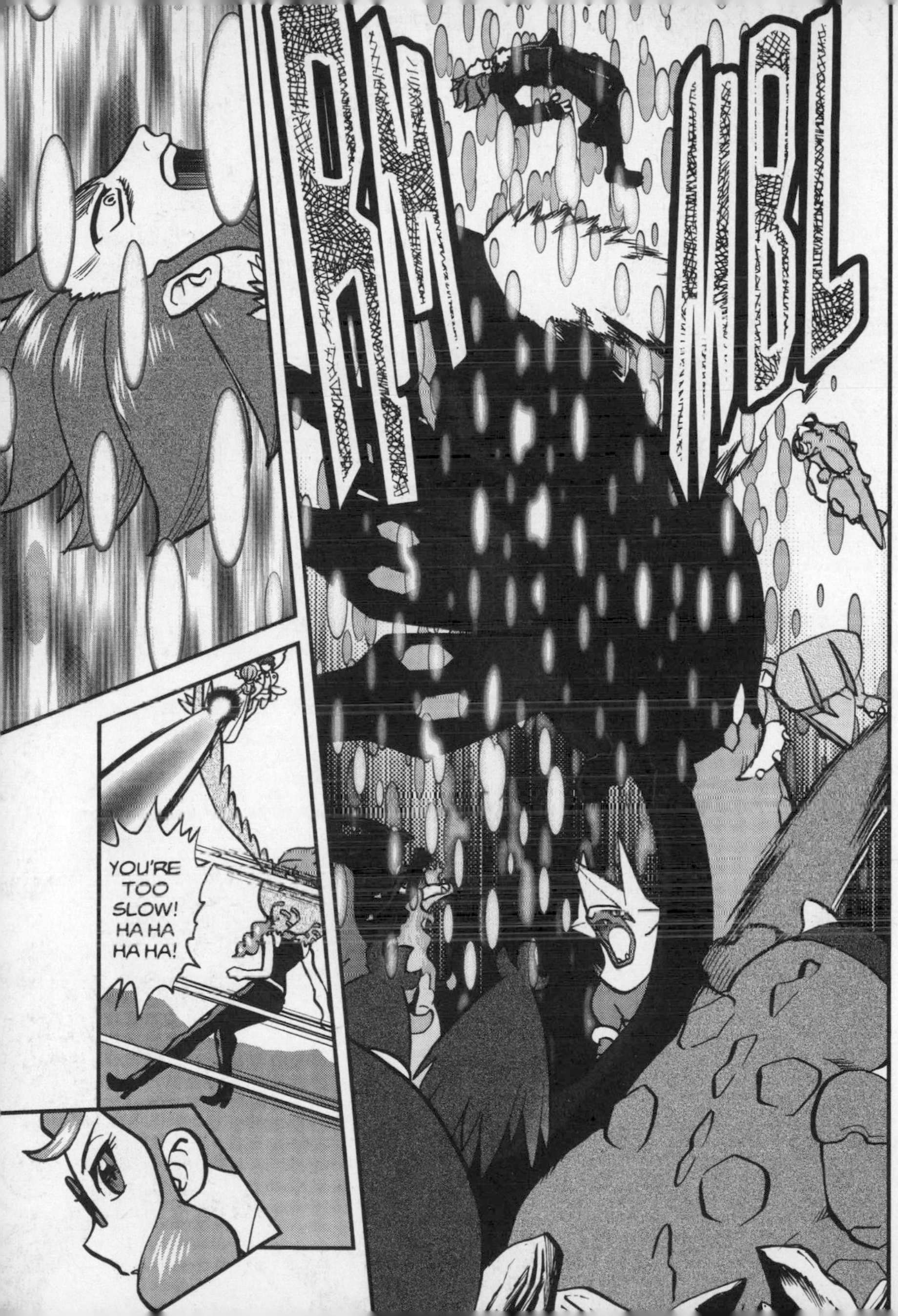
YOU'RE TOO SLOW! HA HA HA HA!

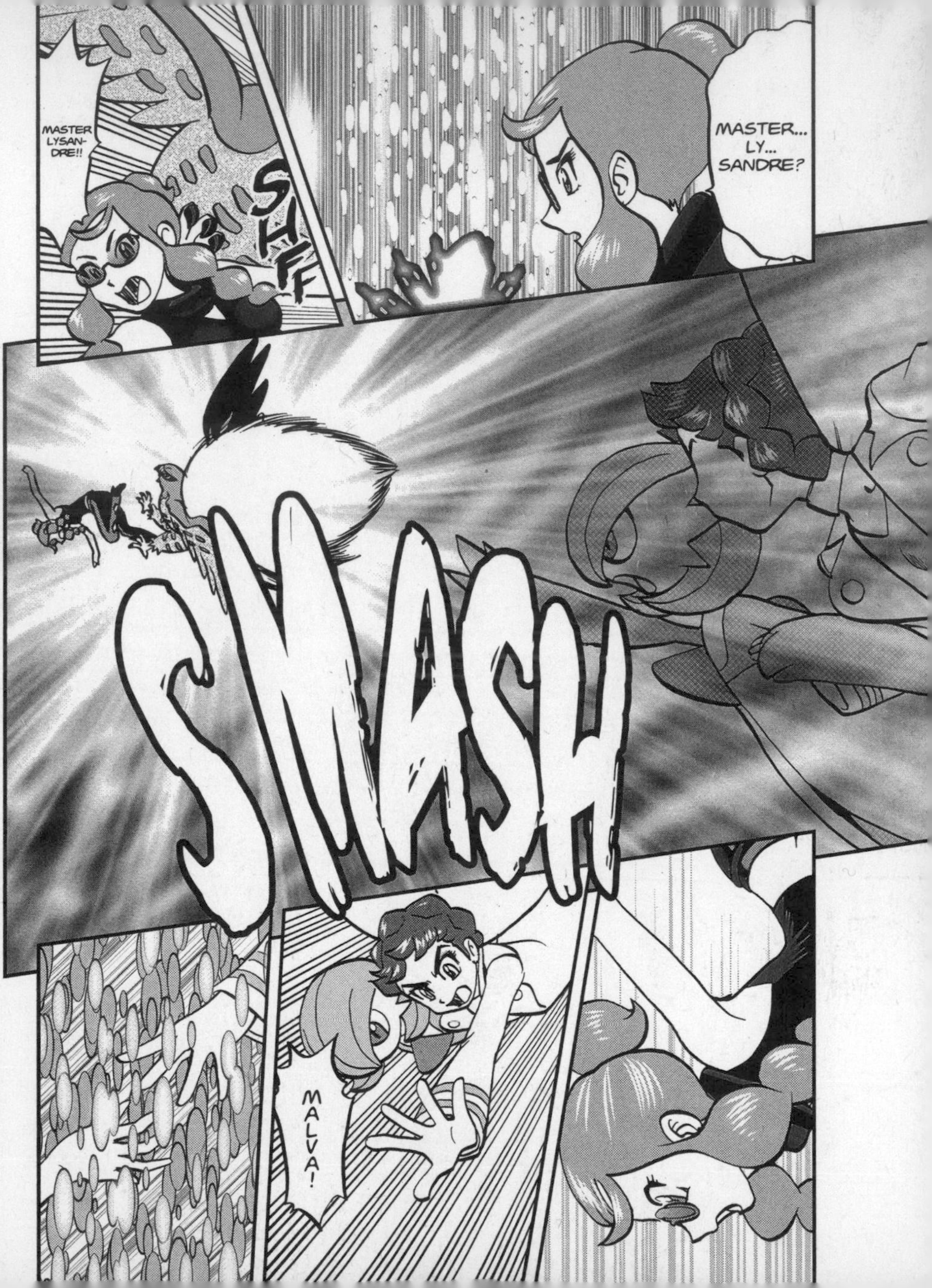
MASTER... LY... SANDRE?
MASTER LYSAN-DRE!!
SHFF
SMASH
MALVA!

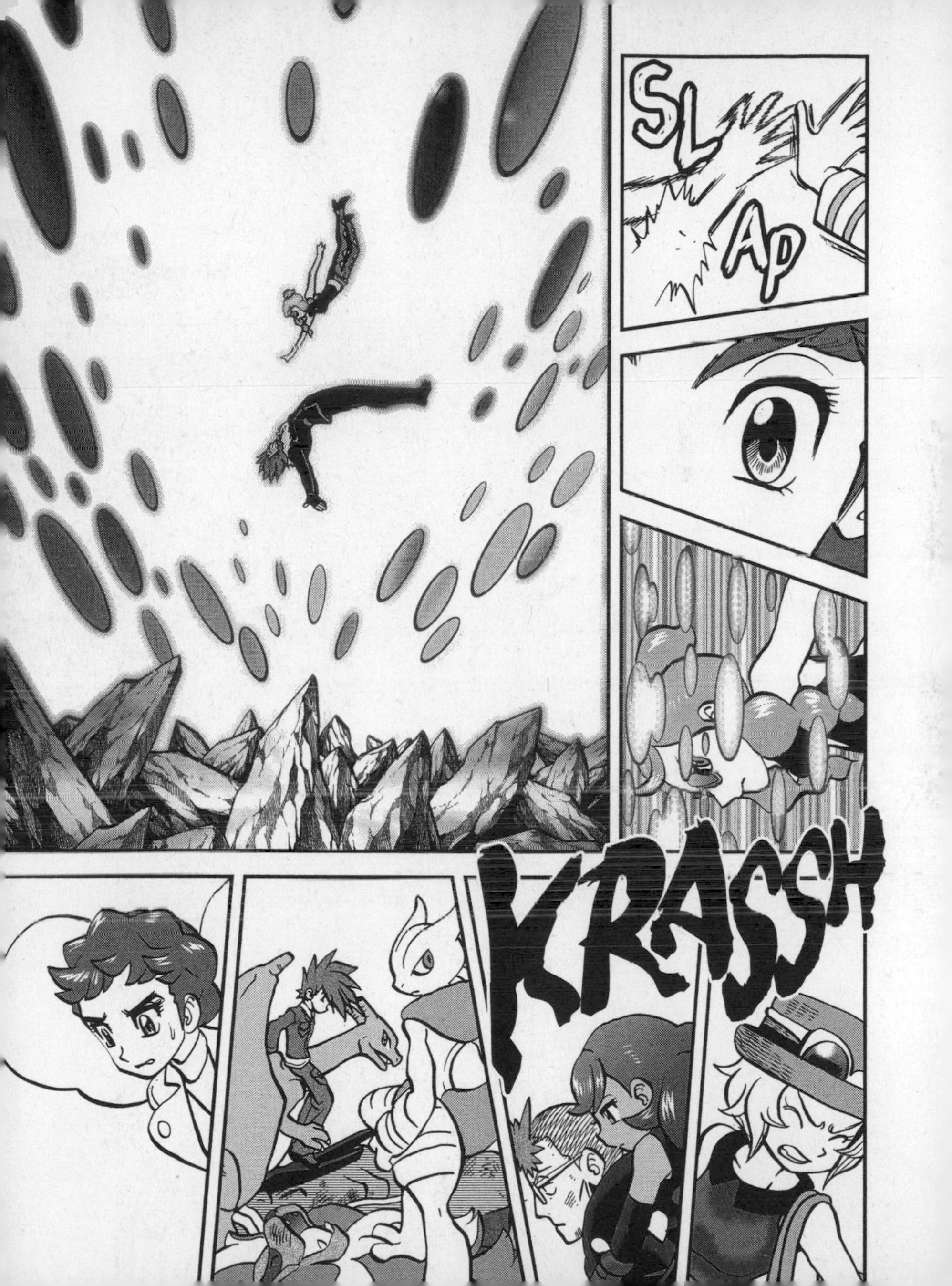
SLAP
KRASSH

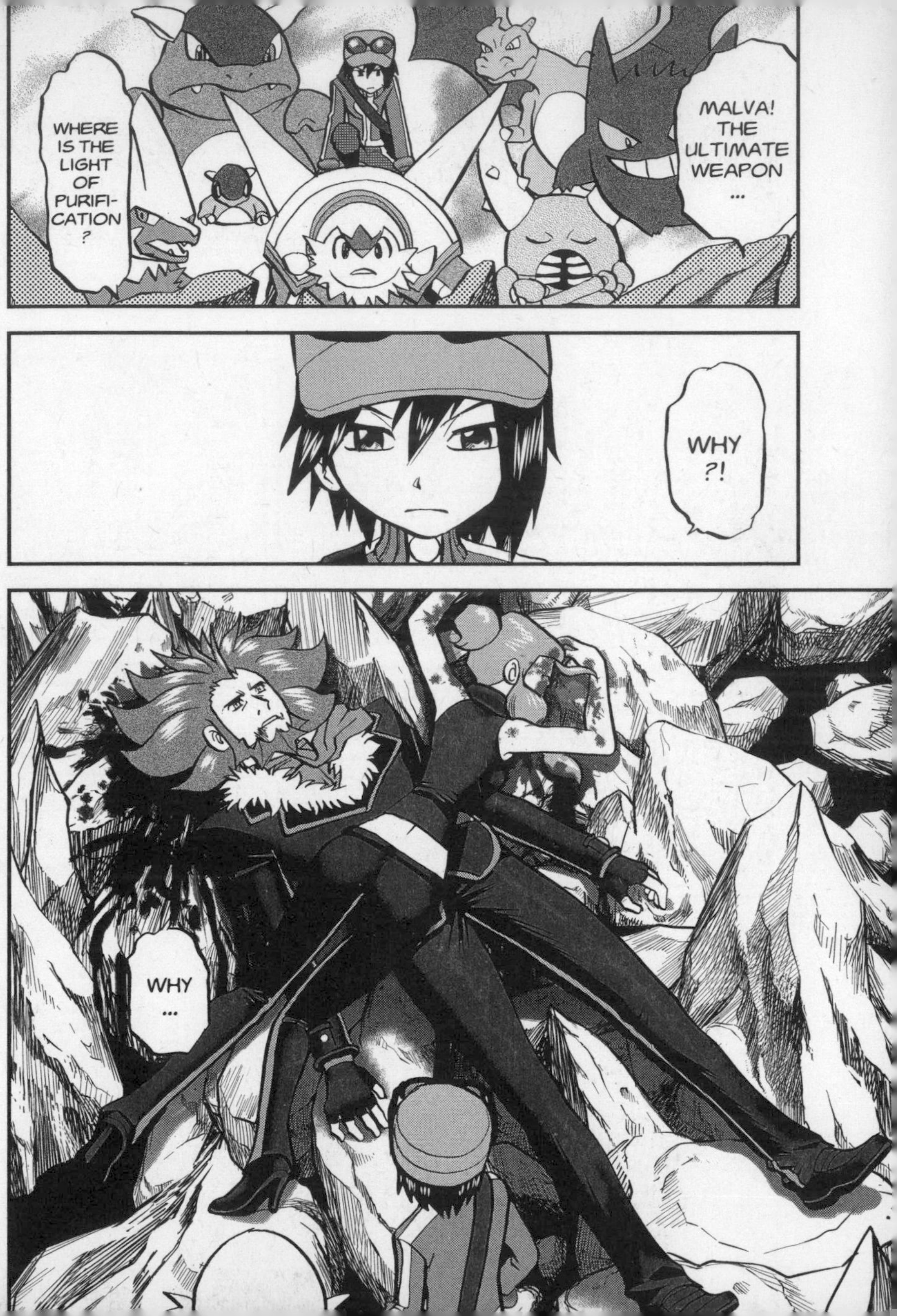
MALVA! THE ULTIMATE WEAPON ...
WHERE IS THE LIGHT OF PURIFICATION ?
WHY ?!
WHY ...

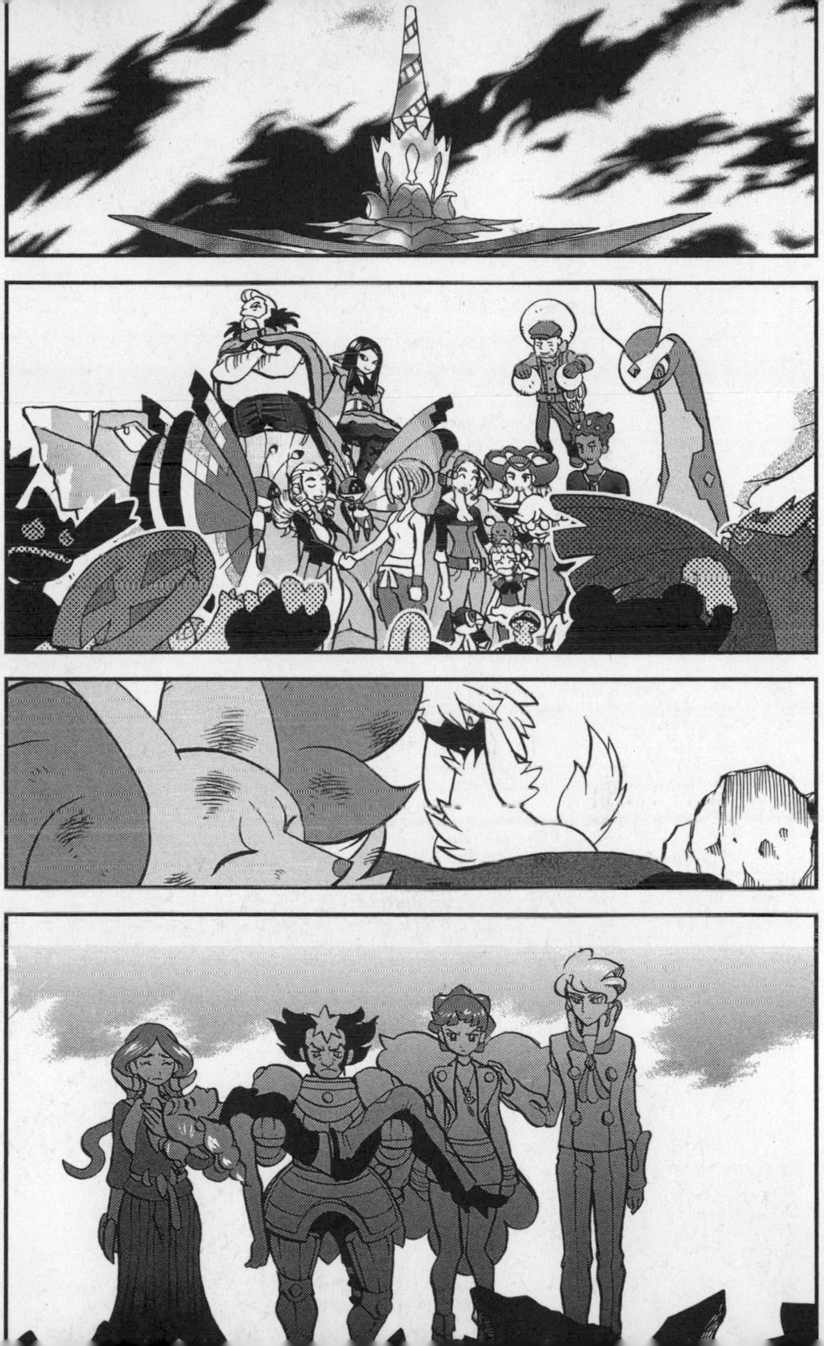

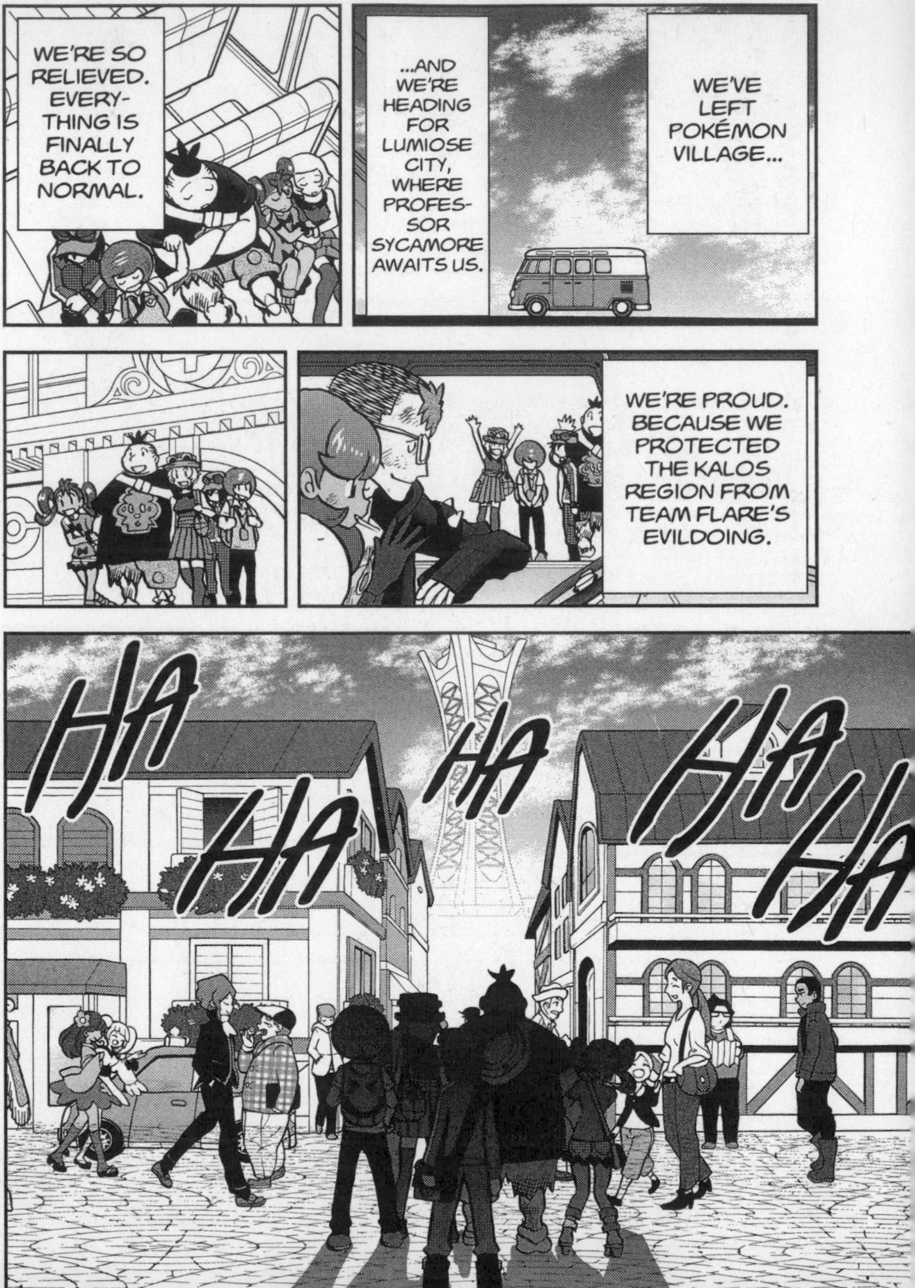
WE'VE LEFT POKÉMON VILLAGE...
...AND WE'RE HEADING FOR LUMIOSE CITY, WHERE PROFESSOR SYCAMORE AWAITS US.
WE'RE SO RELIEVED. EVERYTHING IS FINALLY BACK TO NORMAL.
WE'RE PROUD. BECAUSE WE PROTECTED THE KALOS REGION FROM TEAM FLARE'S EVILDOING.
HA HA HA HA HA HA

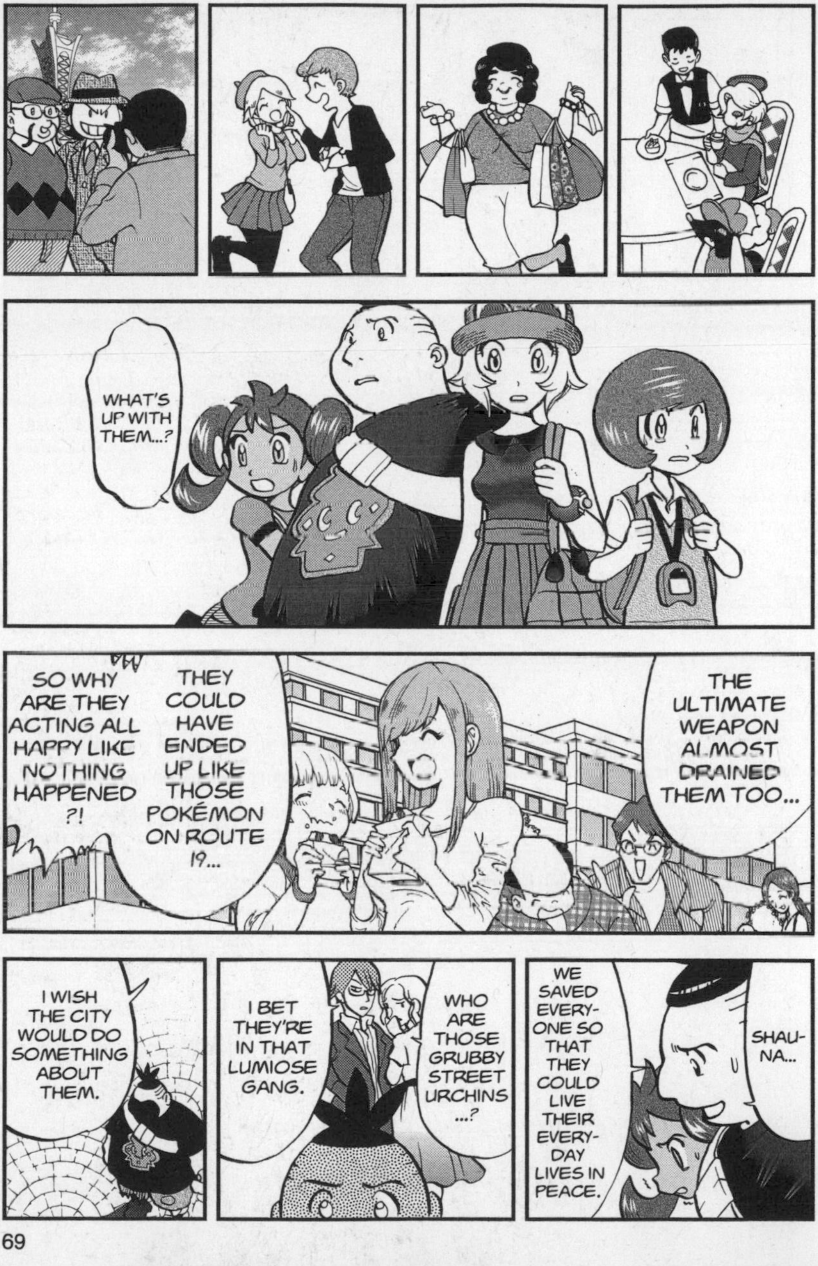
WHAT'S UP WITH THEM...?
THE ULTIMATE WEAPON ALMOST DRAINED THEM TOO...
THEY COULD HAVE ENDED UP LIKE THOSE POKÉMON ON ROUTE 19...
SO WHY ARE THEY ACTING ALL HAPPY LIKE NOTHING HAPPENED?!
SHAUNA...
WE SAVED EVERYONE SO THAT THEY COULD LIVE THEIR EVERYDAY LIVES IN PEACE.
WHO ARE THOSE GRUBBY STREET URCHINS...?
I BET THEY'RE IN THAT LUMIOSE GANG.
I WISH THE CITY WOULD DO SOMETHING ABOUT THEM.

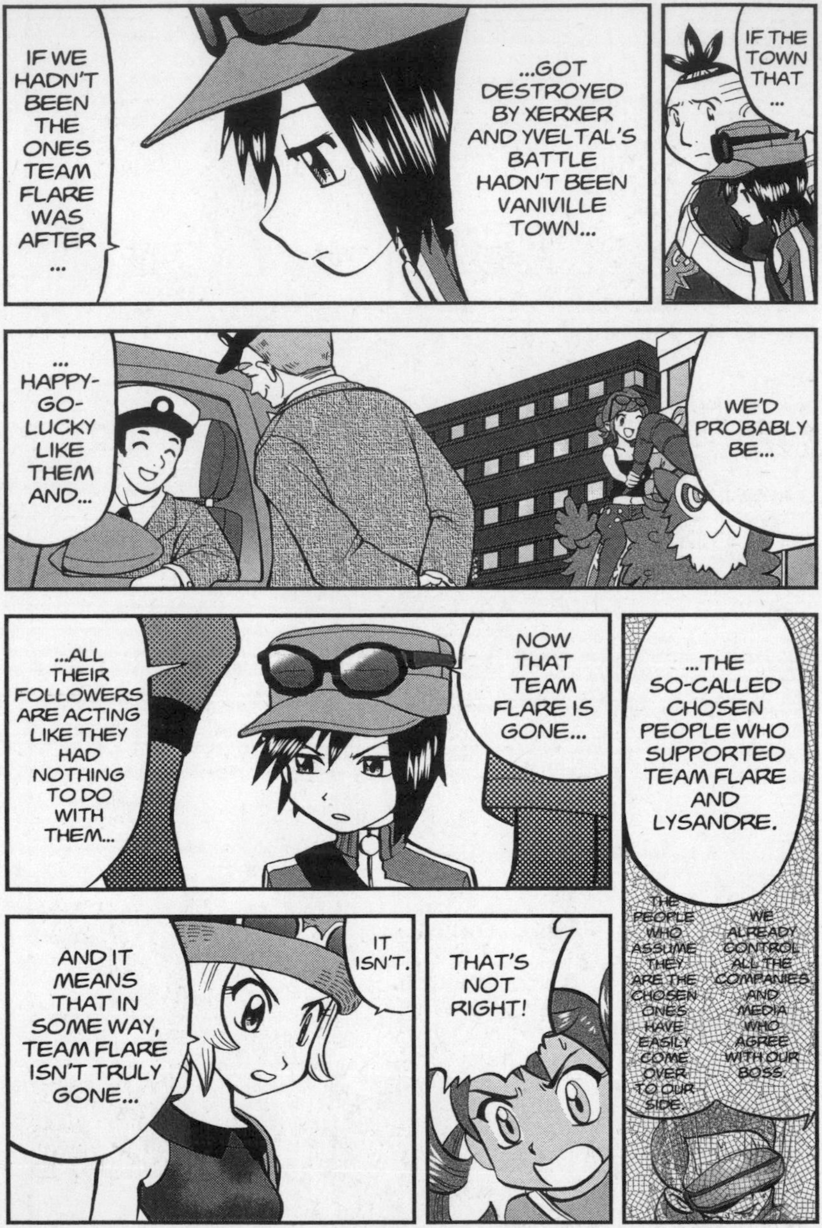
IF THE TOWN THAT ...
...GOT DESTROYED BY XERXER AND YVELTAL'S BATTLE HADN'T BEEN VANIVILLE TOWN...
IF WE HADN'T BEEN THE ONES TEAM FLARE WAS AFTER ...
WE'D PROBABLY BE...
... HAPPY-GO-LUCKY LIKE THEM AND...
...THE SO-CALLED CHOSEN PEOPLE WHO SUPPORTED TEAM FLARE AND LYSANDRE.
WE ALREADY CONTROL ALL THE COMPANIES AND MEDIA WHO AGREE WITH OUR BOSS.
THE PEOPLE WHO ASSUME THEY ARE THE CHOSEN ONES HAVE EASILY COME OVER TO OUR SIDE.
NOW THAT TEAM FLARE IS GONE...
...ALL THEIR FOLLOWERS ARE ACTING LIKE THEY HAD NOTHING TO DO WITH THEM...
THAT'S NOT RIGHT!
IT ISN'T.
AND IT MEANS THAT IN SOME WAY, TEAM FLARE ISN'T TRULY GONE...

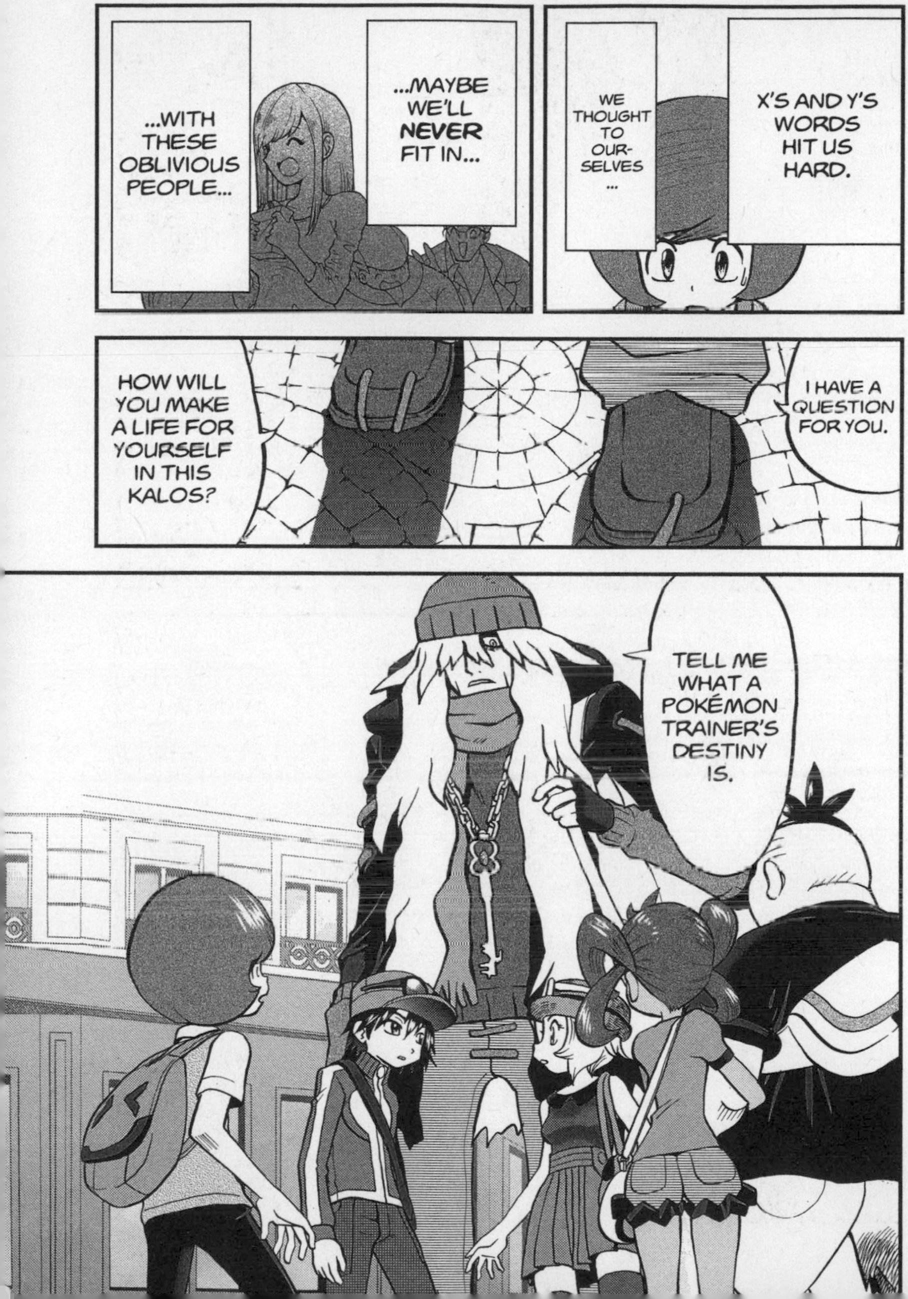
X'S AND Y'S WORDS HIT US HARD.
WE THOUGHT TO OUR-SELVES ...
...MAYBE WE'LL **NEVER** FIT IN...
...WITH THESE OBLIVIOUS PEOPLE...
I HAVE A QUESTION FOR YOU.
HOW WILL YOU MAKE A LIFE FOR YOURSELF IN THIS KALOS?
TELL ME WHAT A POKÉMON TRAINER'S DESTINY IS.

Current Location

Lumiose City

A dazzling metropolis of art and artifice, located in the very heart of the Kalos region.

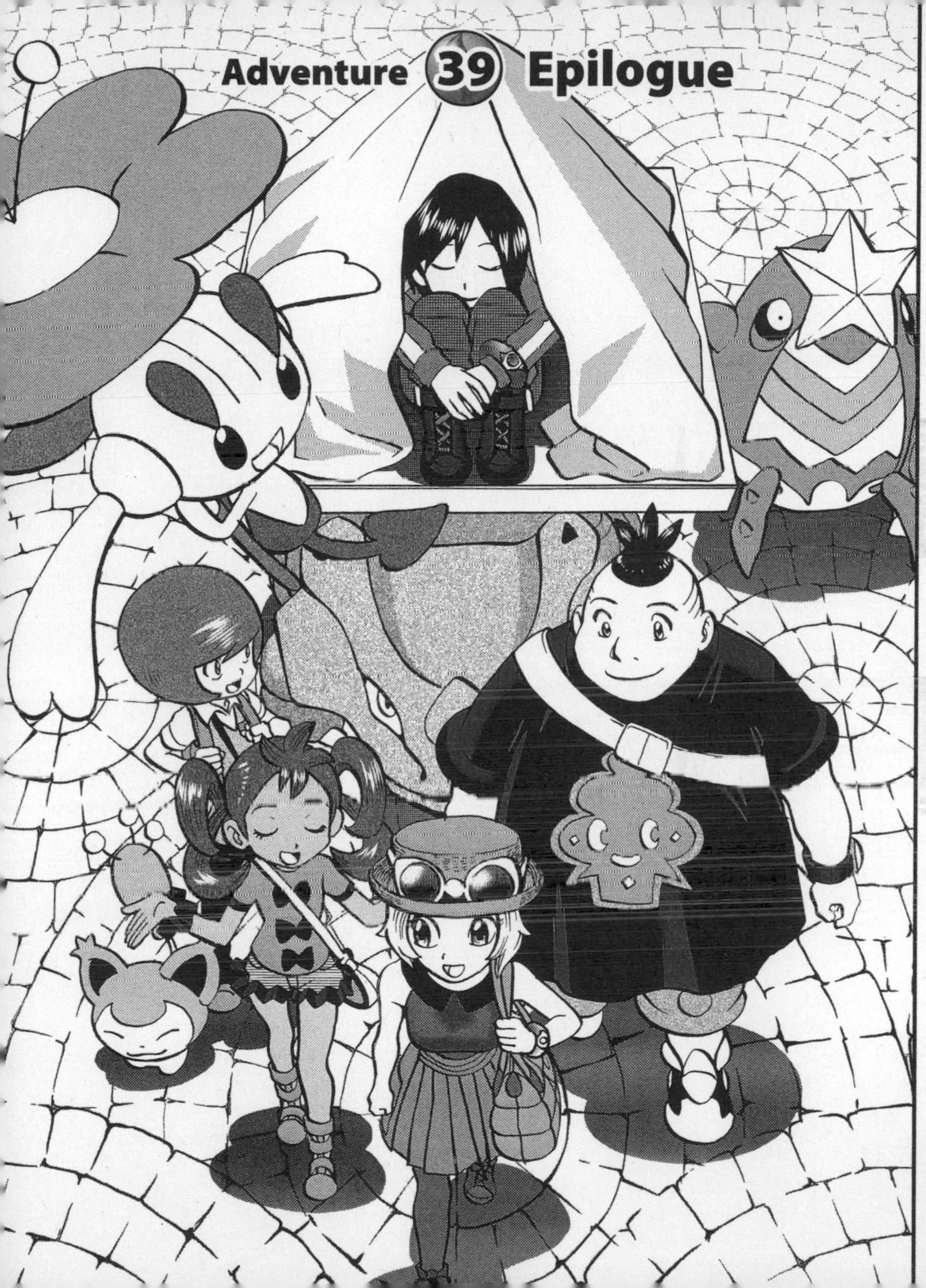
Adventure 39 Epilogue

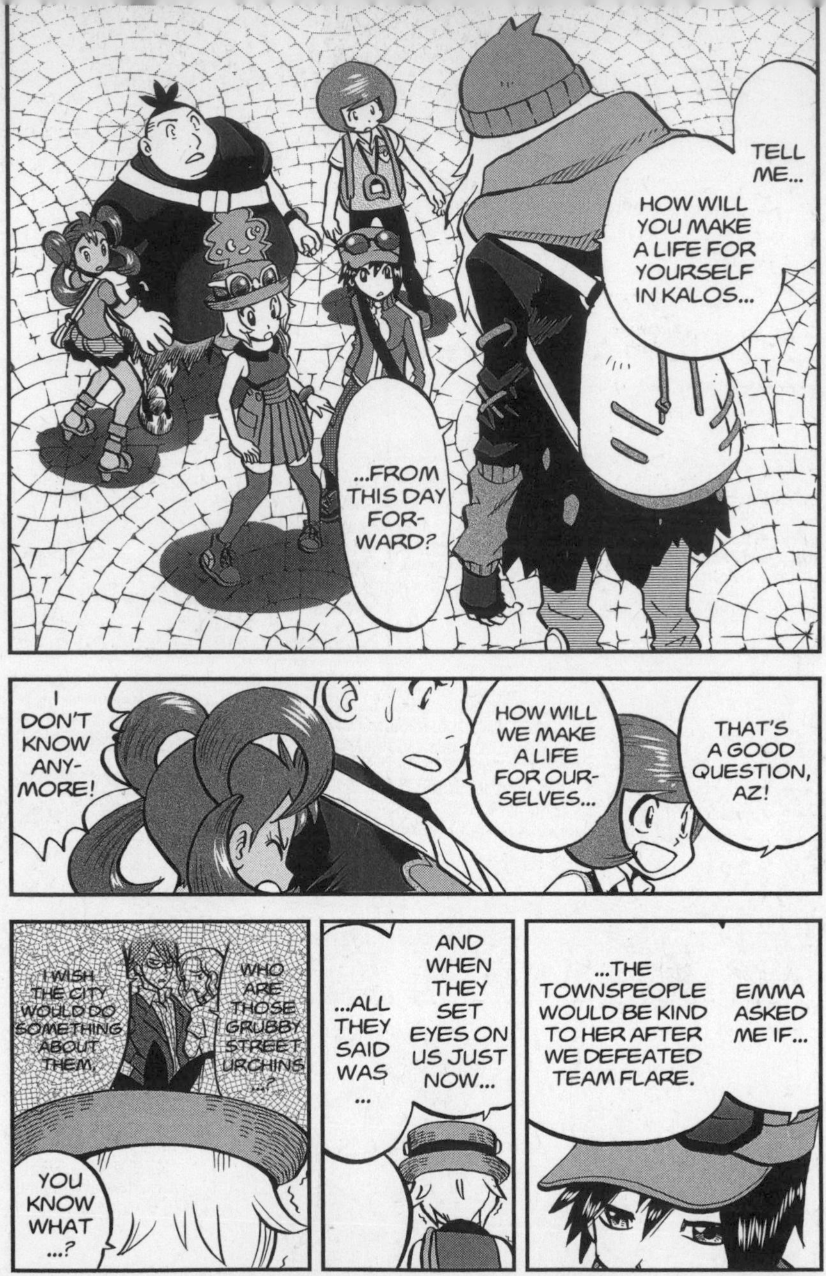
TELL ME...
HOW WILL YOU MAKE A LIFE FOR YOURSELF IN KALOS...
...FROM THIS DAY FOR-WARD?
THAT'S A GOOD QUESTION, AZ!
HOW WILL WE MAKE A LIFE FOR OUR-SELVES...
I DON'T KNOW ANY-MORE!
EMMA ASKED ME IF...
...THE TOWNSPEOPLE WOULD BE KIND TO HER AFTER WE DEFEATED TEAM FLARE.
AND WHEN THEY SET EYES ON US JUST NOW...
...ALL THEY SAID WAS ...
WHO ARE THOSE GRUBBY STREET URCHINS ...?
I WISH THE CITY WOULD DO SOMETHING ABOUT THEM.
YOU KNOW WHAT ...?

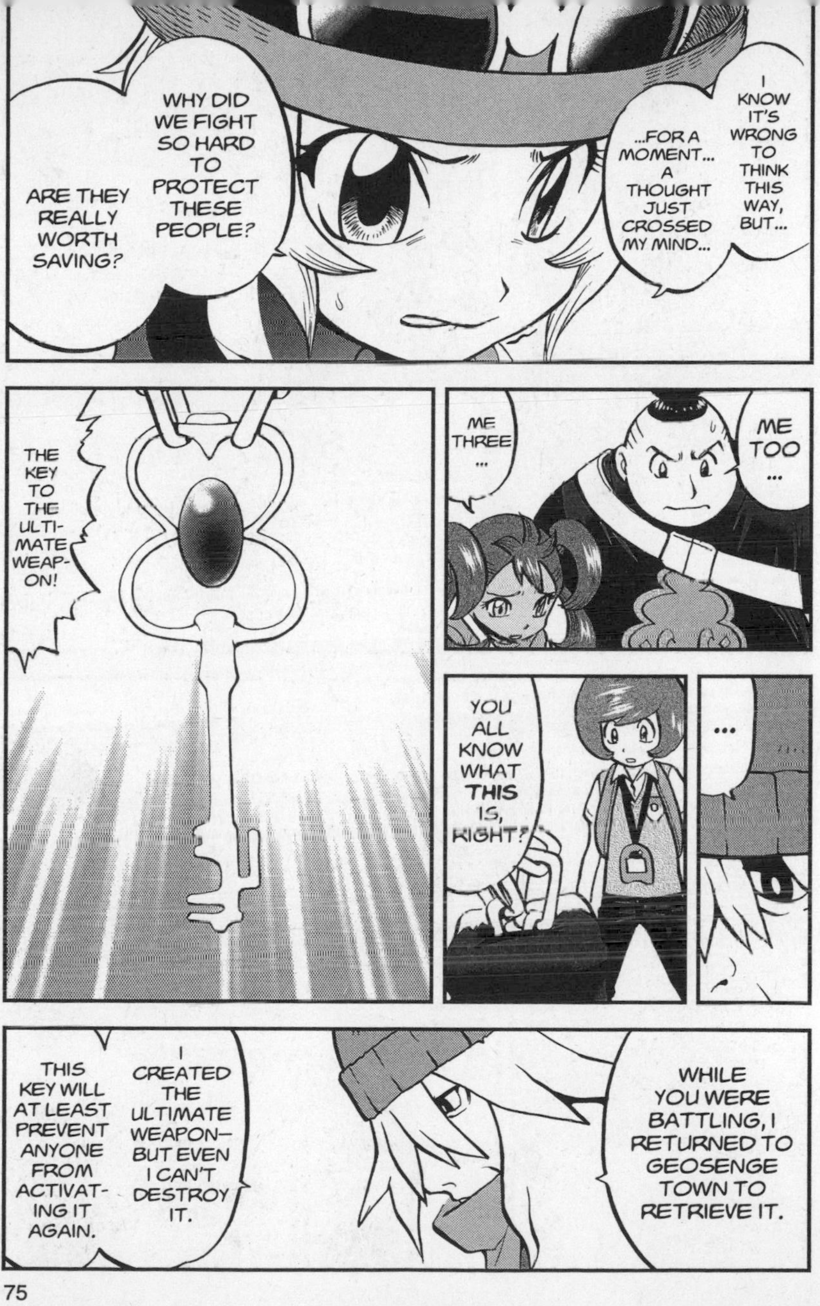
I KNOW IT'S WRONG TO THINK THIS WAY, BUT...
...FOR A MOMENT... A THOUGHT JUST CROSSED MY MIND...
WHY DID WE FIGHT SO HARD TO PROTECT THESE PEOPLE?
ARE THEY REALLY WORTH SAVING?
ME TOO...
ME THREE...
...
YOU ALL KNOW WHAT THIS IS, RIGHT?
THE KEY TO THE ULTIMATE WEAPON!
WHILE YOU WERE BATTLING, I RETURNED TO GEOSENGE TOWN TO RETRIEVE IT.
I CREATED THE ULTIMATE WEAPON—BUT EVEN I CAN'T DESTROY IT.
THIS KEY WILL AT LEAST PREVENT ANYONE FROM ACTIVATING IT AGAIN.

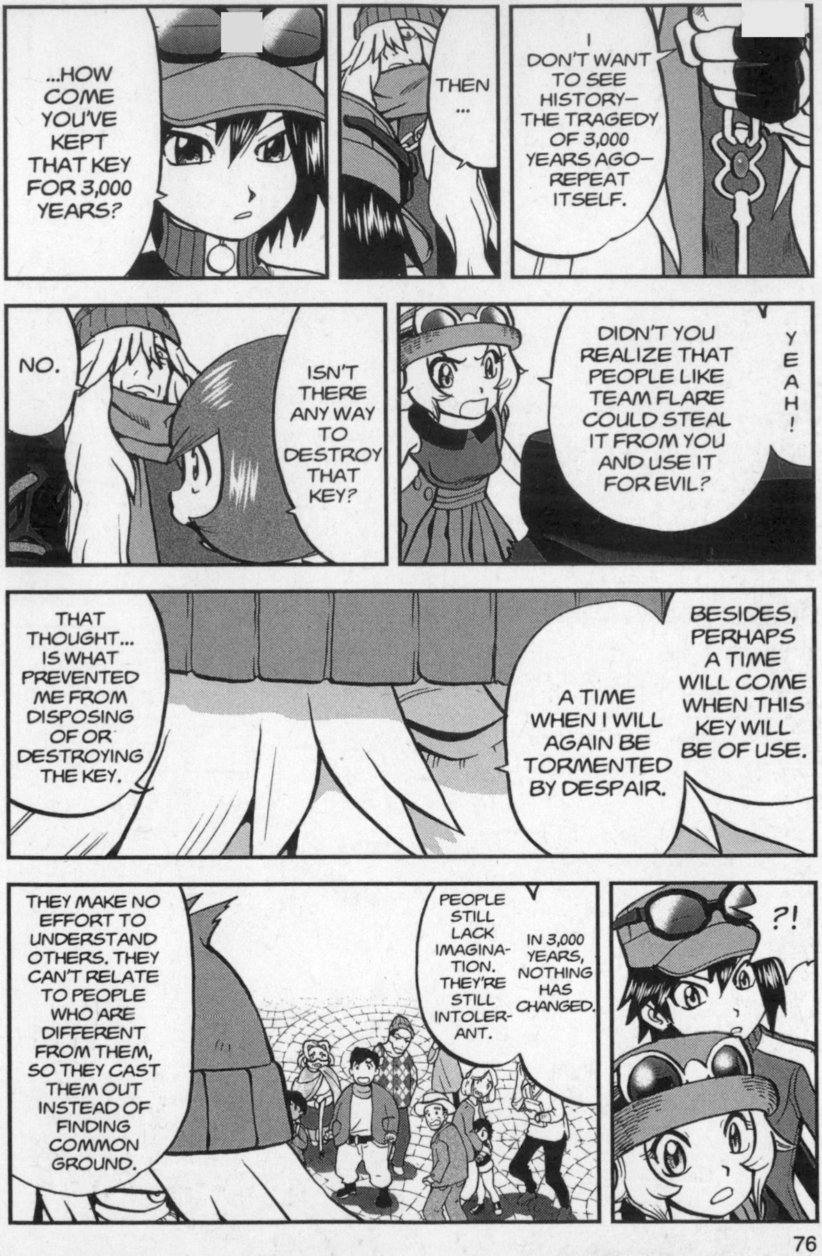
I DON'T WANT TO SEE HISTORY— THE TRAGEDY OF 3,000 YEARS AGO— REPEAT ITSELF.
THEN ...
...HOW COME YOU'VE KEPT THAT KEY FOR 3,000 YEARS?
YEAH!
DIDN'T YOU REALIZE THAT PEOPLE LIKE TEAM FLARE COULD STEAL IT FROM YOU AND USE IT FOR EVIL?
ISN'T THERE ANY WAY TO DESTROY THAT KEY?
NO.
BESIDES, PERHAPS A TIME WILL COME WHEN THIS KEY WILL BE OF USE.
A TIME WHEN I WILL AGAIN BE TORMENTED BY DESPAIR.
THAT THOUGHT... IS WHAT PREVENTED ME FROM DISPOSING OF OR DESTROYING THE KEY.
?!
IN 3,000 YEARS, NOTHING HAS CHANGED.
PEOPLE STILL LACK IMAGINATION. THEY'RE STILL INTOLERANT.
THEY MAKE NO EFFORT TO UNDERSTAND OTHERS. THEY CAN'T RELATE TO PEOPLE WHO ARE DIFFERENT FROM THEM, SO THEY CAST THEM OUT INSTEAD OF FINDING COMMON GROUND.

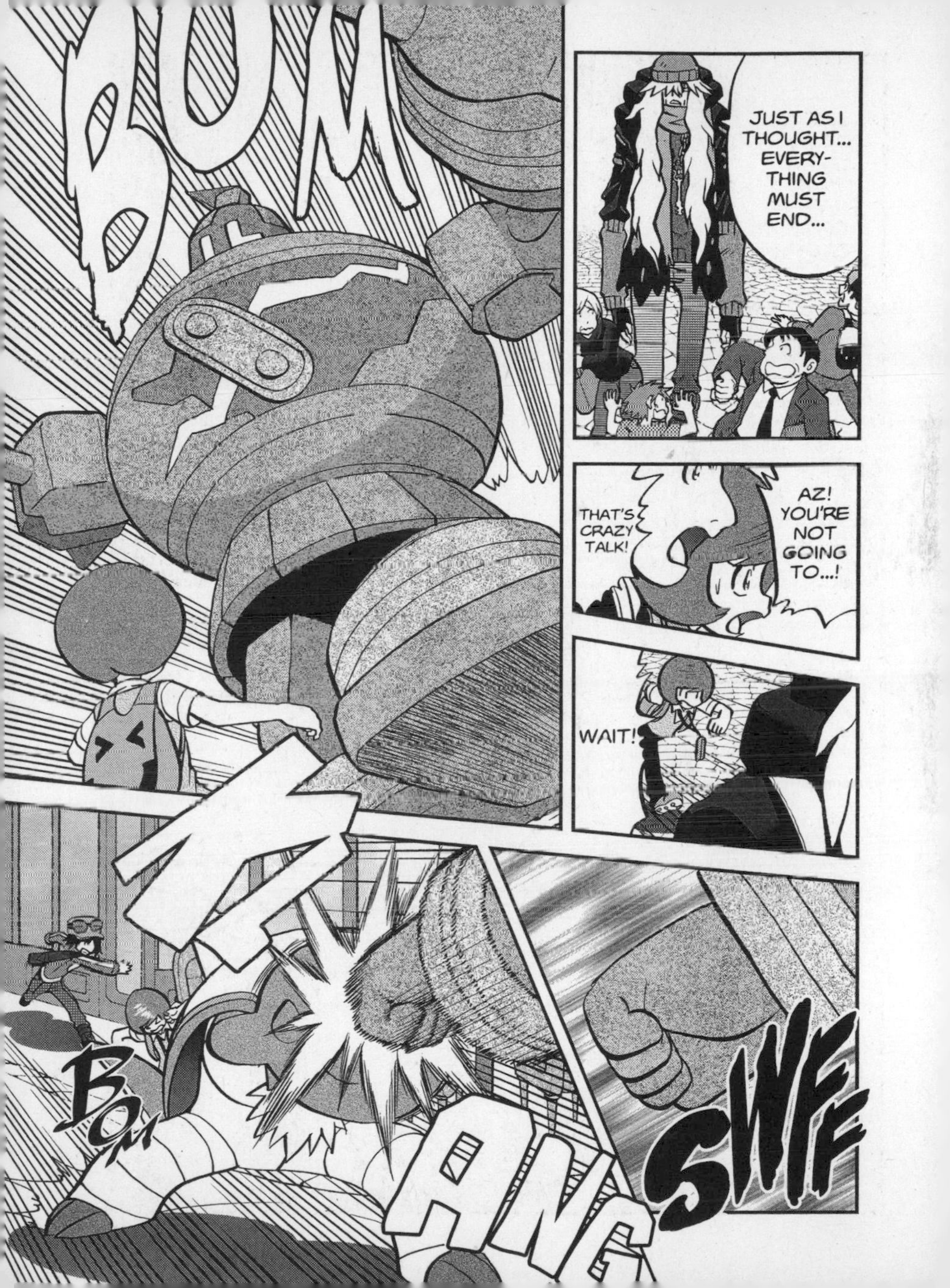
JUST AS I THOUGHT... EVERYTHING MUST END...
AZ! YOU'RE NOT GOING TO...!
THAT'S CRAZY TALK!
WAIT!
BOOM
SWF
BOOM

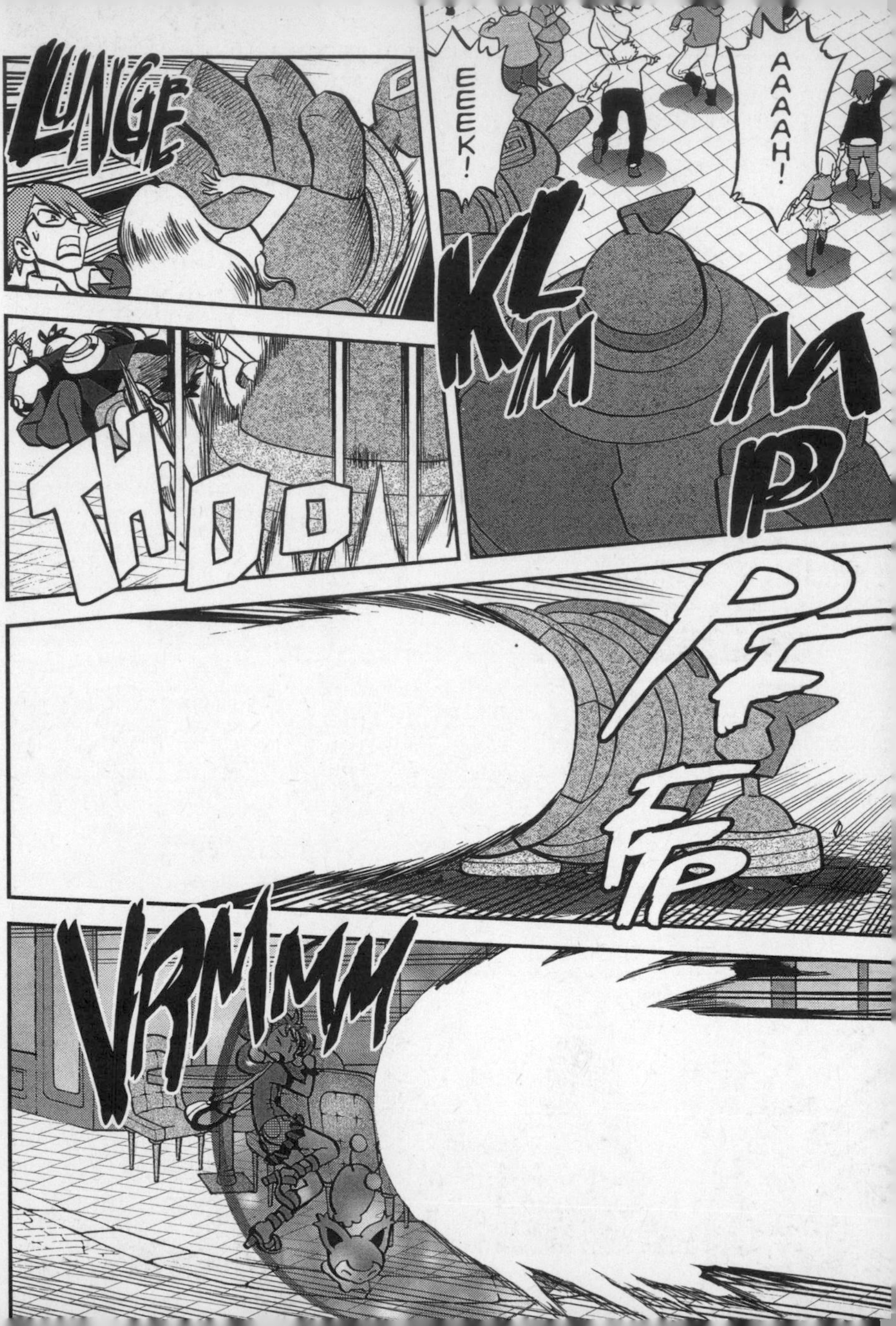
AAAAH!
EEEK!
KLMMP
LUNGE
THOOM
PFFP
VRMMM

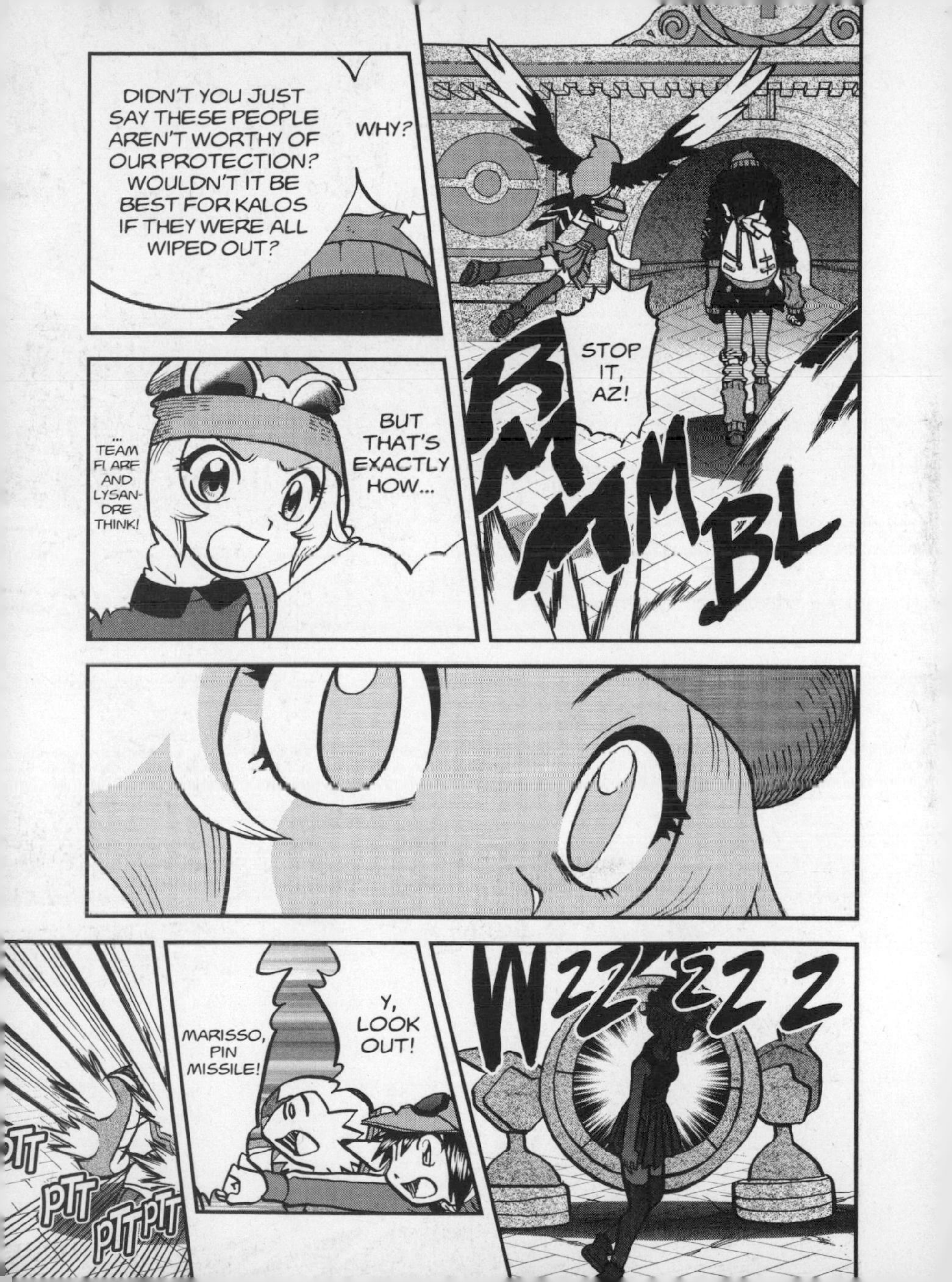
STOP IT, AZ!
RMMMBL
WHY?
DIDN'T YOU JUST SAY THESE PEOPLE AREN'T WORTHY OF OUR PROTECTION? WOULDN'T IT BE BEST FOR KALOS IF THEY WERE ALL WIPED OUT?
BUT THAT'S EXACTLY HOW...
...TEAM FLARE AND LYSANDRE THINK!
WZZZ ZZZ
Y, LOOK OUT!
MARISSO, PIN MISSILE!
PTT
PTT
PTTPTT

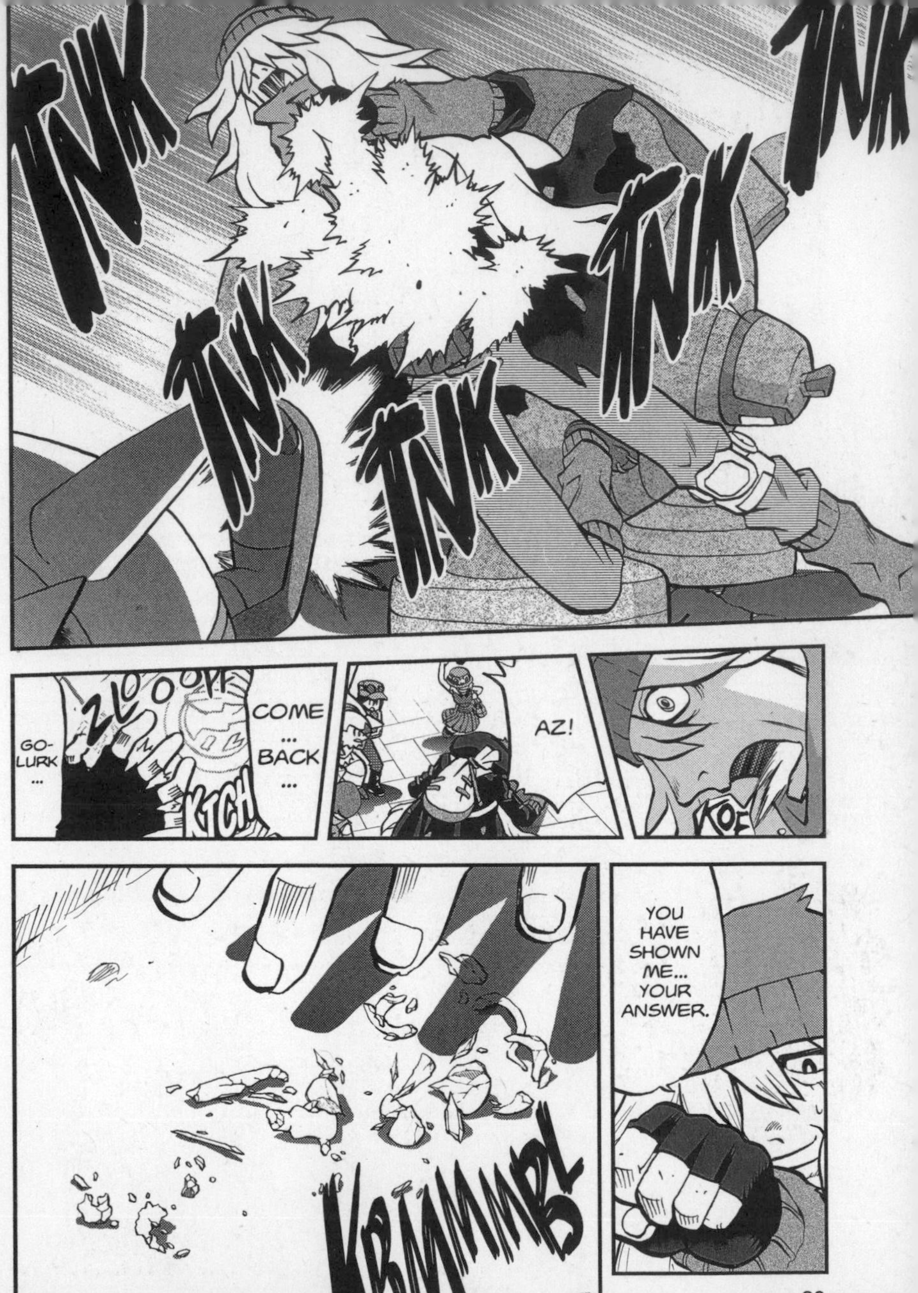
TINK
TINK
TINK
TINK
TINK
TINK
KOF
AZ!
COME ... BACK ...
ZLOOOPF
GO-LURK ...
KTCH
YOU HAVE SHOWN ME... YOUR ANSWER.
KRMMMBL

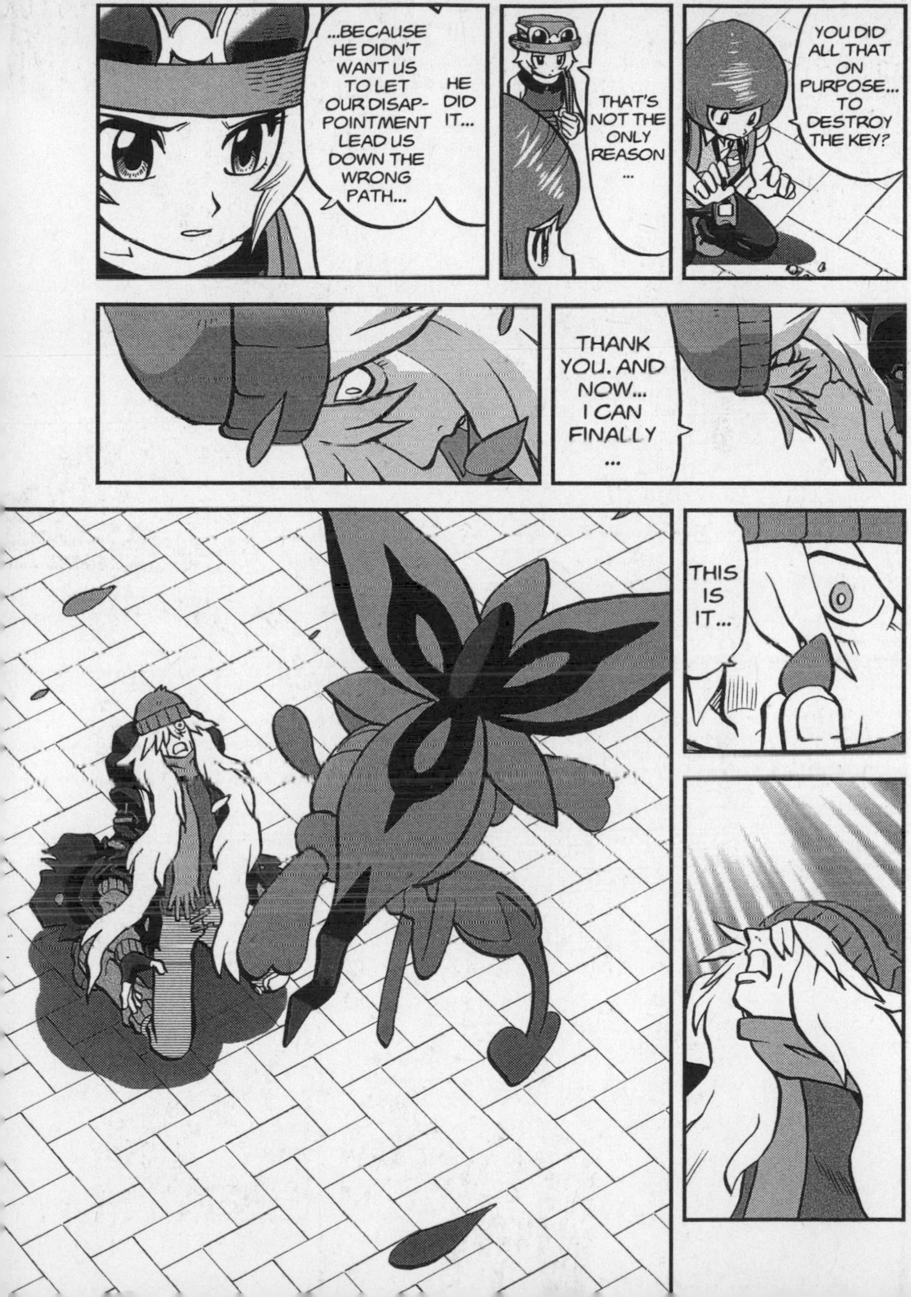
YOU DID ALL THAT ON PURPOSE... TO DESTROY THE KEY?
THAT'S NOT THE ONLY REASON ...
HE DID IT...
...BECAUSE HE DIDN'T WANT US TO LET OUR DISAP-POINTMENT LEAD US DOWN THE WRONG PATH...
THANK YOU. AND NOW... I CAN FINALLY ...
THIS IS IT...

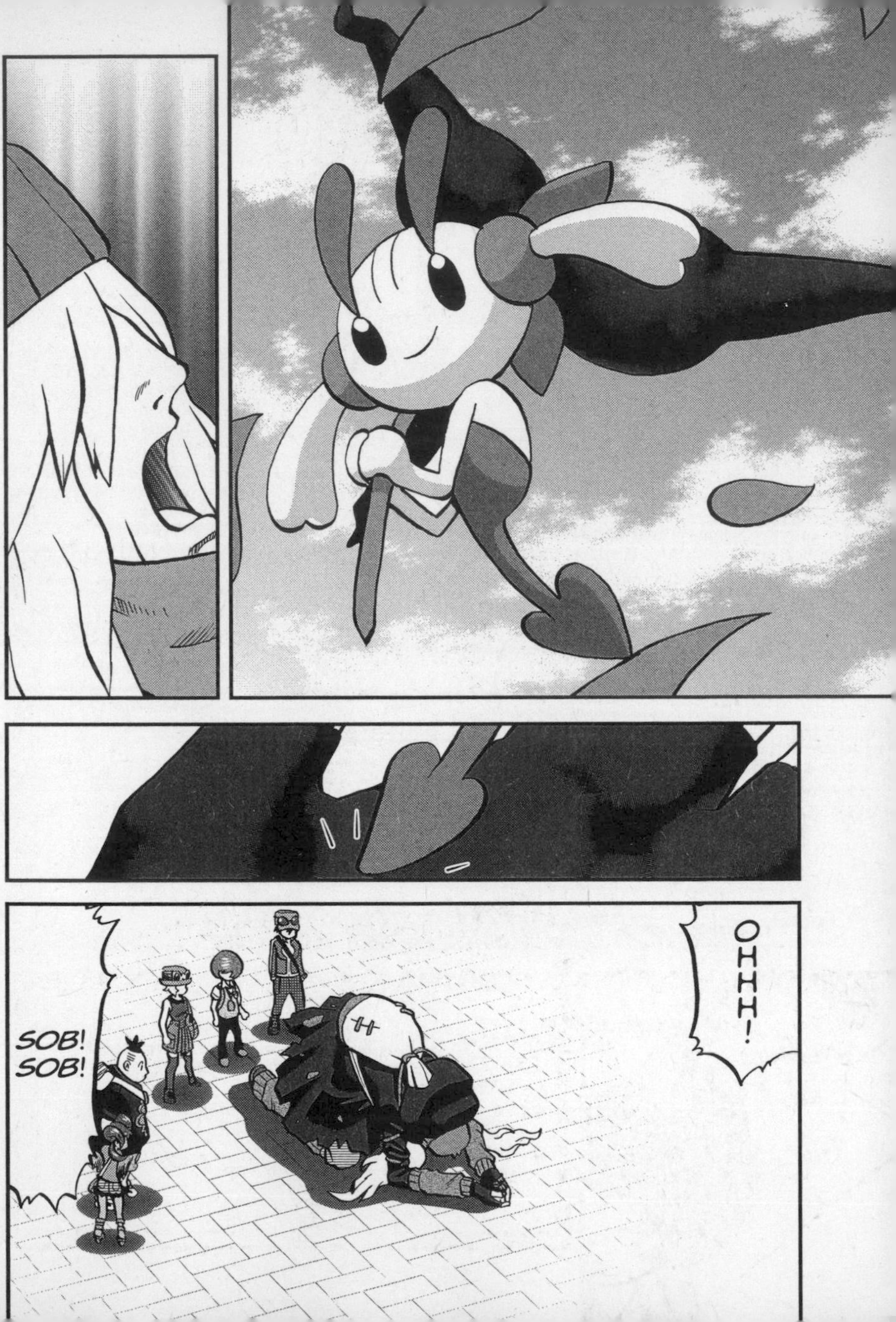
OHHH!
SOB! SOB!

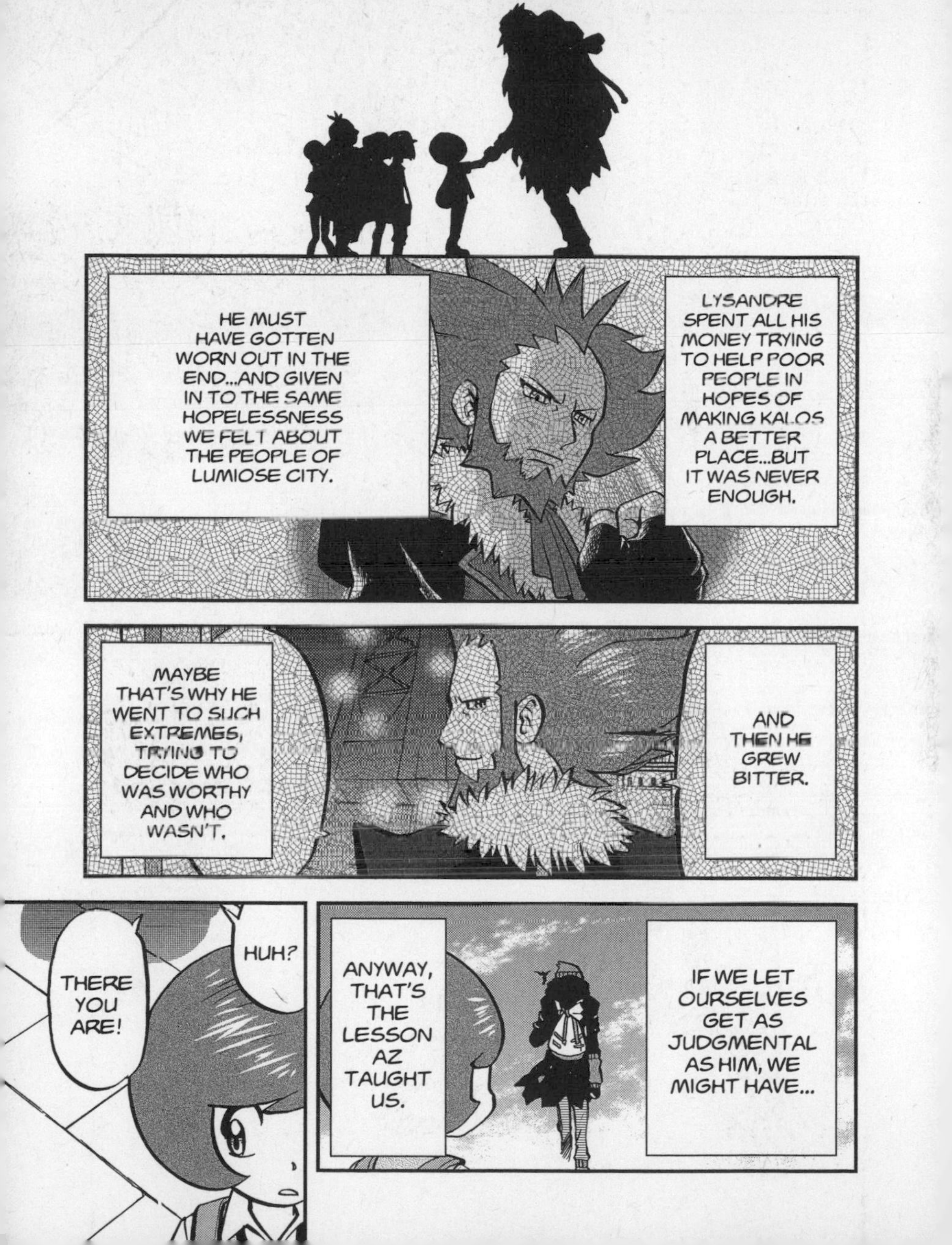
LYSANDRE SPENT ALL HIS MONEY TRYING TO HELP POOR PEOPLE IN HOPES OF MAKING KALOS A BETTER PLACE...BUT IT WAS NEVER ENOUGH.
HE MUST HAVE GOTTEN WORN OUT IN THE END...AND GIVEN IN TO THE SAME HOPELESSNESS WE FELT ABOUT THE PEOPLE OF LUMIOSE CITY.
AND THEN HE GREW BITTER.
MAYBE THAT'S WHY HE WENT TO SUCH EXTREMES, TRYING TO DECIDE WHO WAS WORTHY AND WHO WASN'T.
IF WE LET OURSELVES GET AS JUDGMENTAL AS HIM, WE MIGHT HAVE...
ANYWAY, THAT'S THE LESSON AZ TAUGHT US.
HUH?
THERE YOU ARE!

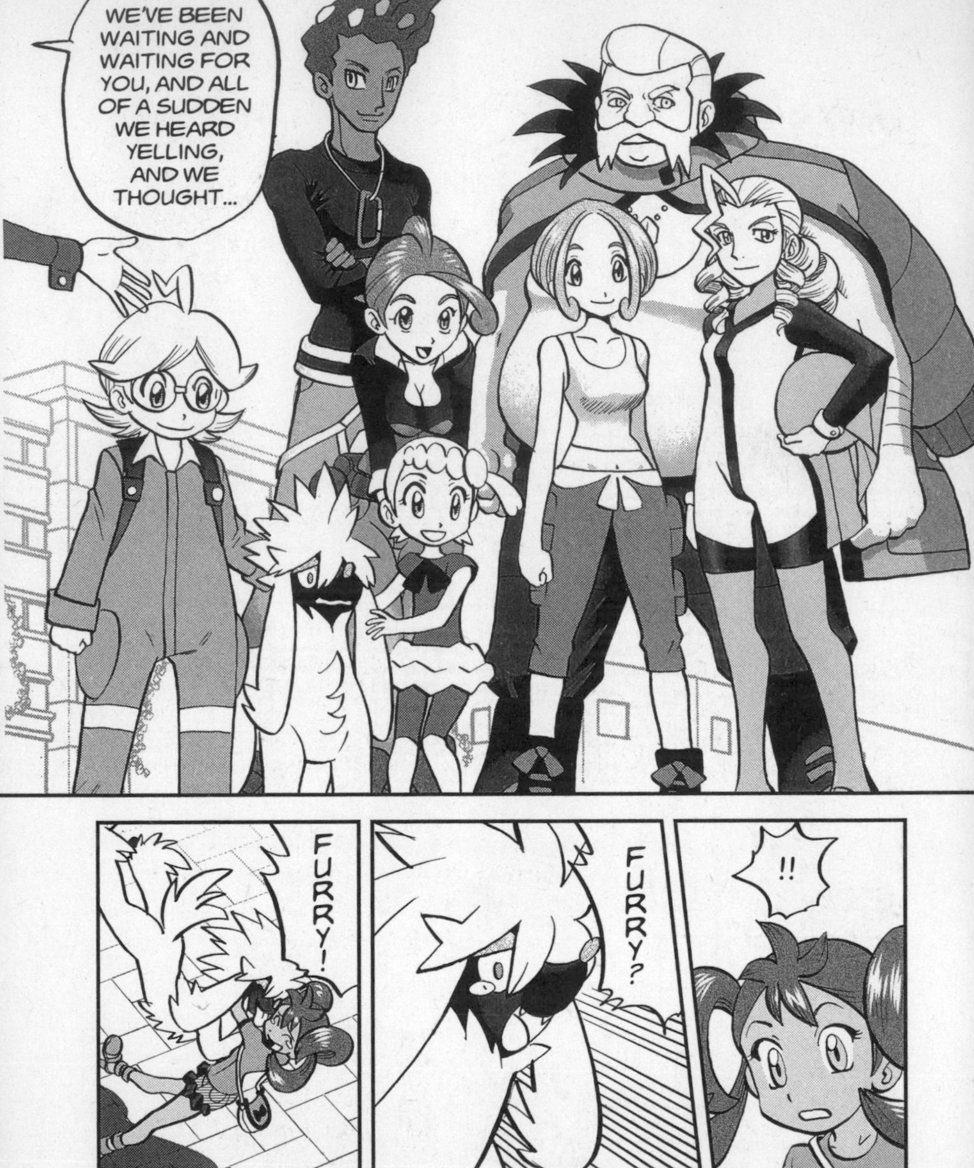
WE'VE BEEN WAITING AND WAITING FOR YOU, AND ALL OF A SUDDEN WE HEARD YELLING, AND WE THOUGHT...
!!
FURRY?
FURRY!

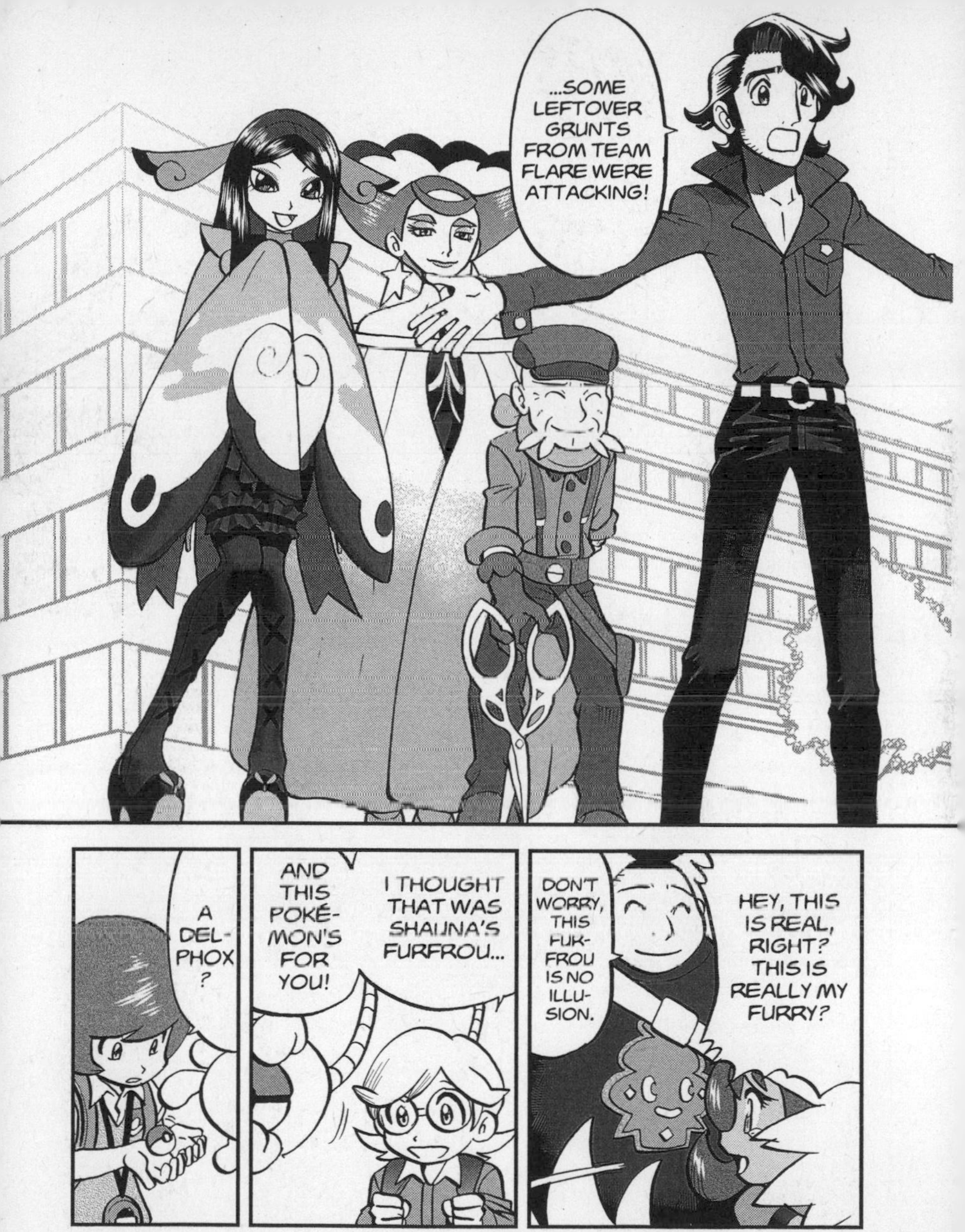
...SOME LEFTOVER GRUNTS FROM TEAM FLARE WERE ATTACKING!
HEY, THIS IS REAL, RIGHT? THIS IS REALLY MY FURRY?
DON'T WORRY, THIS FUR-FROU IS NO ILLU-SION.
I THOUGHT THAT WAS SHAUNA'S FURFROU...
AND THIS POKÉ-MON'S FOR YOU!
A DEL-PHOX?

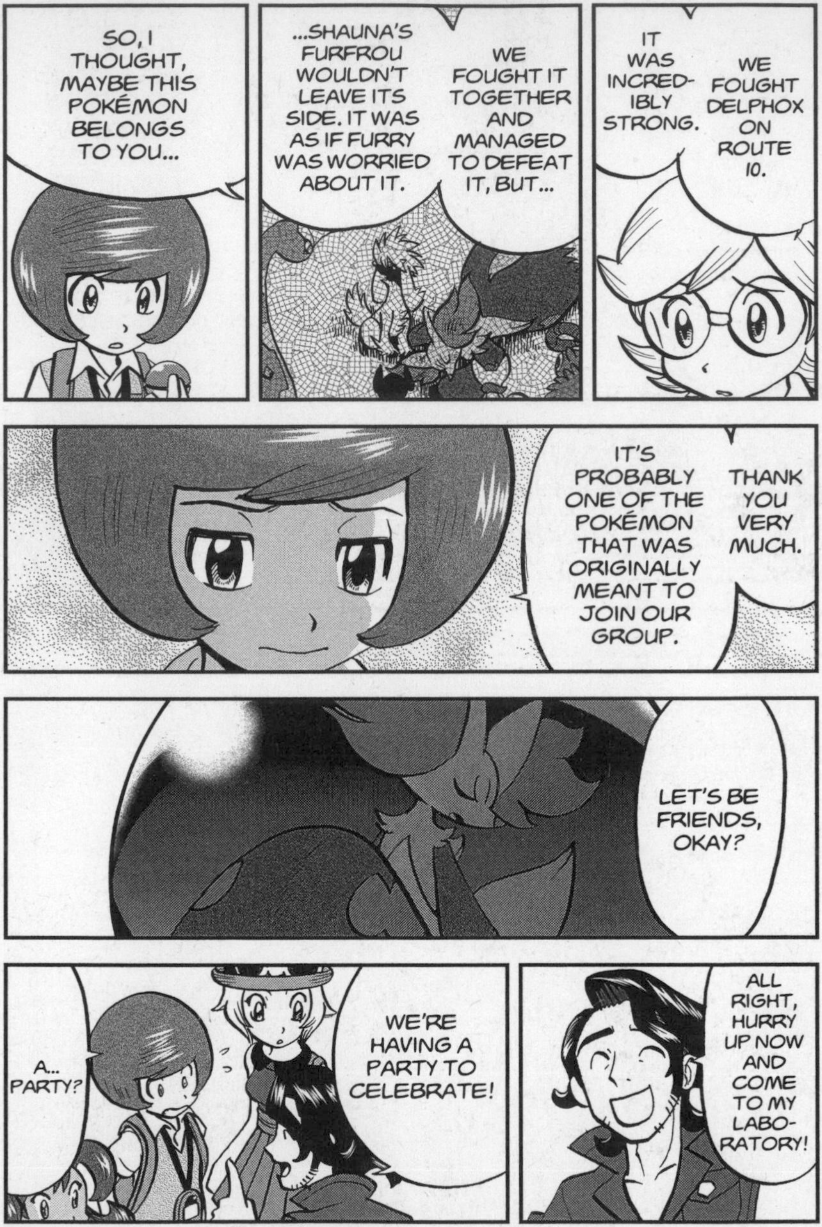
WE FOUGHT DELPHOX ON ROUTE 10.
IT WAS INCREDIBLY STRONG.
WE FOUGHT IT TOGETHER AND MANAGED TO DEFEAT IT, BUT...
...SHAUNA'S FURFROU WOULDN'T LEAVE ITS SIDE. IT WAS AS IF FURRY WAS WORRIED ABOUT IT.
SO, I THOUGHT, MAYBE THIS POKÉMON BELONGS TO YOU...
THANK YOU VERY MUCH.
IT'S PROBABLY ONE OF THE POKÉMON THAT WAS ORIGINALLY MEANT TO JOIN OUR GROUP.
LET'S BE FRIENDS, OKAY?
ALL RIGHT, HURRY UP NOW AND COME TO MY LABORATORY!
WE'RE HAVING A PARTY TO CELEBRATE!
A... PARTY?

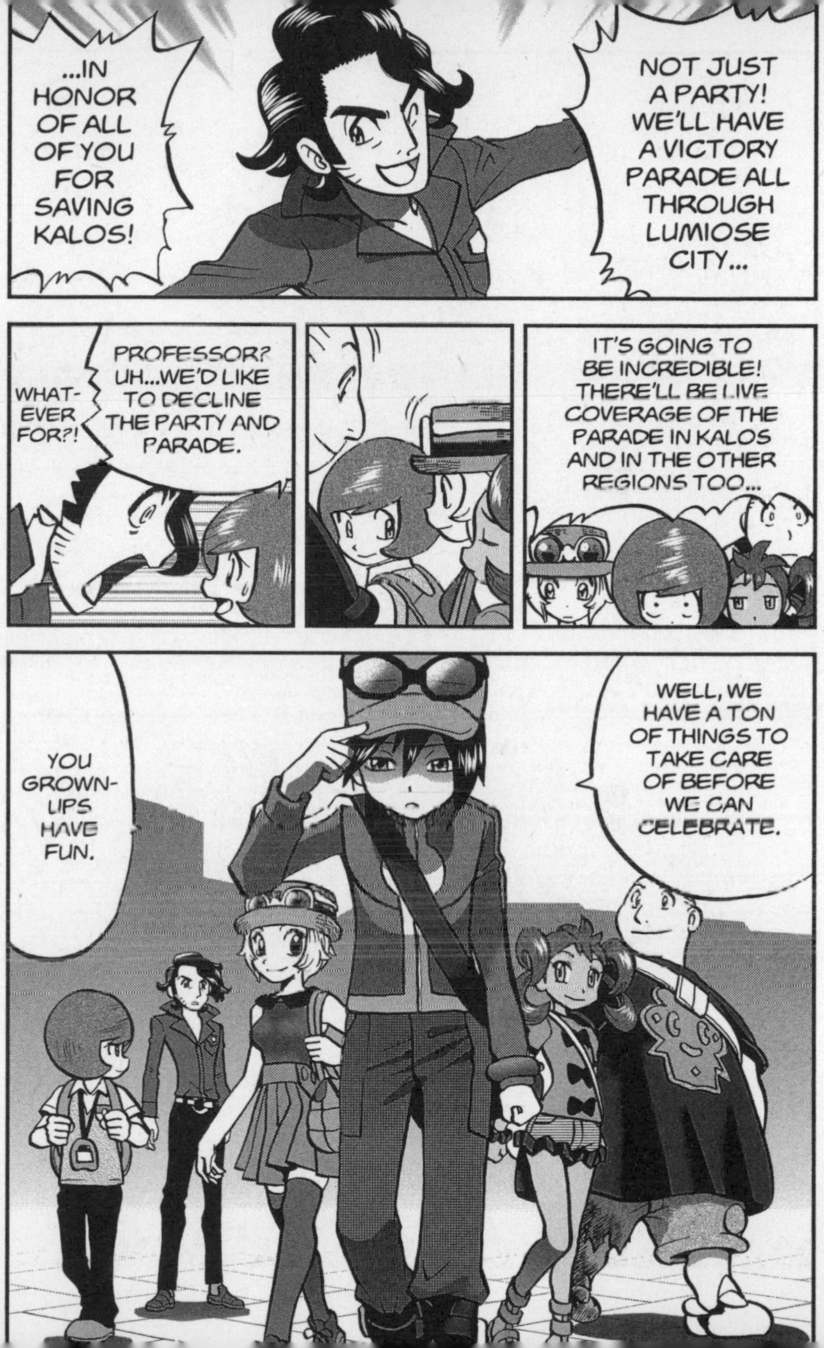
NOT JUST A PARTY! WE'LL HAVE A VICTORY PARADE ALL THROUGH LUMIOSE CITY...
...IN HONOR OF ALL OF YOU FOR SAVING KALOS!
IT'S GOING TO BE INCREDIBLE! THERE'LL BE LIVE COVERAGE OF THE PARADE IN KALOS AND IN THE OTHER REGIONS TOO...
PROFESSOR? UH...WE'D LIKE TO DECLINE THE PARTY AND PARADE.
WHAT-EVER FOR?!
WELL, WE HAVE A TON OF THINGS TO TAKE CARE OF BEFORE WE CAN CELEBRATE.
YOU GROWN-UPS HAVE FUN.

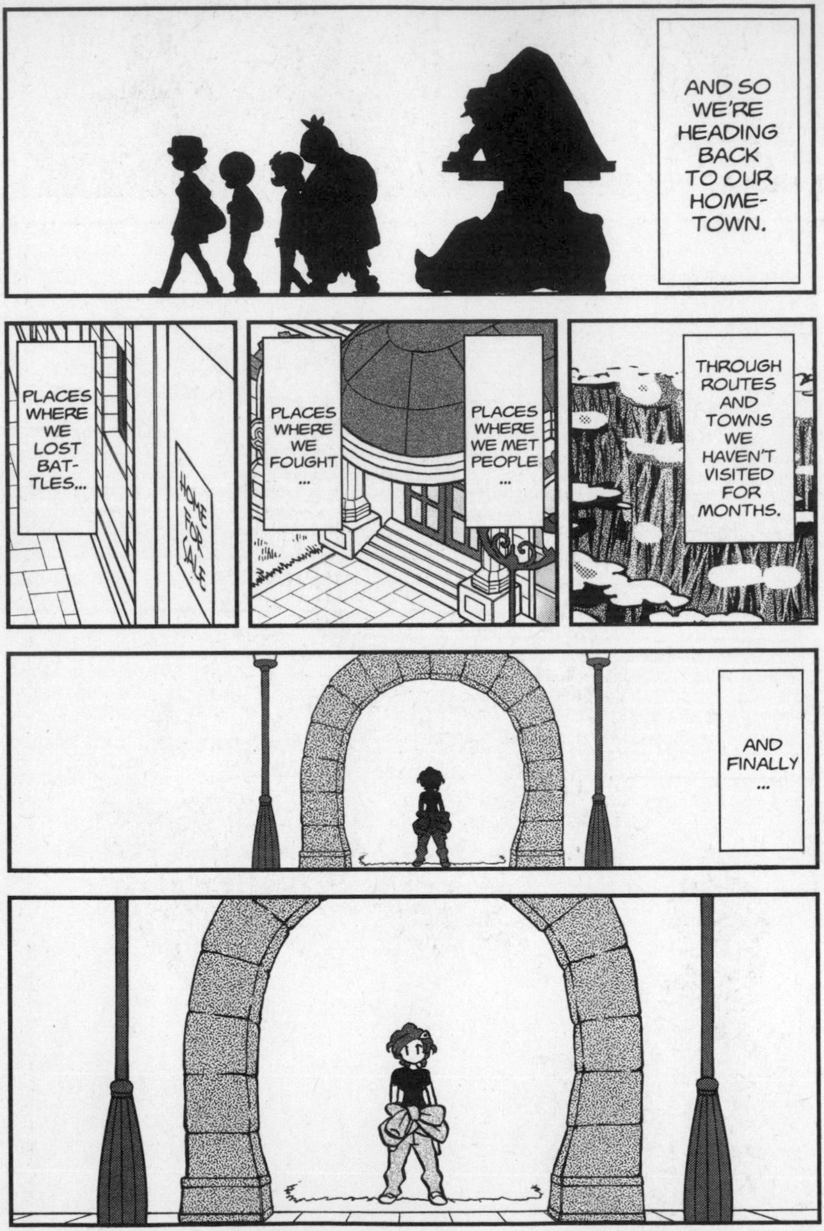
AND SO WE'RE HEADING BACK TO OUR HOME-TOWN.
THROUGH ROUTES AND TOWNS WE HAVEN'T VISITED FOR MONTHS.
PLACES WHERE WE MET PEOPLE ...
PLACES WHERE WE FOUGHT ...
PLACES WHERE WE LOST BAT-TLES...
HOME FOR SALE
AND FINALLY ...

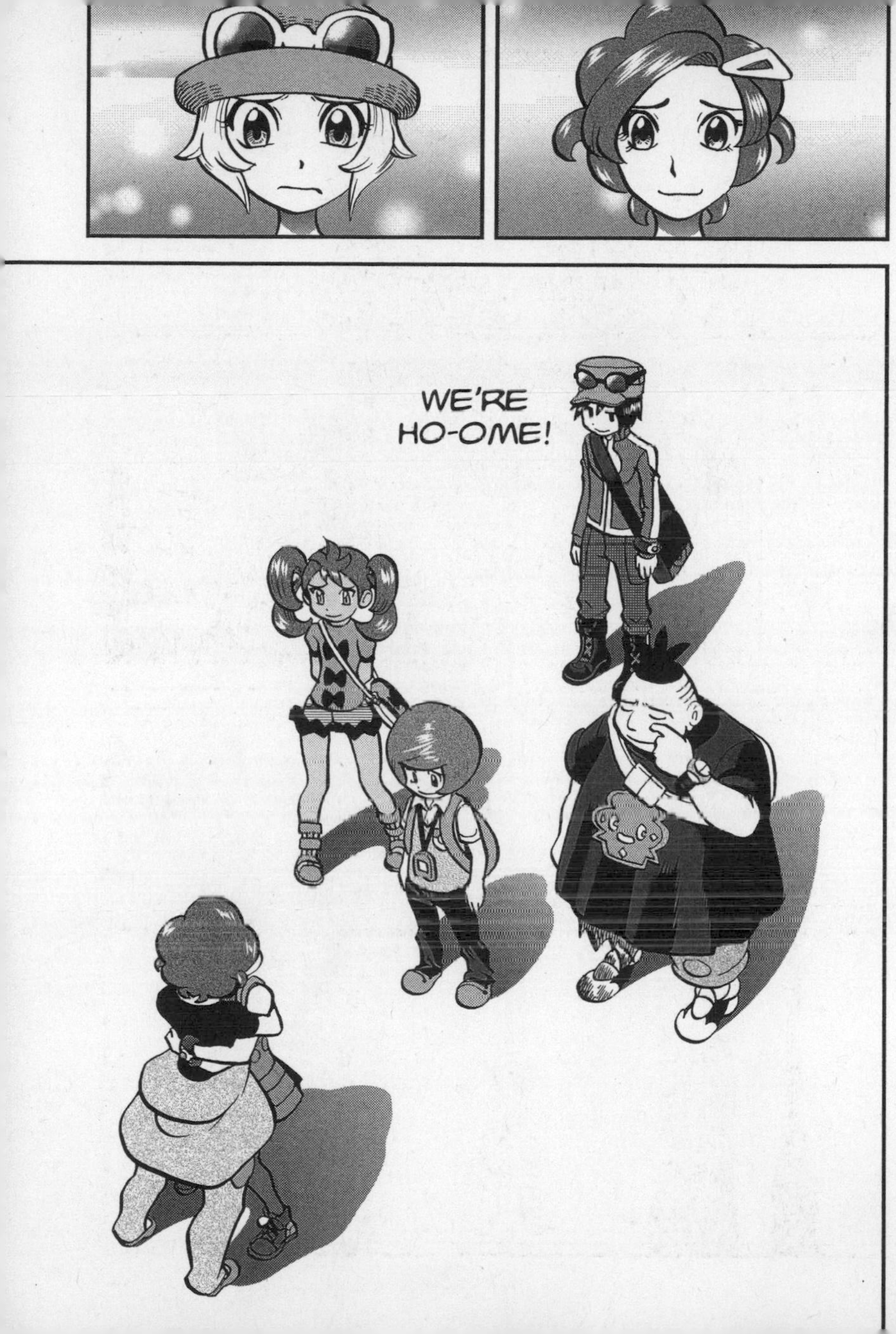
WE'RE HO-OME!

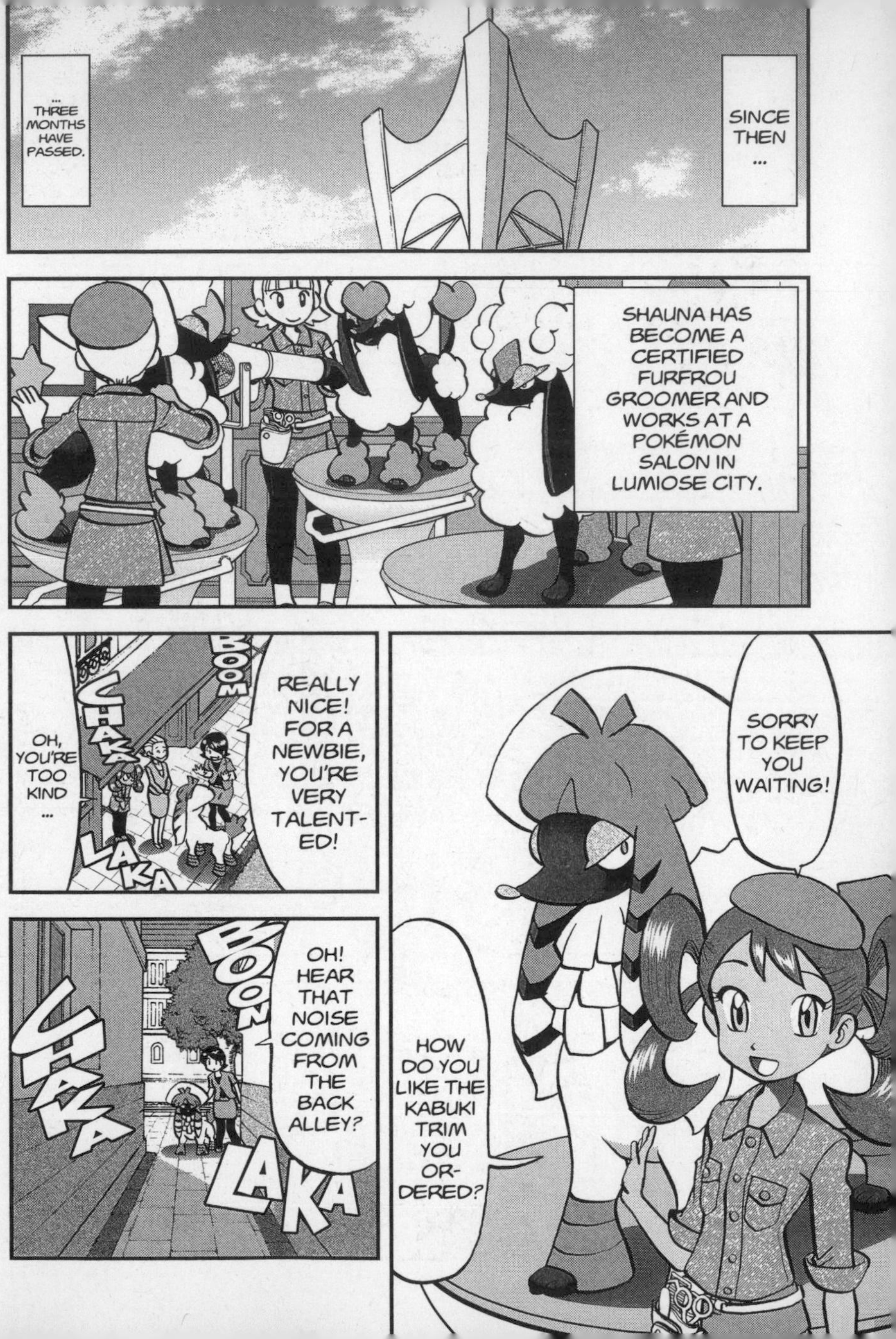
SINCE THEN ...
... THREE MONTHS HAVE PASSED.
SHAUNA HAS BECOME A CERTIFIED FURFROU GROOMER AND WORKS AT A POKÉMON SALON IN LUMIOSE CITY.
SORRY TO KEEP YOU WAITING!
HOW DO YOU LIKE THE KABUKI TRIM YOU ORDERED?
BOOM
REALLY NICE! FOR A NEWBIE, YOU'RE VERY TALENT-ED!
CHAKA
OH, YOU'RE TOO KIND ...
LAKA
BOOM
OH! HEAR THAT NOISE COMING FROM THE BACK ALLEY?
CHAKA
LAKA

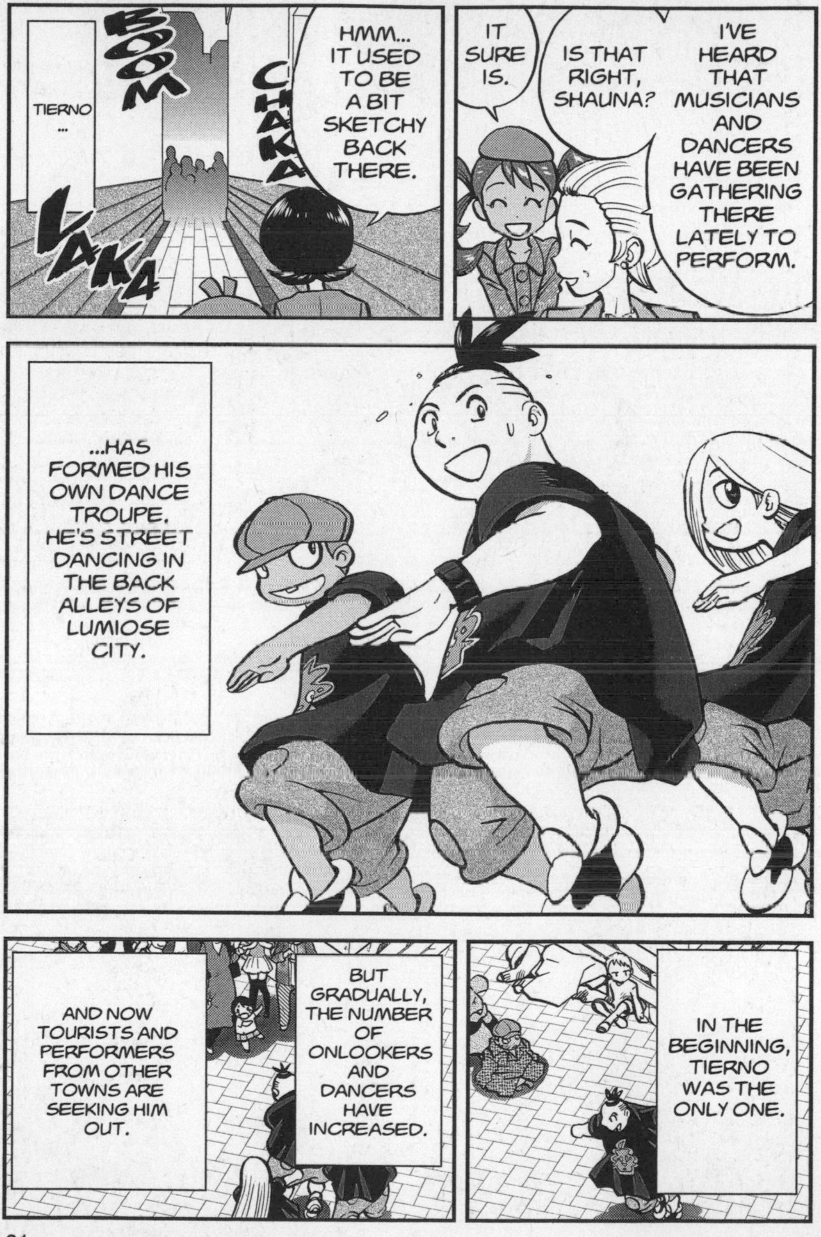

I'VE HEARD THAT MUSICIANS AND DANCERS HAVE BEEN GATHERING THERE LATELY TO PERFORM.
IS THAT RIGHT, SHAUNA?
IT SURE IS.
HMM... IT USED TO BE A BIT SKETCHY BACK THERE.
CHAKA
BOOM
TIERNO ...
LAKA
...HAS FORMED HIS OWN DANCE TROUPE. HE'S STREET DANCING IN THE BACK ALLEYS OF LUMIOSE CITY.
IN THE BEGINNING, TIERNO WAS THE ONLY ONE.
BUT GRADUALLY, THE NUMBER OF ONLOOKERS AND DANCERS HAVE INCREASED.
AND NOW TOURISTS AND PERFORMERS FROM OTHER TOWNS ARE SEEKING HIM OUT.

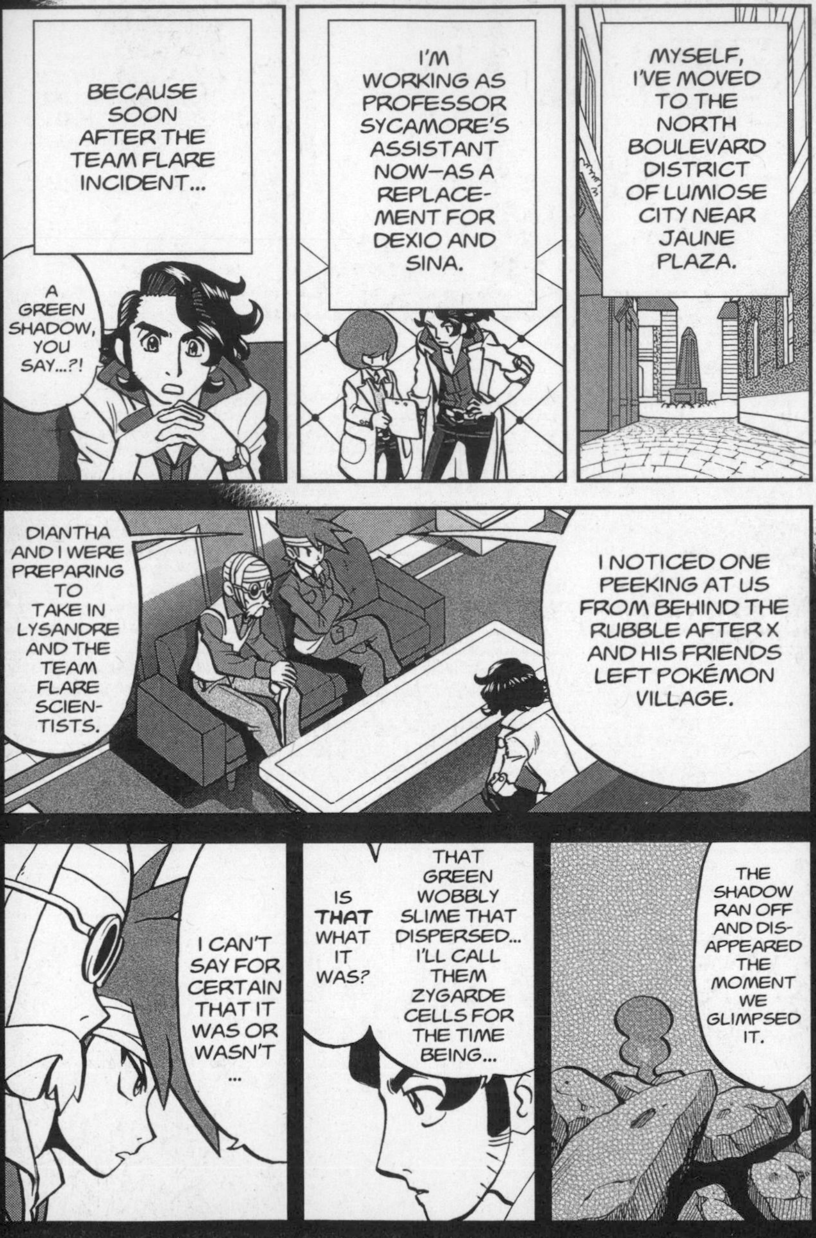
MYSELF, I'VE MOVED TO THE NORTH BOULEVARD DISTRICT OF LUMIOSE CITY NEAR JAUNE PLAZA.
I'M WORKING AS PROFESSOR SYCAMORE'S ASSISTANT NOW—AS A REPLACEMENT FOR DEXIO AND SINA.
BECAUSE SOON AFTER THE TEAM FLARE INCIDENT...
A GREEN SHADOW, YOU SAY...?!
I NOTICED ONE PEEKING AT US FROM BEHIND THE RUBBLE AFTER X AND HIS FRIENDS LEFT POKÉMON VILLAGE.
DIANTHA AND I WERE PREPARING TO TAKE IN LYSANDRE AND THE TEAM FLARE SCIENTISTS.
THE SHADOW RAN OFF AND DISAPPEARED THE MOMENT WE GLIMPSED IT.
THAT GREEN WOBBLY SLIME THAT DISPERSED... I'LL CALL THEM ZYGARDE CELLS FOR THE TIME BEING...
IS **THAT** WHAT IT WAS?
I CAN'T SAY FOR CERTAIN THAT IT WAS OR WASN'T ...

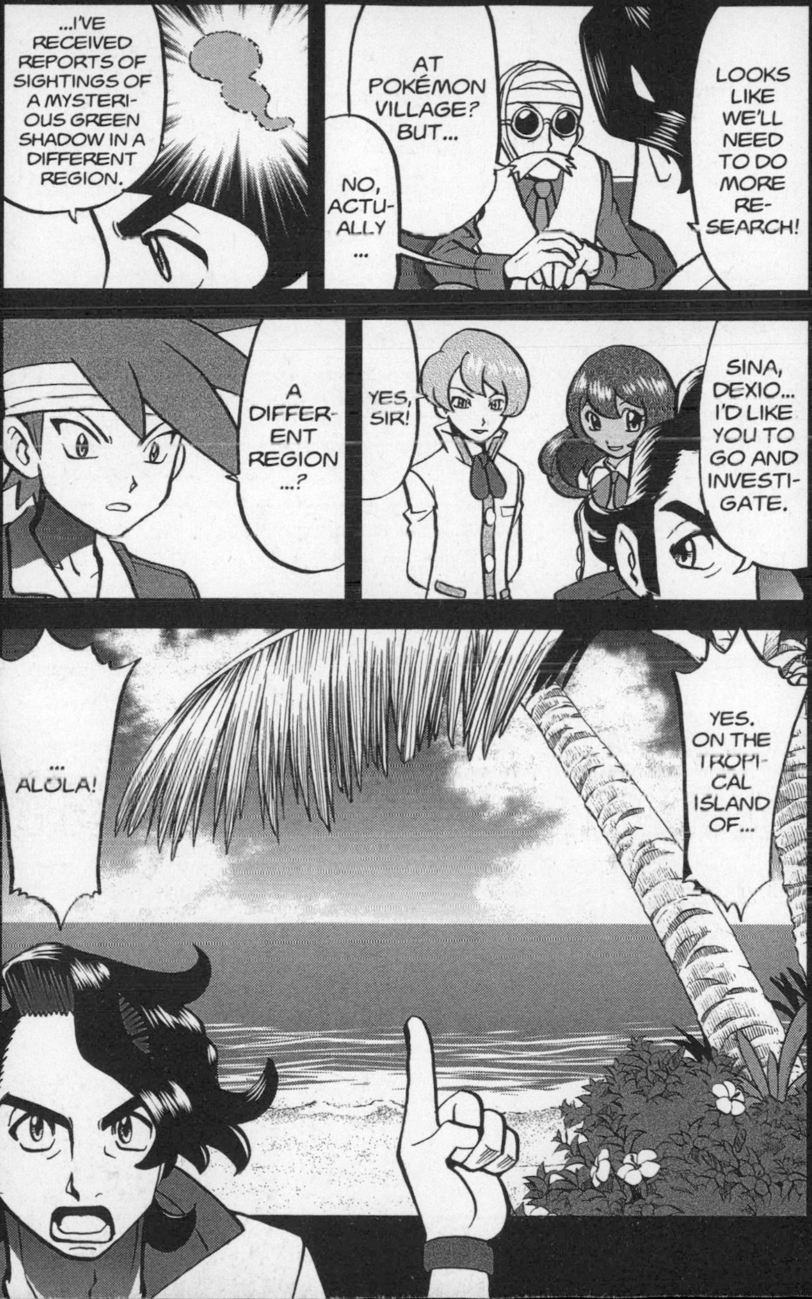
LOOKS LIKE WE'LL NEED TO DO MORE RE-SEARCH!
AT POKÉMON VILLAGE? BUT...
NO, ACTUALLY...
...I'VE RECEIVED REPORTS OF SIGHTINGS OF A MYSTERIOUS GREEN SHADOW IN A DIFFERENT REGION.
SINA, DEXIO... I'D LIKE YOU TO GO AND INVESTIGATE.
YES, SIR!
A DIFFERENT REGION...?
YES. ON THE TROPICAL ISLAND OF...
...ALOLA!

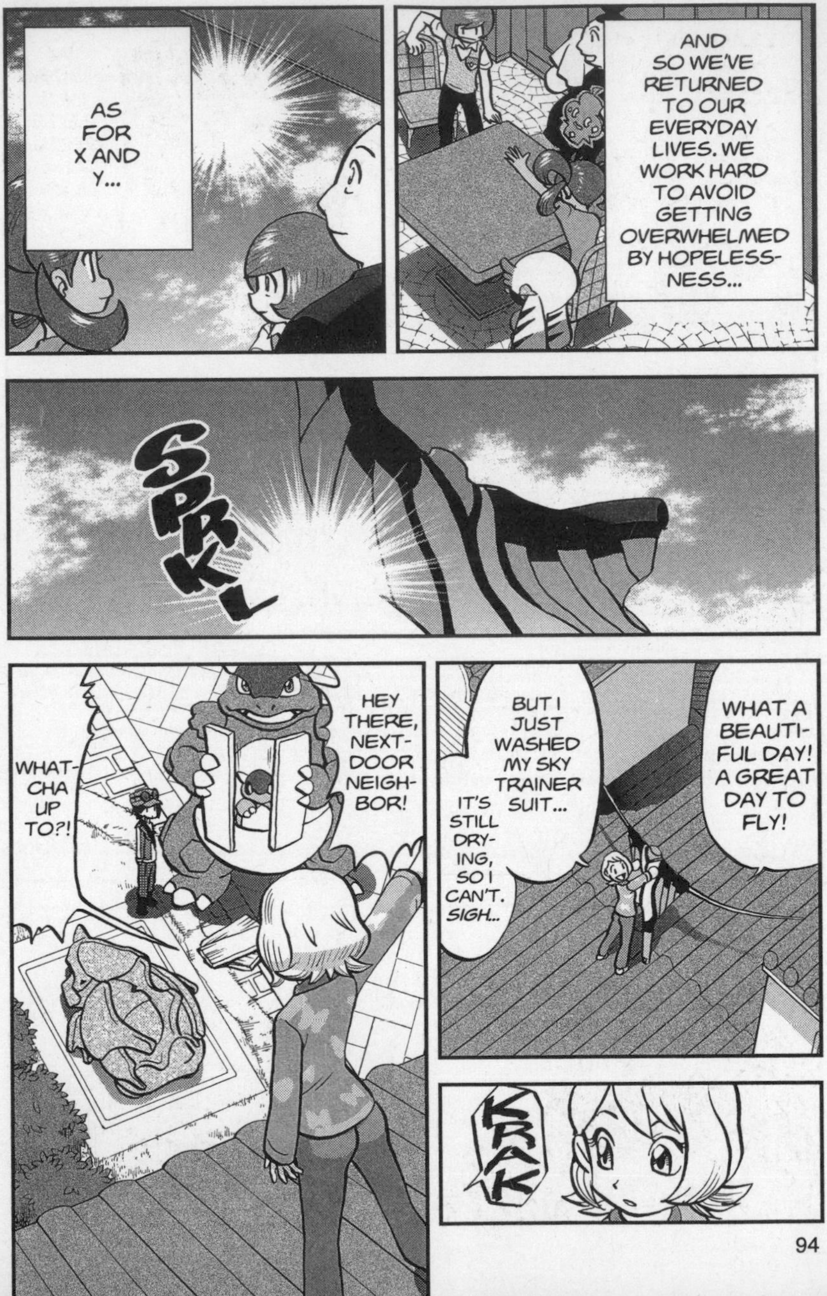
AND SO WE'VE RETURNED TO OUR EVERYDAY LIVES. WE WORK HARD TO AVOID GETTING OVERWHELMED BY HOPELESSNESS...
AS FOR X AND Y...
SPRKL
WHAT A BEAUTIFUL DAY! A GREAT DAY TO FLY!
BUT I JUST WASHED MY SKY TRAINER SUIT...
IT'S STILL DRYING, SO I CAN'T. SIGH...
KRAK
HEY THERE, NEXT-DOOR NEIGHBOR!
WHATCHA UP TO?!

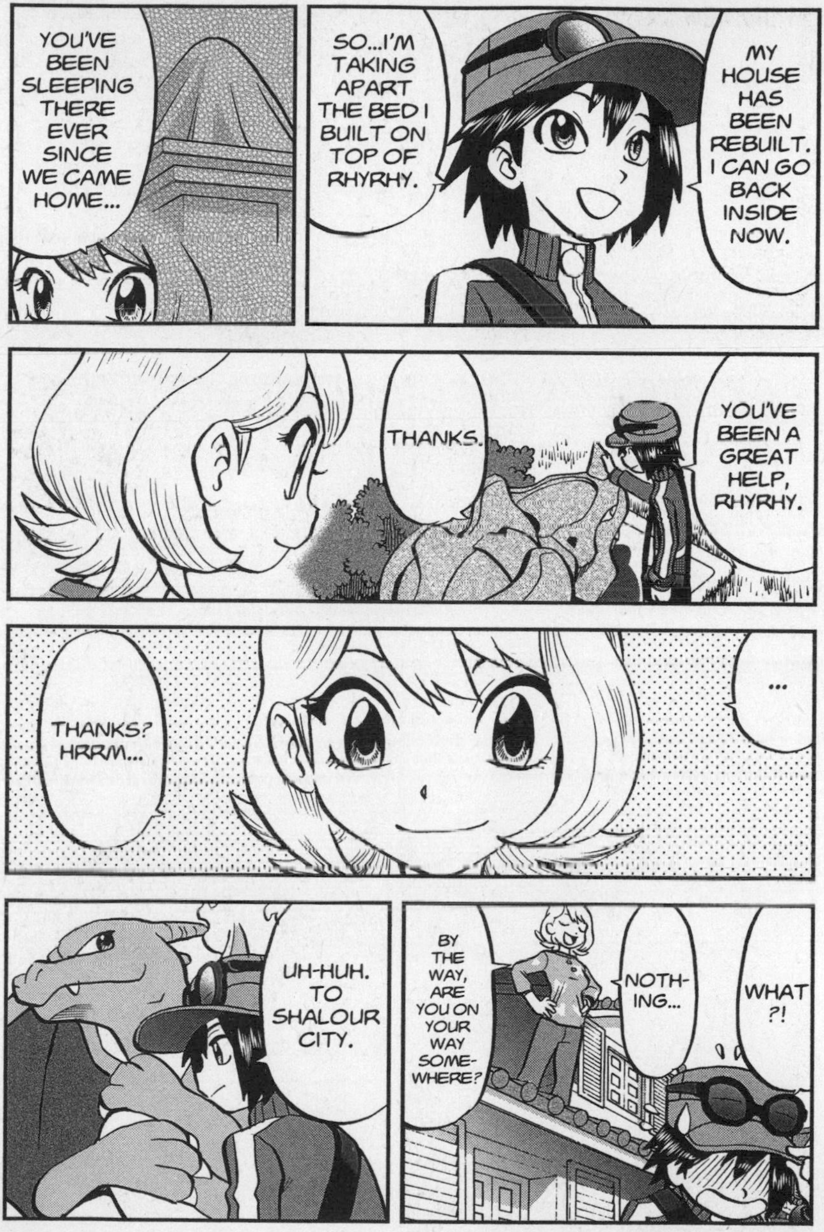
MY HOUSE HAS BEEN REBUILT. I CAN GO BACK INSIDE NOW.
SO...I'M TAKING APART THE BED I BUILT ON TOP OF RHYRHY.
YOU'VE BEEN SLEEPING THERE EVER SINCE WE CAME HOME...
YOU'VE BEEN A GREAT HELP, RHYRHY.
THANKS.
...
THANKS? HRRM...
WHAT?!
NOTH-ING...
BY THE WAY, ARE YOU ON YOUR WAY SOME-WHERE?
UH-HUH. TO SHALOUR CITY.

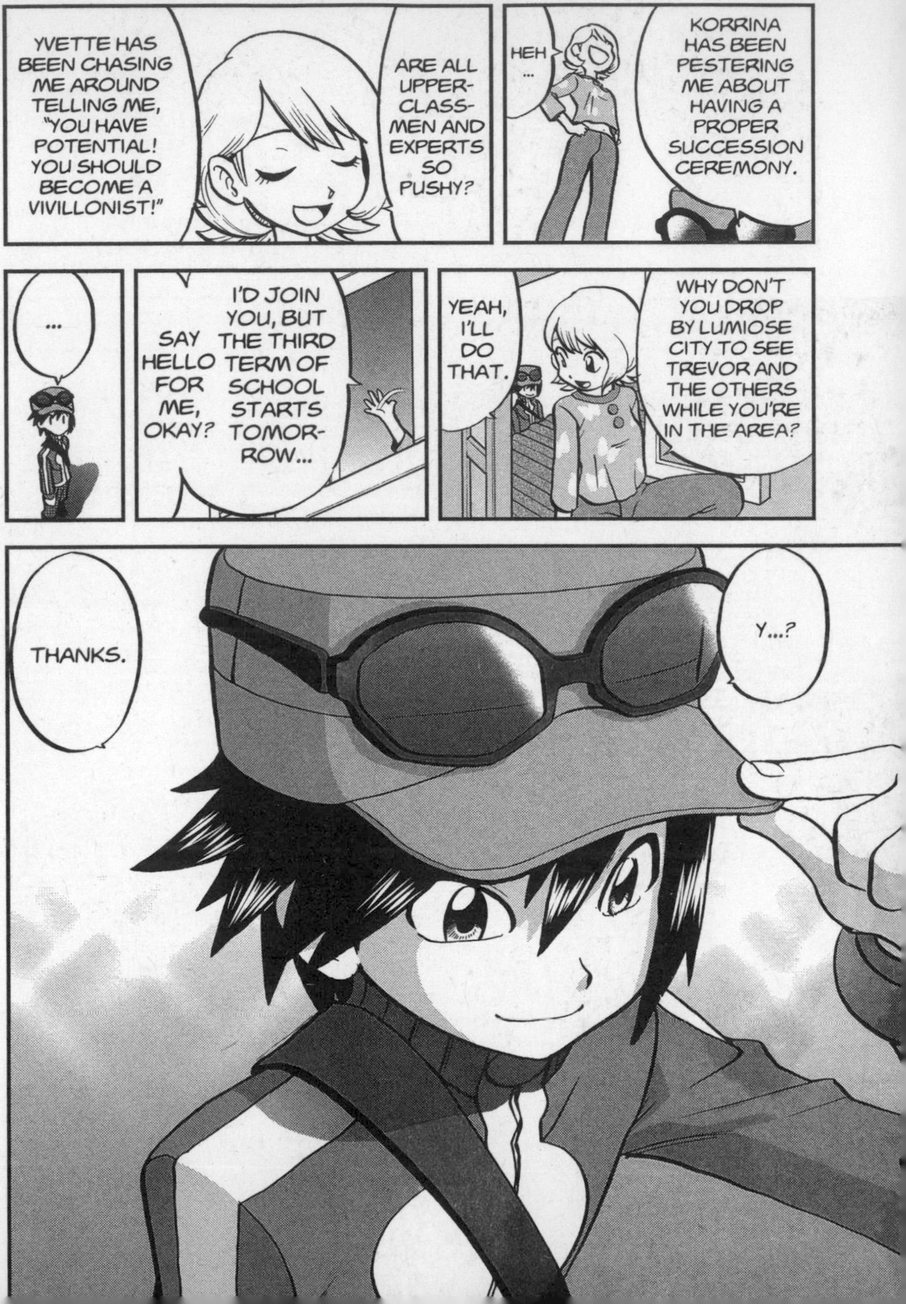
KORRINA HAS BEEN PESTERING ME ABOUT HAVING A PROPER SUCCESSION CEREMONY.
HEH ...
ARE ALL UPPER-CLASS-MEN AND EXPERTS SO PUSHY?
YVETTE HAS BEEN CHASING ME AROUND TELLING ME, "YOU HAVE POTENTIAL! YOU SHOULD BECOME A VIVILLONIST!"
WHY DON'T YOU DROP BY LUMIOSE CITY TO SEE TREVOR AND THE OTHERS WHILE YOU'RE IN THE AREA?
YEAH, I'LL DO THAT.
I'D JOIN YOU, BUT THE THIRD TERM OF SCHOOL STARTS TOMOR-ROW...
SAY HELLO FOR ME, OKAY?
...
Y...?
THANKS.

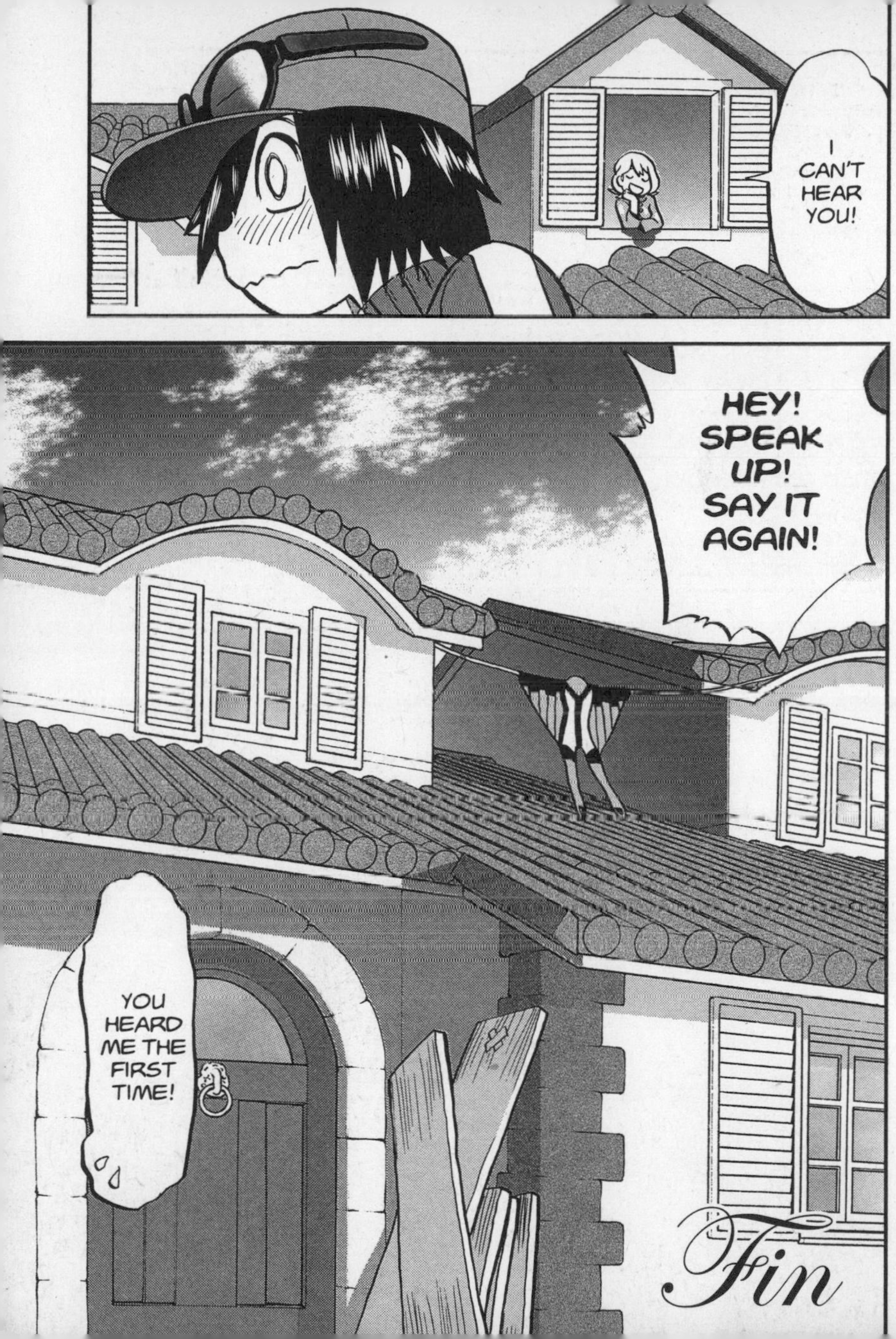
I CAN'T HEAR YOU!
HEY! SPEAK UP! SAY IT AGAIN!
YOU HEARD ME THE FIRST TIME!
Fin

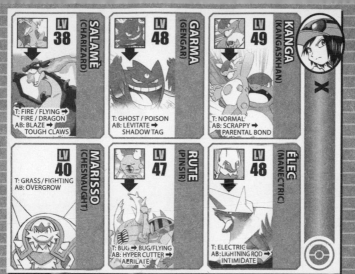

POKÉMON DATA

LV: LEVEL (AS OF ADVENTURE 39)
AB: ABILITY
T: TYPE

*Types and Abilities that change after Mega Evolution are indicated by ➡

X

KANGA (KANGASKHAN)
LV 49
T: NORMAL
AB: SCRAPPY ➡ PARENTAL BOND

ÉLEC (MANECTRIC)
LV 48
T: ELECTRIC
AB: LIGHTNING ROD ➡ INTIMIDATE

GARMA (GENGAR)
LV 48
T: GHOST / POISON
AB: LEVITATE ➡ SHADOW TAG

RUTE (PINSIR)
LV 47
T: BUG ➡ BUG/FLYING
AB: HYPER CUTTER ➡ AERILATE

SALAMÈ (CHARIZARD)
LV 38
T: FIRE / FLYING ➡ FIRE / DRAGON
AB: BLAZE ➡ TOUGH CLAWS

MARISSO (CHESNAUGHT)
LV 40
T: GRASS / FIGHTING
AB: OVERGROW

Y

FLETCHY (FLETCHINDER)
LV 34
T: FIRE / FLYING
AB: FLAME BODY

CROAKY (GRENINJA)
LV 47
T: WATER / DARK
AB: BATTLE BOND

RHYRHY (RHYHORN)
LV 41
T: GROUND / ROCK
AB: ROCK HEAD

VEEVEE (SYLVEON)
LV 47
T: FAIRY
AB: CUTE CHARM

SOLSOL (ABSOL)
LV 49
T: DARK
AB: SUPER LUCK ➡ MAGIC BOUNCE

XERXER/XERXEY (XERNEAS)
LV 55
T: FAIRY
AB: FAIRY/AURA

TIERNO

CRAWDAUNT
LV 32
T: WATER / DARK
AB: SHELL ARMOR

SHAUNA

KITTY (SKITTY)
LV 30
T: NORMAL
AB: NORMALIZE

TREVOR

FLOETTE
LV 21
T: FAIRY
AB: FLOWER VEIL

TREVOR'S REPORT 1

OBSERVATIONS ON THE VARIABILITY IN SIZE AND APPEARANCE OF THE POKÉMON IN THE KALOS REGION

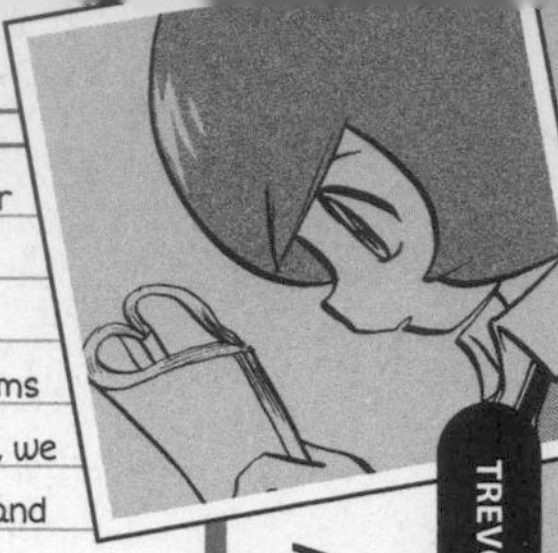

No.

Date

During the battle against Team Flare and over the course of our journey, I have been primarily concerned with Mega Evolution.

○ Mega Evolution is a phenomenon in which a Pokémon transforms its shape and increases its power. However, in the Kalos region, we observed numerous other instances of transforming Pokémon and variations in Pokémon appearance unrelated to Mega Evolution.

○ These variations are a notable feature of the Pokémon of Kalos.

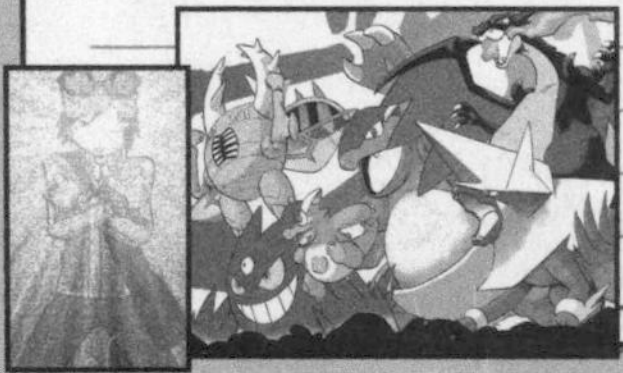

○ Differences range from power-ups to simple variations in markings, but I would like to enumerate them here and participate in further research on these phenomena.

MEGA EVOLUTION

I WAS GIVEN MANY OPPORTUNITIES TO OBSERVE THIS PROCESS BECAUSE X IS NOW ABLE TO WIELD MEGA EVOLUTION AND HAS BEEN ADDING MEGA EVOLVING POKÉMON TO HIS TEAM. THE MOST REMARKABLE MEGA EVOLUTIONS I HAVE OBSERVED ARE AS FOLLOWS...

● TWO TYPES OF MEGA EVOLUTION

I HAVE DETERMINED THAT THE SAME POKÉMON HOLDING DIFFERENT MEGA STONES RESULTS IN DIFFERENT MEGA EVOLUTIONS. I OBSERVED THIS WITH CHARIZARD AND MEWTWO. I WAS ESPECIALLY SURPRISED TO HEAR THAT THE SAME MEWTWO UNDERWENT TWO TYPES OF MEGA EVOLUTION DURING A SINGLE BATTLE SIMPLY BY SWITCHING THE MEGA STONE IT WAS HOLDING.

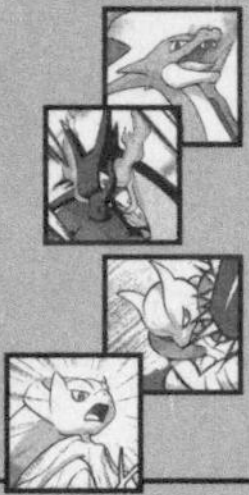

● FIVE SIMULTANEOUS MEGA EVOLUTIONS

THIS WAS POSSIBLE BECAUSE X HAD OBTAINED FIVE MEGA STONES. BUT THE STRAIN UPON THE TRAINER WIELDING FIVE AT ONCE IS MUCH HIGHER THAN WITH JUST ONE.

MODES

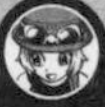

XERNEAS

I HAD THE OPPORTUNITY TO OBSERVE THIS PHENOMENON AT CLOSE RANGE BECAUSE Y CAPTURED XERNEAS. XERNEAS'S HORN CAN CHANGE COLOR FROM A RAINBOW HUE TO BLUE. THE SCIENTIFIC TERM FOR THIS VARIABILITY IS "MODE."

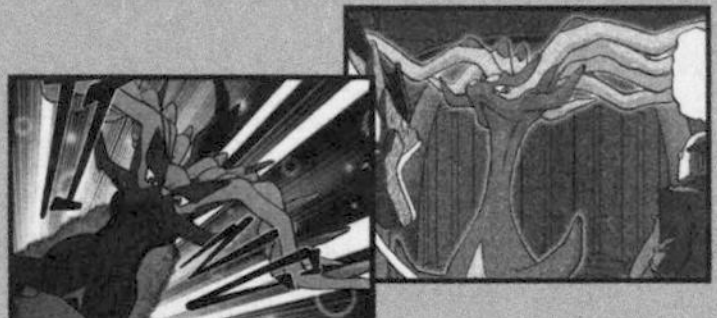

▲THE BLUE HORN REPRESENTS A DORMANT STATE AND IS CALLED NEUTRAL MODE. THE RAINBOW HORN REPRESENTS A HOSTILE STATE AND IS CALLED ACTIVE MODE.

DIFFERENT TRIMS

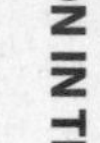

FURFROU

I ASKED SHAUNA—NOW A PROFESSIONAL FURFROU GROOMER—TO EXPLAIN THIS. IT TURNS OUT THE DIFFERENCES IN FURFROU'S APPEARANCE ARE SIMPLY A MATTER OF STYLE AND ARE CREATED BY A GROOMER THROUGH A SKILLFUL APPLICATION OF SCISSORS.

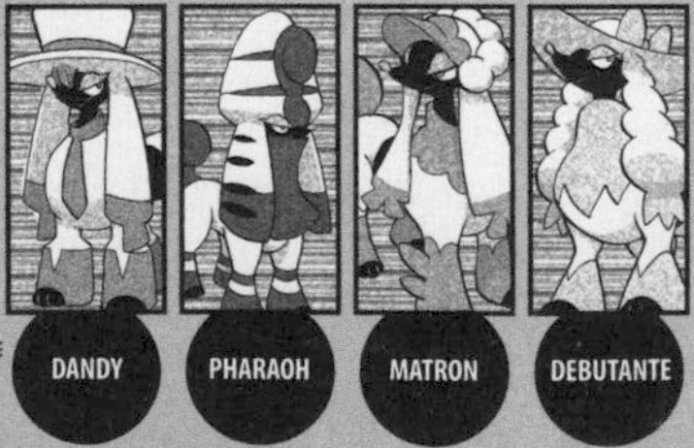
DANDY
PHARAOH
MATRON
DEBUTANTE

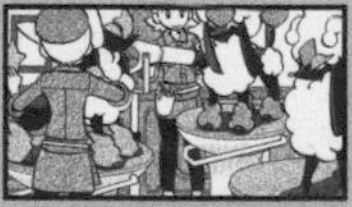

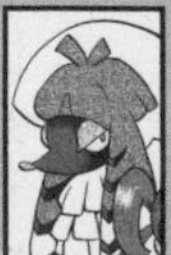

▲STYLISH TRIMS AVAILABLE AT SPECIALTY GROOMING SHOPS INCLUDE STAR, HEART, DIAMOND AND KABUKI TRIMS.

PATTERN VARIATIONS

VIVILLON

I INTERVIEWED YVETTE—A SKY TRAINER TRAINEE AND VIVILLONIST—ABOUT THESE VARIATIONS. SHE REPORTS THAT SHE HAS COLLECTED VIVILLON WITH EIGHTEEN OF THE POSSIBLE WING PATTERNS.

WFF WFF WFF WFF

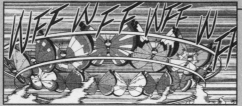

▲ SHE HAS YET TO OBTAIN THE POKÉ BALL PATTERN AND FANCY PATTERN. THERE ARE 20 TYPES OF WING PATTERNS IN ALL.

SIZE VARIATION

PUMPKABOO GOURGEIST

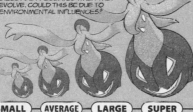

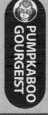

CASSIUS'S GOURGEIST IS A LARGE SIZE. I AM STILL INVESTIGATING THE DIFFERENCES IN SIZE, BUT THE ACADEMY HAS CURRENTLY DIVIDED THEM INTO FOUR CATEGORIES: SMALL, AVERAGE, LARGE AND SUPER.

▼ SURPRISINGLY, THE DIFFERENT SIZES ARE PRESERVED WHEN THEY EVOLVE. COULD THIS BE DUE TO ENVIRONMENTAL INFLUENCES?

SMALL
AVERAGE
LARGE
SUPER

FLOWER VARIATIONS

FLABÉBÉ FLOETTE FLORGES

I PERSONALLY NURTURED MY FLABÉBÉ INTO A FLOETTE. MY FLOETTE CHOSE A YELLOW FLOWER. THEIR FLOWERS BECOME A PART OF THEIR BODY, SO THE POKÉMON ACADEMY VIEWS THIS AS AN APPEARANCE VARIATION. THERE ARE CURRENTLY FIVE FLOWER COLORS.

▶ FLABÉBÉ, FLOETTE AND FLORGES. EACH CHOOSE BETWEEN FIVE COLORS WHICH RESULTS IN FIFTEEN POSSIBLE VARIATIONS. THAT'S A LOT!

WHITE
RED
YELLOW
BLUE
ORANGE

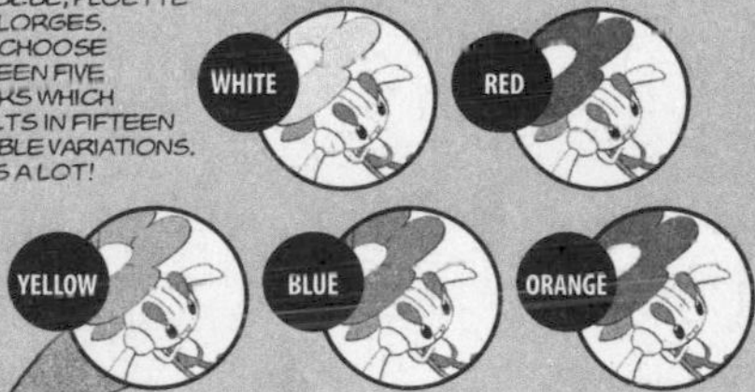

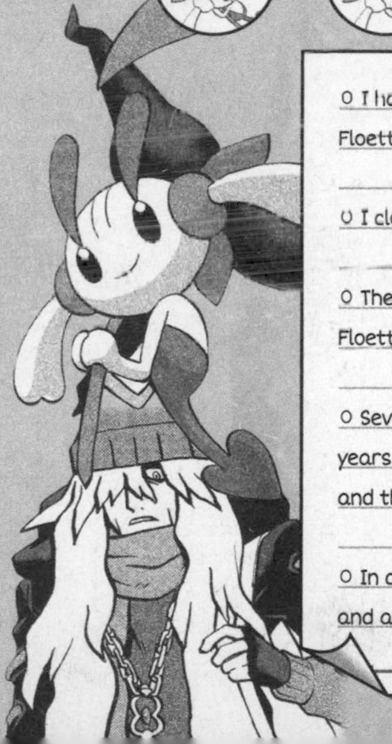

○ I have also identified a unique variation in the case of one Floette.

○ I closely observed the Floette that was reunited with AZ.

○ The shape of its flower is quite different from a typical Floette.

○ Several factors may have contributed to this: its demise 3,000 years ago, exposure to unusual radiation, getting resurrected, and the subsequent length of time spent wandering the world.

○ In conclusion, there are many variations in Pokémon size and appearance.

No.

Date

○ We've met Zygarde twice thus far: during the battle at the Anistar Sundial and during the final battle at Pokémon Village.

○ What intrigues me is Zygarde's absorption and dispersion behavior, which we witnessed right before it disappeared.

○ Since Zygarde is a Legendary Pokémon of equal or greater status than Yveltal and Xerneas, it likely harbors a secret we have yet to discover. I would like to use the data we've gathered thus far to investigate this possibility.

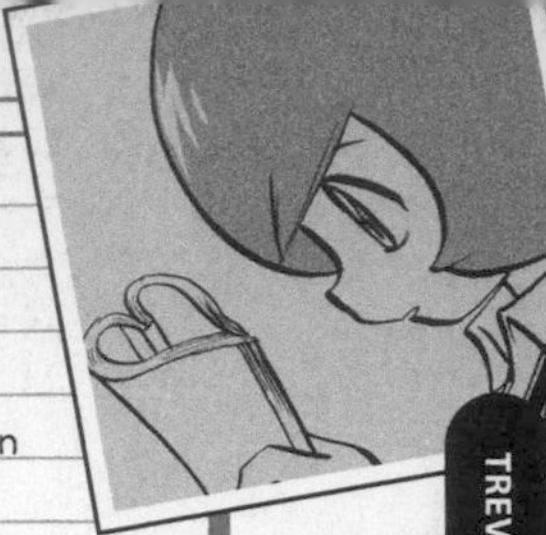

TREVOR'S REPORT 2

OBSERVATIONS ON ZYGARDE'S CELL ABSORPTION AND TRANSFORMATION.

ZYGARDE CELLS

ZYGARDE IS SAID TO HAVE DISPERSED INTO LITTLE BLOBS AFTER THE BATTLE AT POKÉMON VILLAGE. OUR HYPOTHESIS IS THAT ZYGARDE IS ACTUALLY A COLLECTIVE LIFE FORM COMPOSED OF MANY CELL-LIKE UNITS.

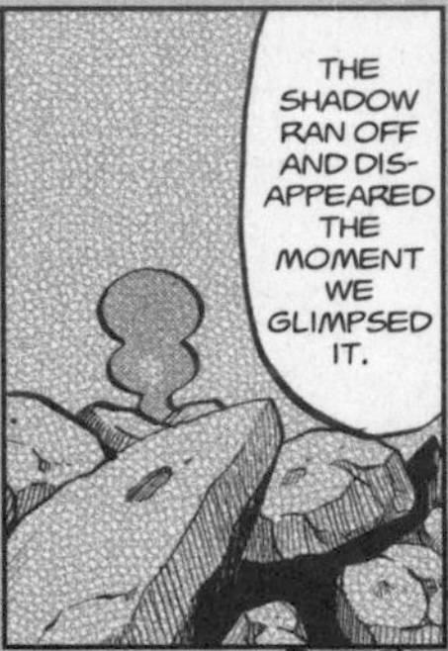
THE SHADOW RAN OFF AND DIS-APPEARED THE MOMENT WE GLIMPSED IT.

▶ THE GREEN SHADOW WE SAW, CURRENTLY REFERRED TO AS A ZYGARDE CELL.

▼ COME TO THINK OF IT, POKÉMON VILLAGE IS A HAVEN FOR HURT POKÉMON. THERE MIGHT WELL HAVE BEEN A DISRUPTION IN THE ECOSYSTEM THERE THAT IMPACTED THEM.

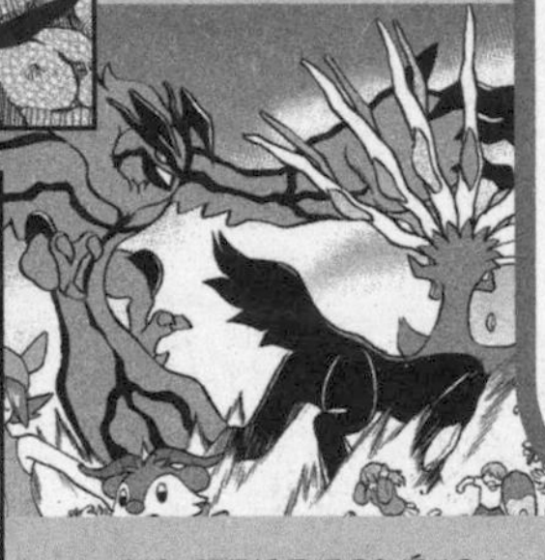

THE POSSIBILITY OF BECOMING SOMETHING GREATER THAN THE OVERSEER.

ZYGARDE IS THE POKÉMON OF ORDER, WHO OVERSEES THE WORLD FROM DEEP BENEATH THE SURFACE OF THE GROUND. WHEN SOMETHING DISRUPTS THE ECOSYSTEM, IT RISES OUT OF ITS CAVE TO WIELD ITS POWER AND RESTORE BALANCE. THAT'S WHAT WE'VE BEEN TOLD ABOUT ZYGARDE UP TILL NOW. SO WHAT IS THE MEANING OF THE ABSORPTION PROCESS WE SAW IT UNDERGO IN WHICH IT SEEMED TO ADD MORE CELLS TO ITS FORM? I SUSPECT IT WAS TRYING TO BECOME SOMETHING MORE THAN AN OVERSEER..

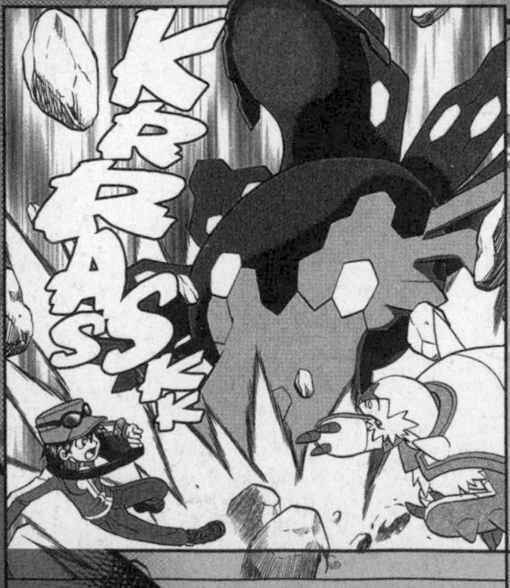
KRRRASSSK

A COMMENT FROM PROFESSOR SYCAMORE

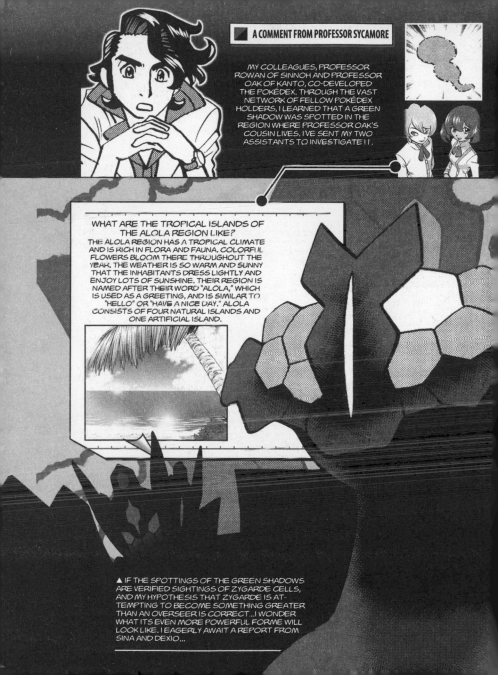

MY COLLEAGUES, PROFESSOR ROWAN OF SINNOH AND PROFESSOR OAK OF KANTO, CO-DEVELOPED THE POKÉDEX. THROUGH THE VAST NETWORK OF FELLOW POKÉDEX HOLDERS, I LEARNED THAT A GREEN SHADOW WAS SPOTTED IN THE REGION WHERE PROFESSOR OAK'S COUSIN LIVES. I'VE SENT MY TWO ASSISTANTS TO INVESTIGATE IT.

WHAT ARE THE TROPICAL ISLANDS OF THE ALOLA REGION LIKE?

THE ALOLA REGION HAS A TROPICAL CLIMATE AND IS RICH IN FLORA AND FAUNA. COLORFUL FLOWERS BLOOM THERE THROUGHOUT THE YEAR. THE WEATHER IS SO WARM AND SUNNY THAT THE INHABITANTS DRESS LIGHTLY AND ENJOY LOTS OF SUNSHINE. THEIR REGION IS NAMED AFTER THEIR WORD "ALOLA," WHICH IS USED AS A GREETING, AND IS SIMILAR TO "HELLO" OR "HAVE A NICE DAY." ALOLA CONSISTS OF FOUR NATURAL ISLANDS AND ONE ARTIFICIAL ISLAND.

▲ IF THE SPOTTINGS OF THE GREEN SHADOWS ARE VERIFIED SIGHTINGS OF ZYGARDE CELLS, AND MY HYPOTHESIS THAT ZYGARDE IS ATTEMPTING TO BECOME SOMETHING GREATER THAN AN OVERSEER IS CORRECT...I WONDER WHAT ITS EVEN MORE POWERFUL FORME WILL LOOK LIKE. I EAGERLY AWAIT A REPORT FROM SINA AND DEXIO...

Pokémon X • Y
Volume 12
Perfect Square Edition

Story by HIDENORI KUSAKA
Art by SATOSHI YAMAMOTO

©2017 The Pokémon Company International.
©1995–2017 Nintendo / Creatures Inc. / GAME FREAK inc.
TM, ®, and character names are trademarks of Nintendo.
POCKET MONSTERS SPECIAL X•Y Vol. 6
by Hidenori KUSAKA, Satoshi YAMAMOTO
© 2014 Hidenori KUSAKA, Satoshi YAMAMOTO
All rights reserved.
Original Japanese edition published by SHOGAKUKAN.
English translation rights in the United States of America, Canada, the United
Kingdom, Ireland, Australia, New Zealand and India arranged with SHOGAKUKAN.

English Adaptation—Bryant Turnage
Translation—Tetsuichiro Miyaki
Touch-up & Lettering—Annaliese Christman
Design—Alice Lewis
Editor—Annette Roman

Printed in the U.S.A.

Published by
VIZ Media, LLC
P.O. Box 77010
San Francisco, CA 94107

10 9 8 7 6 5 4 3 2 1
First printing, October 2017

www.perfectsquare.com   www.viz.com

Begin your Pokémon Adventure here in the Kanto region!

POKÉMON™ ADVENTURES

RED & BLUE BOX SET

Story by HIDENORI KUSAKA Art by MATO

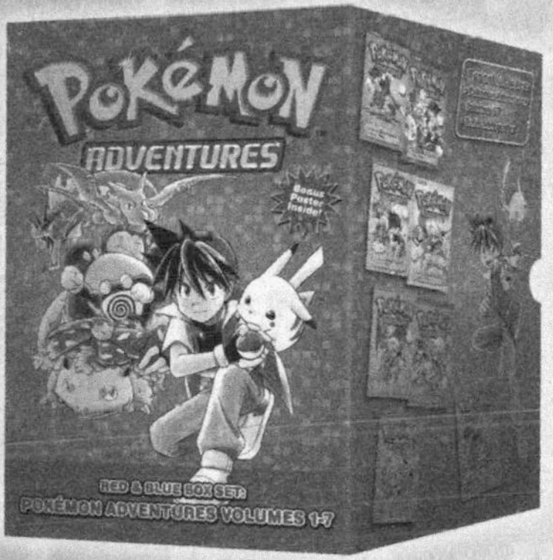

POKÉMON
ADVENTURES
Bonus Poster Inside!
RED & BLUE BOX SET:
POKÉMON ADVENTURES VOLUMES 1-7

Includes POKÉMON ADVENTURES Vols. 1-7 and a collectible poster!

All your favorite Pokémon game characters jump out of the screen into the pages of this action-packed manga!

Red doesn't just want to train Pokémon, he wants to be their friend too. Bulbasaur and Poliwhirl seem game. But independent Pikachu won't be so easy to win over!

And watch out for Team Rocket, Red... They only want to be your enemy!

Start the adventure today!

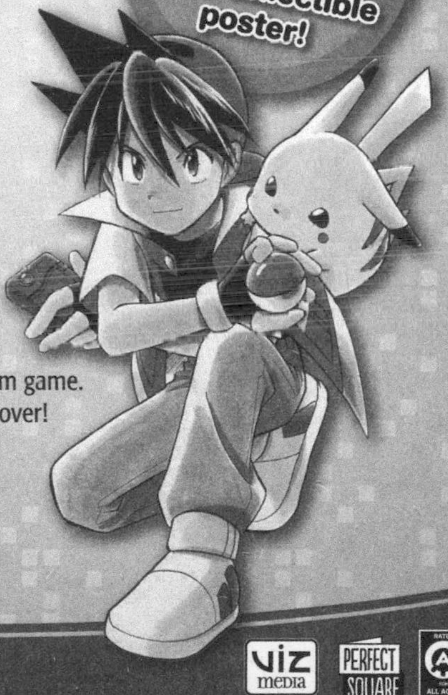

Pokémon ADVENTURES™

HeartGold & SoulSilver

ory by **HIDENORI KUSAKA**
t by **SATOSHI YAMAMOTO**

In this **two-volume** thriller, troublemaker Gold and feisty Silver must team up again to find their old enemy Lance and the Legendary Pokémon Arceus!

Available now!

POCKET COMICS

STORY & ART BY SANTA HARUKAZE

BLACK & WHITE
$9.99 US / $10.99 CAN

LEGENDARY POKÉMON
$9.99 US / $10.99 CAN

X•Y
$12.99 US / $13.99 CAN

A Pokémon pocket-sized book chock-full of four-panel gags, Pokémon trivia and fun quizzes based on the characters you know and love!

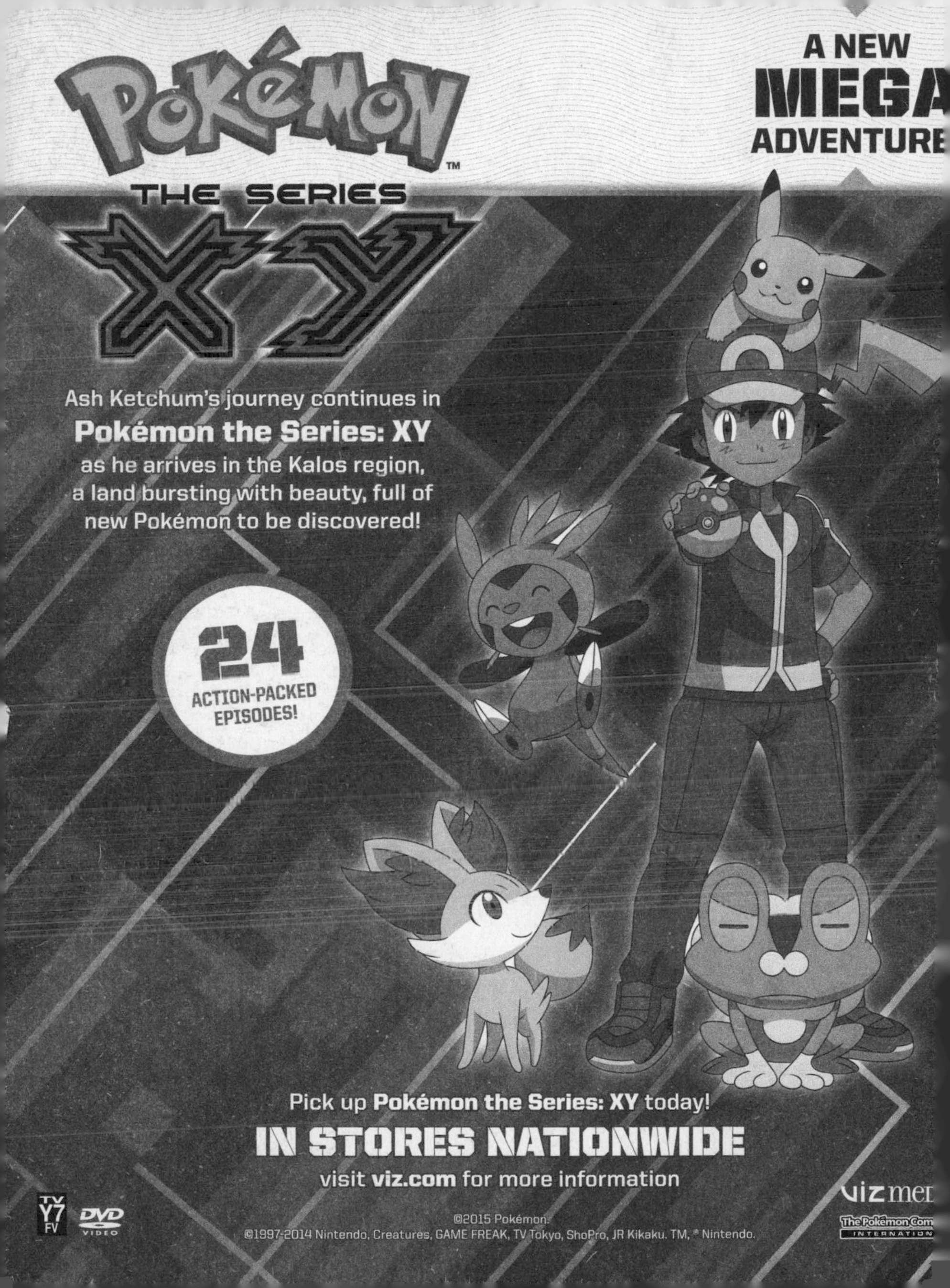
A NEW
MEGA
ADVENTURE
POKÉMON™
THE SERIES
XY
Ash Ketchum's journey continues in
Pokémon the Series: XY
as he arrives in the Kalos region,
a land bursting with beauty, full of
new Pokémon to be discovered!
24
ACTION-PACKED
EPISODES!
Pick up Pokémon the Series: XY today!
IN STORES NATIONWIDE
visit viz.com for more information
TV Y7 FV
DVD VIDEO
©2015 Pokémon.
©1997-2014 Nintendo, Creatures, GAME FREAK, TV Tokyo, ShoPro, JR Kikaku. TM, ® Nintendo.

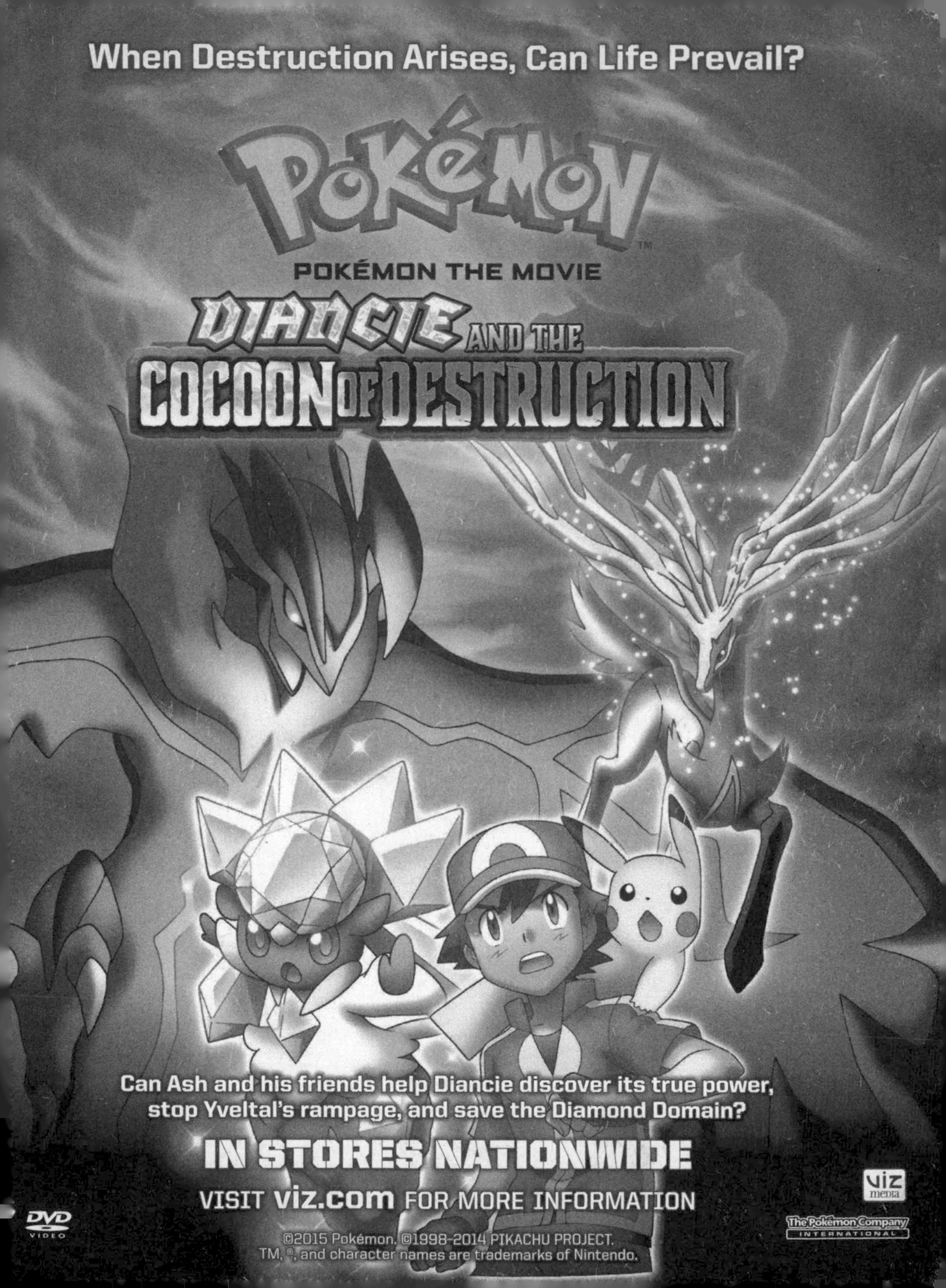
When Destruction Arises, Can Life Prevail?
POKéMON
TM
POKÉMON THE MOVIE
DIANCIE AND THE COCOON OF DESTRUCTION
Can Ash and his friends help Diancie discover its true power, stop Yveltal's rampage, and save the Diamond Domain?
IN STORES NATIONWIDE
VISIT viz.com FOR MORE INFORMATION
DVD VIDEO
VIZ media
The Pokémon Company INTERNATIONAL
©2015 Pokémon. ©1998-2014 PIKACHU PROJECT.
TM, ®, and character names are trademarks of Nintendo.

⟨⟨⟨ READ THIS WAY!

THIS IS THE END OF THIS GRAPHIC NOVEL!

To properly enjoy this VIZ Media graphic novel, please turn it around and begin reading from right to left.

This book has been printed in the original Japanese format in order to preserve the orientation of the original artwork. Have fun with it!

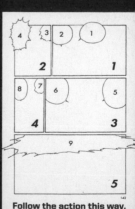

Follow the action this way.